Praise for the Dream Club Mysteries

"A dream come true for cozy readers everywhere."
—Lorna Barrett, *New York Times* bestselling author of
the Booktown Mysteries

"A wry and clever debut. Huge fun."
—Carolyn Hart, *New York Times* bestselling author of
the Death on Demand Mysteries

"A fun series that goes where no sleuth has gone before.
Once you pick this book up, you won't look at dreams in the
same way. Or mysteries."
—Carolyn Haines, award-winning author of
the Sarah Booth Delaney Mysteries

"Balancing a murder plot with humorous characters and a
genteel Southern setting, this is a terrific start to a new series."
—*Library Journal*

own dreams after reading
pens a lively mystery."
—*RT Book Reviews*

—*Kings River Life Magazine*

found the club members'
ons thought provoking . . .
. . . populated with charac-
—MyShelf.com

retation to impressive new
heights . . . An engrossing plot with enough twists and turns
to keep the reader as an active participant in the murder
investigation."
—Open Book Society

A Premonition of Murder

* * *
*   *
*   *
*   *

Mary Kennedy

BERKLEY PRIME CRIME, NEW YORK

F
KEN
M

BERKLEY PRIME CRIME

An imprint of Penguin Random House LLC
375 Hudson Street, New York, New York 10014

A PREMONITION OF MURDER

A Berkley Prime Crime Book / published by arrangement with the author

ISBN: 978-0-425-26807-0

PUBLISHING HISTORY
Berkley Prime Crime mass-market edition / June 2016

PRINTED IN THE UNITED STATES OF AMERICA

10 9 8 7 6 5 4 3 2 1

Cover art by Bill Bruning.
Cover design by Leslie Worrell.
Interior text design by Kelly Lipovich.

Penguin
Random
House

To the Kennedy cats,
Oliver, Oscar, Henry, Eliza, Fur-Face, and Calpurnia,
for all the love, loyalty, and joy you bring to our lives.

Acknowledgments

I want to thank Michelle Vega for her wonderful enthusiasm and endless patience. And a big shout-out to Bethany Blair and all the folks at Penguin Random House for bringing this book to life. My agent, Holly Root, has been my champion, my cheerleader, and my inspiration for all my books and I'm eternally grateful to her. And where would I be without my devoted readers? I'm thrilled beyond words that you enjoy my books and happy that I can connect with you on social media.

Something was off about the outdoor luncheon, but I couldn't quite put my finger on it.

On the surface, everything was perfect. The "tablescape" was pure Sandra Lee—snowy white table linens, cut-glass goblets filled with a nice Chablis, and a lush centerpiece of blue hydrangeas and yellow daylilies.

I tilted my head back, enjoying the warm sunshine. It was a lovely afternoon in Savannah; the air was soft, filled with the intoxicating scent of gardenias, and we were shaded by a magnificent live oak. It enveloped us, almost like a canopy. Our hostess, Abigail Marchand, caught me looking up at the sprawling branches and smiled. "One of my ancestors planted that tree," she said in her soft voice. "It was here when Sherman made his march into Georgia."

"So it dates back to the Civil War," I commented. "It's beautiful."

She raised her eyebrows. "You mean 'The War of

Northern Aggression,' my dear," she corrected me. Abigail was old-school, Old South, no doubt about it. And old money.

There were five of us seated at the round table on the flagstone patio and our hostess looked over the plates and cutlery with a keen eye. At eighty-seven, a famously reclusive heiress, she was used to perfection and had the money and taste to make it happen. And she didn't miss a trick.

"Lucy," she called out in a voice that had suddenly turned to steel, "have you forgotten something?" The housekeeper, who'd been hovering nearby, raced over with two wine bottles, one red, one white.

"More wine, Senora?" Her tone was anxious, deferential.

"Not more wine," Abigail snapped. "The cheese straws, where are they? You know we always serve cheese straws with wine."

"I'll get them right now. And Mr. Osteroff stopped by. He wants to leave some papers for you to sign, okay?" She pointed to a dour-looking man standing at the base of the steps leading into the back entrance of the house. I noticed a black Jaguar parked near the patio. He must have pulled up silently.

"Yes, of course, he can leave them on the hall table." Abigail stopped and waved at the man. "Norman, you are a dear; thank you! Want to join us for a glass of wine?" He gave a thin smile, followed by a dismissive little wave of his hand, and continued up the steps. "That's my lawyer," Abigail said. "A genius at legal issues but no social skills whatsoever. Now, where were we?"

The maid was still standing there, hands clasped in front of her, as if she was awaiting further instructions. "For heaven's sake, Lucy, show Mr. Osteroff inside and then bring us the cheese straws."

As the maid nodded and scurried away, Abigail gave a

world-weary sigh. "I have to check and double-check everything these days. Lucy's been with me thirty years, and I think she's getting forgetful." She playfully tapped her head. "Of course, at our age, that's not unusual. Present company excluded, of course." She grinned at the Harper sisters, Rose and Minerva, who exchanged a look and chuckled. "How many years have we been friends?" she asked her elderly guests.

"It's got to be over fifty years," Minerva said promptly.

"All the way back to the founding of the Magnolia Society," her sister Rose chimed in. The two sisters could have been twins, dressed in flowery dresses, with curly white hair framing their faces. They were wearing matching pearl earrings, little white socks, and orthopedic shoes. The Harper sisters were some of the first neighbors to welcome me when I moved to Savannah last year to help my sister Ali with her failing business. The two sisters run a flower shop down the street from Ali's candy store and are members of our Dream Club.

"The Magnolia Society," Abigail went on in a wistful tone. She turned her bright blue eyes on me. "Taylor, you may have suspected that I invited you and Ali here today to talk about the Society and our plans for the future."

"I wasn't really sure why you invited us, Abigail, but we're very happy to be here."

It was true. Ali and I had been stunned when Minerva and Rose said we were invited for lunch at Beaux Reves, the fabulous estate at the edge of town. I'd always been curious about it, but almost no one got past the wrought iron gates.

Beaux Reves has been written up in dozens of guide books, and I read that it has twenty rooms, twelve bedrooms, and fifteen baths, plus a wine cellar, a stable, and a king's ransom in furnishings and artwork. I glanced up at the white stucco mansion with its graceful balustrades and porticos looming over us and wondered if we'd get to see the inside. Abigail had met us at the flagstone patio and after a peremptory look at the gardens, we'd been ushered over to the luncheon table. I had the feeling this was going to be the extent of the tour.

Sara Rutledge, a journalist friend, told us that Abigail never gave interviews, steadfastly refused to allow the local papers to photograph the mansion, and never opened it for fund-raising events or garden tours. According to local rumors, she hadn't left the house for years. Yet she'd invited us over for lunch today. Why? Our octogenarian friends, the Harper sisters, had hinted that Abigail was looking for "new blood" for the Magnolia Society; the few remaining members were getting up into their nineties.

"I've always been curious about your home," Ali said, reaching for a cheese straw from the silver platter Lucy placed in front of us. In my short time in Savannah, I'd learned that cheese straws are practically a Southern staple and a popular hostess gift. "So it's really a treat for us to be here today."

"My pleasure, my dear," Abigail said. She paused for a moment while Lucy served our lunch: a delicate mixture of spring greens with lobster salad and marinated asparagus tips. The plates were chilled, and there was a basket of buttery dinner rolls on the table. "Now," she added briskly, "let me tell you why you're really here."

She paused and closed her eyes for a moment, taking a sip of wine. Even though she was in her late eighties, her porcelain skin was unlined and her silvery hair was swept up in a chic French twist. She was wearing a simple—yet expensive— sleeveless white linen shift with pale blue enameled earrings and delicate silver bands on her wrist.

Suddenly, her eyes flew open and she rested her hands on the table. "I just learned that I'm going to die." She swallowed hard. "I probably only have a few days left."

My stomach clenched, and I felt the same little frisson of fear that I'd noticed when I'd first sat down. I hadn't imagined my feeling of foreboding. The dark cloud was real. The Angel of Death was among us, and his dark wings were grazing the sun-splashed patio.

"Good heavens," Minerva said, her voice catching in her throat. "Oh, my poor dear, I had no idea you were ill." She glanced at her sister Rose, whose eyes were misting over. "You're always so energetic, and you've been such an inspiration to us with the Society."

Rose reached over and laid her hand gently over Abigail's. "Abigail, this can't be true. You know, doctors don't know everything. Why, they told Lois Albritton she had only a few months to live, and she was with us for another twenty years."

Abigail smiled and gently removed Rose's hand. "Please, everyone, it's not the end of the world. I've had a wonderful life, and all good things must come to an end." She picked up the basket of dinner rolls and handed it to me. "Taylor, pass this around, will you? Lucy's spent all morning preparing this lunch, and she'll be disappointed if we don't clean our plates." She put her napkin on her lap and picked up her fork, nodding for everyone else to join in. "Now eat up and I'll explain everything."

She took a bite of lobster salad and said slowly, "I always knew it was time for some new members to carry on the work of the Society, but I thought I had a couple of good years ahead of me. My mother and grandmother lived well into their nineties. I had no idea my time was running out." Minerva gave a soft sob, and Abigail went on softly, "It's not a medical issue; it's fate. Karma, you might say. And we can't fight karma, can we? It all came to me in a dream last week."

A dream? This was the last thing I'd expected to hear. Ali and I locked eyes for a moment. My sister and I are so close we can practically read each other's thoughts, and I knew she was as shocked as I was. It was Ali who introduced me to the power of dreams when I moved from Chicago to Savannah. Ali has been fascinated by dreams for years, and she started a Dream Club that meets once a week in our apartment above the candy shop. It's a small, dedicated group of women, and we meet over coffee and desserts to share our dreams and analyze them.

I've gone from being a die-hard skeptic to a reluctant believer. Recently we helped the police solve three murders right here in Savannah. A popular dance instructor was killed, soon followed by a second, related murder. The third victim was a famous chef, in town for a book signing. In both cases, the Dream Club provided invaluable clues that helped uncover the killers.

I forced my attention back to Abigail, who was recounting her dream. "There was a dark vortex and I felt myself falling, falling into the blackness . . . There was no hope, no escape." Her voice wobbled a little, and I knew she was trying to keep her emotions in check. Minerva and Rose were listening raptly, and Minerva was dabbing at her eyes with an embroidered white handkerchief.

I listened carefully and uncovered several familiar symbols and images that could signify death. Abigail's voice trembled as she recounted being engulfed in a whirlpool of pitch-black water, pulling her inevitably toward the bottom.

"Something was crushing me, some evil force . . ."

I wished I'd brought a tape recorder. She described a tight feeling in her chest, a weakness in her limbs. She felt like her lungs were exploding, her throat was closing, and she couldn't call for help. She was alone and terrified, feeling the life force seep out of her. It was certainly a vivid description of a death-by-drowning nightmare, but it wasn't unfamiliar to me.

And it didn't necessarily signify death. There were other possibilities, and I wondered if Abigail would be open to them.

"You've never had this dream before?" Ali asked.

"I never dream, my dear," Abigail replied. "My head hits the pillow and I'm out like a light." I wondered if that was true. Sleep studies have shown that almost everyone dreams, but some people simply don't remember their dreams.

"And you associate this dream with death?" Minerva asked gently.

"Well, of course I do. Wouldn't you?" Abigail replied, her eyebrows shooting up in surprise. "I was gasping like a fish on a line. I couldn't breathe and I was being pulled downward to some shadowy depth. Probably the netherworld," she added grimly.

"The reason Minerva asked," Ali interjected, "is that dreams can have many interpretations. Even nightmares, like the one you just described. It's impossible to know the subtext in a dream—the meaning beneath the surface—unless you have a complete picture of what's going on in the person's life."

Abigail blinked. "I never thought there would be more than one interpretation," she said quietly.

"There can be many, my dear friend," Minerva offered. She told Abigail about our work in the Dream Club and asked if she would like to get some feedback from the club members.

"I would like that very much," Abigail said, brightening. She gave a gay little laugh. "Well, now I feel a bit silly because I thought I was a goner."

"If you'd like," Rose offered, "I'll call you later, and we can discuss the dream in more detail before I present it at the next Dream Club meeting. And then I'll get back to you with the members' interpretations."

Abigail nodded. "That sounds wonderful." She sat back in her chair and blew out a little puff of air. "I feel like the governor has just called and I've been granted a reprieve," she joked. "This is really one for the book. I'll have to jot it down tonight. Oh, and I suppose I should tell you another bit of a dream I remembered from that same night. It's a happy dream. I dreamt that I reconnected with a distant relative, someone I hadn't seen in decades. And then a few days later, this person popped up in my life! The dream came true. I was so grateful to find her that I talked to my lawyer about changing my will and leaving her my entire estate. Of course, I haven't made up my mind yet. There are so many worthy causes here in Savannah." She gestured to the manicured pathways, the formal rose garden, the endless stretch of green lawn.

Minerva and Rose exchanged a look. "That's quite a legacy," Minerva said gently. "Are you sure you even want to consider leaving it to someone you just met?"

"But I didn't just meet her," Abigail insisted. "I reconnected with her. She's part of the family—the European side—and we've been out of touch for years and years. And in the end, family is everything, you know."

"Well, just don't act hastily," Rose advised.

"Oh, I won't." Abigail gave a girlish laugh. "Now that I know I'm not going to be pushing up daisies anytime soon, I can take my time deciding what to do with the estate. And dear fuddy-duddy old Norman cautioned me, too. He wants me to leave my will exactly as it is and not make any rash changes. But I suppose that's the way lawyers are. Mired in the past. You can't teach an old dog new tricks." She paused and looked around the table. "You ladies have given me a new lease on life. So finish up, everyone." She raised her glass in a toast. Her mood suddenly turned as bright and sunny as the Savannah sky. "Lucy's made peach pie with crème fraîche for dessert, and I don't know about you, but I plan on indulging!"

"Well, that was unexpected," Minerva said a couple of hours later. "Abigail is certainly full of surprises. I had no idea she'd drop a bombshell like that."

"I knew she wanted to interest you and Ali in the Magnolia Society," Rose said to me, "but I had no idea there was such a sense of urgency."

"She had a premonition about her own death," Ali said softly. "How sad. I'm so glad she reached out to us."

We'd lingered over coffee and dessert at Beaux Reves but never managed to get inside the mansion. Now we were back at Oldies But Goodies, sitting in our comfortable apartment right above the shop. It was a large, airy living space with glossy white woodwork, creamy taupe walls, and a vintage brick fireplace with a marble mantelpiece. The décor was shabby chic, Savannah style, and my sister Ali had covered the fussy antique furniture with white cotton slipcovers. She'd made throw pillows from scraps of blue-and-white gingham, and the room looked fresh and inviting.

I'd brewed a pot of sweet tea—another Savannah staple, I'd discovered—and placed the enameled drink tray on an old wicker chest Ali had found in a thrift store. She'd spray-painted it white, and it made a lovely coffee table.

"How much do you know about Abigail?" I asked Minerva as she reached for a piece of shortbread. I'd quickly pulled a package of homemade Scottish shortbread cookies out of the freezer and defrosted them in the microwave.

"Probably more than most people, but it isn't very much."

"What we know about Abigail would fit into a thimble,"

Rose added. "She's very selective in what she shares with people. Most of our contact with her over the years has been about the Magnolia Society, and now that we have e-mail, we usually communicate that way. Rarely by phone or in person. I was surprised that she opened her home to a stranger for the summer. That was completely out of character."

"A stranger?" Ali asked.

"A young man from the university, a graduate student, I believe. His name is Angus Morton, and she hired him to catalog everything at Beaux Reves. I suppose she thought it was time to get her affairs in order, and this would be a good place to start."

"She didn't say much about the Society," I said thoughtfully. "It's a philanthropic group, isn't it?"

"Oh my, yes," Minerva said, "it's a nonprofit. Abigail is absolutely devoted to the idea of preserving all that is good in Savannah: our parks, our monuments, our historic places. Rose and I are on the outer edges of the group; we help with mailings, contacting city councilmen, that sort of thing. There are only a handful of the original founders left, and Abigail is one of them. They set the policies and the agenda on how the organization should move forward."

"It sounds almost like a secret society, "Ali offered. She plopped down on the sofa and scooped Barney into her lap. Barney and Scout are two highly pampered cats who rule the roost. They're both rescues, and Ali adopted them as kittens from a no-kill shelter. They adore Ali, and they seem to know that she pulled them from a cage into a wonderful life.

When I first moved in with Ali, there was a period of adjustment, but I won them over with tuna fish packed in water and organic cat treats. The way to a cat's heart is through his stomach, as Ali always says. Barney curled against her, purring contentedly. Scout was snoozing on the windowsill, one of her favorite spots.

"A secret society? Oh, it's nothing that mysterious, my dear," Minerva said. She paused. "I don't mean to sound morbid, but I always did wonder what would happen to the Society and to Beaux Reves if Abigail passed away."

"Beaux Reves is a magnificent place," I said, wishing we could have taken a peek inside.

Rose nodded. "That it is. We stopped by once to drop off a Christmas gift for Abigail and made it as far as the front parlor. It looked like a room in a museum! Beautiful Oriental rugs, an enormous chandelier she had imported from Paris, Impressionist paintings—"

"I'm positive I spotted a Monet," Minerva interjected. "It was a field of lilies, with a pale blue sky. It was lovely."

"You don't suppose it was a copy?" Ali asked.

"Never!" Rose gave a delicate snort. "Abigail believes in buying the best or buying nothing at all. That's one of her favorite sayings."

"You were telling us you wondered what would happen to the house," I gently reminded Minerva. Sometimes Rose and Minerva have trouble staying on track.

"Oh yes, the house, sorry," Minerva said with a little flutter of her hands. "It would cost a small fortune to keep it up, I suppose, but I wonder if Abigail has willed it to some charitable organization? She'd have to leave a large amount of money for them to maintain it, of course. Right now, she manages with a live-in housekeeper, Lucy Dargos, and an estate manager, Jeb Arnold. He's a sort of jack-of-all-trades and lives in the guesthouse. Lucy has her own apartment on the top floor of the mansion."

"I'm surprised she can manage a place that size with such a tiny staff," Ali said.

"I think she keeps most of the rooms closed off," Minerva added. "That's the only way she can cope. And she hires an outside landscaping service to handle the gardens. She always says she likes to live simply, and I believe she often dines alone in front of the television. She's a news junkie, you see," she added with a smile. "And she loves politics."

"How I wish she had given you a tour," Rose said to me. "Beaux Reves. You know what that means, don't you?"

"Beautiful dreams," I said promptly, remembering my high school French. An odd coincidence since Abigail was preoccupied with a dream, I decided.

"Yes, beautiful dreams," Rose agreed. "Except now it seems poor Abigail is having nightmares. Do you think we can help her? She's such a sweetheart, I'd like to."

"I'm sure we can," Ali said warmly. "I'll call an emergency meeting of the Dream Club for tomorrow night."

2

We had almost a full house the following evening. Detective Sam Stiles was on duty and had to cancel at the last minute, but the rest of the group was there. The Harper sisters arrived first and settled onto a lavender settee that Ali had scored at a flea market. She'd draped a white crocheted throw over it, a gift from the Harper sisters.

Rose and Minerva were quickly followed by Dorien Myers, a prickly woman in her forties whose acid tongue sometimes causes tension in the group, and Lucinda Macavy, a retired school headmistress. We thought romance was in the cards for Lucinda last year, when she developed a brief friendship with a male Dream Club member, but that relationship seemed to have fizzled out, along with his involvement with the group.

At the moment, our membership is all female, although we'd be happy to have a man in the club if a gentleman applied. Etta Mae Beasley took a seat across from me and smiled when she recognized a plate of blueberry scones on the coffee table.

"From my family cookbook?" she asked, her tone ringing with pride.

"Of course," I told her. "It's one of our favorites." A few months ago, Etta Mae had been convinced that a visiting celebrity chef had stolen some of her treasured family recipes and included them in her bestselling cookbook. There was quite a to-do. Etta Mae threatened a lawsuit, and when the chef died under suspicious circumstances at a book signing, she was briefly considered a suspect. Everything was finally smoothed over and Etta Mae is now a valued member of the group. She's new to the field of dream interpretation, but all we ask of our new members is that they be respectful of other points of view and open to the idea that dreams really do have meaning.

By establishing a few ground rules, we've managed to run a fairly harmonious group with little dissension. A couple of our members do tend to "hog the floor," but Ali, our moderator, usually finds a tactful way to step in and redirect the discussion.

Etta Mae looked pleased and settled back happily in her comfy armchair. Sybil Powers and Persia Walker arrived together, and Ali called the group to order. "Help yourselves, everyone," she said. "There's sweet tea and fresh lemonade, and a nice assortment of pastries."

Since we've added a small café to the candy shop, we're always on the lookout for new recipes and we use the Dream Club members as our beta tasters, tweaking the recipes according to their suggestions and deciding which ones will make the final cut. Then we add the item to the menu as half-price specials and gauge customers' reactions.

This night I served a strawberry-rhubarb cobbler that I

thought was delicious but Ali felt was a little too tart, and I was eager to hear the group's take on it. Ali argued that most people would agree that it needed a bit more brown sugar. Southerners like their sweets, she told me. I always scribble the group's comments in a little notebook, and I thank the members for their input. I think they like the idea of being beta tasters and having plenty of free desserts to take home.

"You've outdone yourself, ladies," Minerva said to Ali and me. "I wish you'd let us contribute something. It doesn't seem fair that you two have to do all this baking every week."

"Nonsense. We're glad to do it," Ali told her. "You're the food judges. That can be your contribution. And besides, you bring such lovely flowers," she added, touching a petal on one of the pale pink roses that Minerva had arranged in a hand-painted vase. "These last for days," Ali told her. "We enjoy them all week."

"Then you've been cutting the stems on the diagonal and adding an aspirin as I suggested," Minerva said, beaming.

When everyone was finally settled with plates of goodies, the meeting could begin. "Minerva, Rose, Taylor, and I had an interesting experience this week," Ali began. She described our visit to Beaux Reves and our meeting with the reclusive Abigail Marchand.

"She had a premonition of her own death?" Sybil Powers asked.

"Yes, and it was a terrifying experience for her," Rose murmured. She took a cherry tartlet from the platter and sampled it. Rose takes tiny bites, like a cat, and loves to try every dessert we serve. She doesn't really offer helpful critiques, because she seems to love them all equally and swears she wouldn't change a thing about the recipe.

"The poor thing," Sybil said, shaking her head. "I wish

I could have dropped in on that dream." Sybil was wearing one of her trademark caftans, a beautiful batik in tones of peach and gold. Sybil has an unusual skill—she's a "dream-hopper" and has the ability to "visit" other people's dreams.

Last week, she told us about visiting Marie Antoinette in her final hours. The unlucky monarch was about to meet her gruesome end in the morning, and Sybil visited her dream as the queen slept fitfully, her dreams as dark and threatening as the fate that awaited her. Since time and space have no meaning in the dream world, it's possible for Sybil to slip through the ages and cross continents in her dream-hopping. I once asked her if she had ever accidentally "hopped into" a friend's dream, and she admitted that when that happens, she leaves the dream as fast as she can. She feels it isn't fair or honorable to intrude on a friend's privacy, and I respect her for that.

"So, what shall we tell Abigail as far as interpretations?" Ali said briskly. "The floor is open."

"Well, the first thing to do is to tell her that she may not be at death's door after all," Dorien said acerbically. "Most of us have had those drowning dreams from time to time, and we're still here, aren't we?" She looked around the group, and there was a challenge in her cool stare. "Everyone knows that it's a classic anxiety dream; she's probably drowning all right, but not in the literal sense. She could be drowning from some stressful situation in her life."

"Yes, that's my take, as well. Drowning in problems. Going down for the third time, as they say," Persia murmured.

"Do we know anything about any problems in her life, her health, her finances?" Etta Mae asked. "I'm new in town and I don't know anything about her. I've never even heard of Beaux Reves."

"Well, if you saw that place, you'd know she doesn't have any financial worries, hon," Dorien said harshly. "The place is like a palace, and that woman never had to work a day in her life."

Ali and I exchanged a look. Dorien can be downright unpleasant at times, and both of us wish she'd downplay her cynical tone. She's a bit rough around the edges—although the Harper sisters keep insisting she has a "heart of gold"—and I suppose her own money worries make her a bit envious of someone like Abigail.

Dorien has a tarot-reading business that dropped off a few years ago during the recession and hasn't quite recovered. She does occasional catering jobs and would love to be a personal chef, but there are a few strikes against her.

Her abrasive personality, for one thing. It's hard to imagine she has much in the way of customer service skills. And last year, she was briefly questioned by the police in a murder investigation. She served a catered dinner to a dance instructor who was later found poisoned. A cloud like that is hard to dispel, even though she was innocent. As Ali says, perception is everything.

The meeting moved on to other topics. Etta Mae discussed a recent bout with "sleep paralysis," and the group was sympathetic. Sleep paralysis is a truly terrifying experience, and it's similar to the "locked-in" syndrome that some people have experienced after a neurological event. It's not serious, but it's extremely unpleasant. According to Etta Mae, she has been to several doctors about her problem. One doctor suggested it was "psychological," which annoyed her to no end.

"I was lying in bed with my eyes shut," Etta Mae said, her voice shaky, "and I could hear everyone else in the house stirring. One of the kids tapped on my bedroom door and said they were making pancakes and they were waiting for me to come downstairs. I tried to open my eyes and sit up and I couldn't move. I was absolutely paralyzed."

"How awful," Lucinda murmured. "Did anyone in your family know what was going on?"

"No, they didn't have a clue. I heard someone say that I must be sleeping and then there were footsteps walking down the stairs."

"You haven't told them about your problems with sleep paralysis?" Lucinda asked.

"I don't want to worry them," Etta Mae said quickly. "The kids have enough on their plates as it is." I knew Etta Mae was divorced and struggling to raise three children on her own.

"What happened next?" Persia was perched on the edge of her chair, her expression rapt with interest.

"I felt all my muscles quivering as I struggled to get up and nothing happened. And my eyelids felt like they were glued shut. I couldn't move, but I could hear everything." She let out a big sigh. "I hope nothing like this ever happens to me again. It was like being trapped inside my own body. I felt like I'd been buried alive." She closed her eyes for a moment and her lips quivered.

"Has it happened before?" Ali asked. She reached over to refill everyone's glasses with tea and lemonade.

"Yes. Once, the night before I had surgery. I was terribly worried about going into the hospital and I was under a lot of stress. And the other time"—she paused, twisting her hands in her lap—"was when money was tight and the mortgage was due."

"Do you suppose you're going through something similar right now? Something stressful in your life, I mean?" Rose's tone was kind, but I knew Etta Mae might be offended if someone suggested that it was "all in her head."

"Well"—Etta Mae paused and licked her lips—"I suppose I am, but I'd rather not get into it right now." She gave a little shiver as if she was trying to shrug off the memories of being trapped in her own bed. "Let's move on to someone else. This doesn't really count as a dream, so I suppose I shouldn't have brought it up."

"Of course you should have," Minerva said. "If it's important to you, it's important to us."

"Anything else about Abigail before we finish for the evening?" Ali asked half an hour later.

"I don't think so," Rose said. "Except . . ."

"Except . . ." Ali prompted her.

"Well, I suppose it's nothing, but do you remember what Abigail said about her dream, how she described her impending death as 'fate'?"

"Yes, I do," I spoke up. "I remember she used the word 'fate' a couple of times."

"But there was another word she used," Rose offered. "I was listening very carefully, and she used the word 'karma.' What do you suppose she meant by that?"

There was dead silence for a few moments. And then Dorien said, "'Karma' means 'retribution,' doesn't it? What goes around comes around. That's always been my interpretation of it."

Rose nodded. "I suppose you're right. 'Retribution.' Odd that she would use that word. That sounds as though she's responsible for something and has to make amends. It makes me wonder . . ." Her voice trailed off and when it was obvious she wasn't going to say anything else, Ali stood up and thanked everyone for coming. She packed up the last of the pastries for the Harper sisters to have for breakfast the next day and the meeting ended. We had just ushered the last guest out the door when my cell chirped.

"Sam," I said, checking the readout. "What's up? We missed you tonight. It was a good meeting."

"I'm at a crime scene," she said, her voice tense. Our friend, Detective Sam Stiles, works the homicide division with the Savannah PD. "I don't know if it will make the morning papers, but I thought you'd be interested. You know the victim." My stomach clenched and I sat down. "It's the lady who invited you to lunch the other day. Abigail Marchand," she said softly.

"What happened?" I said over the lump in my throat. I'd only met Abigail once, but sudden death is always shocking and my mind flew to her tragically prophetic dream.

"It seems she took a tumble down the stairs," Sam said. "Her housekeeper found her at the bottom of the landing this morning. She must not have called out for help, because the ME puts the time of death at sometime last night. Maybe between ten and midnight, and she'll know more after the autopsy." *But she might have called for help. Lucy's apartment was way up on the top floor, and she might not have heard a thing.*

There were muffled noises in the background, and I figured that crime scene techs were processing the scene. "Put on those booties," I heard Sam snap at someone. "I don't want you trampling all over the evidence. We may get some footprints here."

"You think you might get footprints?" I asked.

"Probably not." Sam heaved a little sigh. "The whole place is covered in Oriental rugs."

"And you're absolutely sure it wasn't an accident?" My mind was scrabbling for an explanation. "She was elderly and a little unsteady on her feet."

"I think she had some help," Sam said flatly. "I'm calling it a possible homicide, and the ME agrees. She has a hand-print on her back."

I flinched. "A handprint?"

"Her skin was very thin. We definitely have finger marks on the middle of her back. Someone pushed her, I'm sure of it. Gotta go," she said abruptly. "We can talk later."

"Thanks for telling me," I began. She had already switched off the phone.

Ali sat down next to me, her eyes wide, her face pale. "Abigail?"

I nodded. "Someone pushed her down the stairs. They're calling it a homicide."

"So the dream was true," Ali said in a quivery voice. "She dreamt she was going to die."

"Yes, she did," I agreed. *Except she didn't know she was going to be murdered.*

3

My mind raced with possibilities, and I was too shocked and upset to even think about turning in for the night. I sank into a chair at the kitchen table, and after a few minutes, Ali wordlessly placed a cup of hot chocolate in front of me. I smiled my thanks. The drink was a symbolic gesture.

Ali and I are what are known as "adult orphans"; our parents were killed in a car crash ten years ago and ever since, it's been just the two of us against the world. When we lived at home, we used to gather around the family kitchen for a nightly cup of hot chocolate—even in the summertime. Hot chocolate always signifies home, comfort, and happier times for me.

"It's hard to believe, isn't it?" she said softly. She looked very young tonight with her streaky blond hair pulled back into a ponytail. She was wearing white capris with a tie-dyed shirt she'd ordered from an animal rescue group. "We just saw Abigail . . ." she added helplessly. "How could this happen?"

I shook my head. I wished I'd asked Sam more questions, but she'd been stressed and busy at the crime scene. I wanted to know if they suspected an intruder. Had the door been tampered with? Didn't Abigail have an alarm system? It seems odd that anyone living in a mansion with all that valuable artwork and all those antiques wouldn't invest in a good security system. And were the wrought iron gates open or closed when the police arrived at the house?

I remembered the gates were open when we went to Beaux Reves for lunch, but that's because Abigail was expecting us. Was it possible that Abigail knew her killer? But why was someone calling on her so late at night?

"What shall we do?" Ali said, pulling out her cell phone. "Shall I call the Dream Club members and give them the bad news? They probably haven't gone to sleep yet."

"No, let it go till morning," I told her. "There's no sense in upsetting them. We can't settle anything tonight, and we might have more information tomorrow."

Barney jumped onto her lap, and she buried her face for a moment in his soft fur. "I'm going to turn in," she said, scooping him into her arms and standing up. "I feel just awful about poor Abigail." She brushed my hand as she walked by, and Scout trailed after her down the hallway. "Don't stay up too late, okay?"

"I won't," I called after her. I finished the hot chocolate and started turning off the lights. The kitchen suddenly seemed bleak and lonely, and I was eager to hit the sack, but there was one phone call I had to make. Noah Chandler. I let the phone ring a few times, and then his voice mail kicked in. Had he already heard the news? It was very likely. Noah has strong connections with the local police. He works as a PI in Savannah, and his cousin Chris is a rookie cop with the Savannah PD. I quickly left a message, asked if we could meet for lunch tomorrow, and hung up.

Noah and I have a complicated history. We had an intense two-year relationship when we both worked in Atlanta. I was a strategist for a consulting firm and he was with the Atlanta field office of the FBI. We hit it off immediately and had sizzling chemistry, but neither one of us had the time or energy to devote to a relationship.

The timing was off, and we were both workaholics. After one major blowup, I decided to move back to Chicago and tried to put the past—and Noah—behind me. But then I returned to Savannah to help my sister run her store and discovered Noah was here, too. He has family in the area and I learned that he had left the Bureau to open his own detective agency in downtown Savannah.

Was it fate that brought us back together? Or sheer coincidence? Whatever it was, we found ourselves thrown together in a couple of murder investigations. Of course, our relationship is more than professional—it's definitely heading toward being seriously romantic once more—but I'm still not sure how to describe it.

The old attraction is still there, but this time we're both smart enough to take it slow.

At least I hope I am.

The next day, Ali and I sailed into Sweet Caroline's, the charming French bistro owned by our good friend Caroline LaCroix. Caroline is one of those Frenchwomen whose beauty is ageless. With her slender figure, keen fashion sense, and bubbly personality, she could be in her early thirties, although I know she's in her midfifties.

She and her husband used to own a more upscale restaurant in Savannah, but when he passed away, she sold the business and thought briefly about moving back to Paris. Luckily, her loyal friends and customers persuaded her to stay in town and open a smaller place. Her little bistro is flourishing and her homemade soups and freshly baked baguettes make it a favorite lunch spot for the business community.

I'd arranged the lunch with Noah and made sure I invited Sara Rutledge, a friend from Atlanta who's now a journalist here in Savannah. The four of us are close friends, and I didn't want Noah to think this was a "date." As far as I was concerned, this was a working lunch and a chance for us to mull over ideas about Abigail's death.

Noah texted me that he'd be a little late, and I spotted Sara sitting alone, waving to us from a table in the back of the café. "I was planning to do a story on Abigail Marchand next month," Sara said as Ali and I slipped into our seats. Sara immediately reached for a hot, buttery croissant from a wicker basket in the middle of the table. Sara is one of those people who can chomp down on a couple thousand calories a day, but is as slim as a swizzle stick. When I first met her, I decided that she must live on lettuce leaves and Tic Tacs, but that's not the case.

"A story on Abigail?" I asked in surprise. "But she was a recluse. Famously so." I raised my eyebrows. "I can't imagine her opening her door to you. You must have really turned on the charm." I smiled at her. "When we had lunch at Beaux Reves we never even got inside the mansion. We spent the whole time on the patio."

"Well, the piece was going to be more about Beaux Reves than Abigail. It was about the cost of keeping up a Southern mansion and how many of the owners have caved and decided to sell to developers. Abigail was one of the holdouts, of course. She refused to even consider the possibility of selling."

"So she didn't agree to an interview with you," I persisted.

"No, she didn't." Sara's tone was rueful. "I was going to press my luck and try to interview her, but my editor said I was probably wasting my time. We'll have to run the piece with stock photos of the mansion from earlier days and include some quotes from local historians."

I wondered if Sara knew about the Magnolia Society and its mission to save Savannah's historical sites. I tried not to look at the basket of flaky croissants that were calling to me with their little buttery voices. Sara had whipped out a tiny notebook and placed it by the side of her plate, ready to jot down any theories about the case.

She wants to have a career in investigative journalism, but the newspaper market is so tight she takes any assignment she can get—she covers everything from flower shows to Little League games.

The server had just passed around menus when Noah arrived. "Sorry," he said breathlessly, and slid into a chair across from me. Tall and broad-shouldered, with cool, assessing gray eyes, I'm sure he made some female hearts in Caroline's go flutter-flutter.

"An emergency at work?" Ali asked. She reached for one of Caroline's famous handmade potato chips. Caroline has a basket on every table and they are addictive. The first basket is on the house, and after that, you have to order them from the appetizer menu. I could easily eat the whole basket on my own, but I remind myself to put on the brakes.

"I wanted to look into the financials for Abigail," he said, balancing a manila envelope on the table. Noah always believes in "following the money" in any investigation. He says this was drummed into him at Quantico, and I have to admit he's right most of the time. I tend not to look at money as the primary motive in a case, but with Noah, it's his first priority.

"There's a lot of money there," he went on as the server appeared. We quickly ordered our favorites; Ali and I had chef's salads, and Sara and Noah went for grilled chicken and roasted potatoes.

"You mean besides Beaux Reves?" I asked.

"Yes, I do. Abigail made some good investments over the years, and they paid off. I found out the name of her lawyer and financial advisor: Norman Osteroff. Have you heard of him?"

"I've heard he handles a lot of money here in Savannah. Old money," Sara said meaningfully. "How did you get access to her financial records so quickly?" She looked wistful and a bit envious.

As a brand-new journalist in town, Sara is building up her contact list, and she's remarked a couple of times that Savannah is something of a closed society. It's hard to break into, and you have to develop a certain level of trust before people will even talk to you. And even then, many times they refuse to let their names appear in print and insist that the information is off the record. Deep background, Sara calls it.

"A few contacts here and there," Noah said cryptically. I knew he wasn't going to give away his sources. "It's definitely been ruled a homicide, but I guess you already know that?"

"That's what I assumed, but I haven't talked to Sam since last night. When she called me from the crime scene, she was convinced that Abigail was shoved down the stairs; she said it wasn't an accident."

"Who'd want to hurt her?" Sara asked, giving a little shudder. Sara still gets upset by violence and death, and I wonder if she'll ever toughen up enough to make it as an investigative reporter.

"That's what we have to find out," Ali said. She turned to Noah. "Do the police have any suspects?"

"The housekeeper, for starters." He flipped open a notebook. "Lucy Dargos."

"Lucy?" I said, shocked. "She seemed totally devoted to Abigail. She's been with her for over thirty years."

Noah gave a wry smile. "And did you know that Abigail promised her millions in her will?"

"No," I said softly. "I figured Abigail would be generous, but I still don't see how that's a motive for murder. Abigail was in her eighties—"

"But she was in excellent health," Sara cut in. "And her relatives all lived well into their nineties." I could see Sara had done her homework.

"How much do you know about Lucy and her son?" Noah asked. "Did you meet them when you had lunch at Beaux Reves?"

I shook my head. "I didn't even know she had a son. Lucy served lunch, but we really didn't talk much." I remembered Lucy had seemed a little on edge that day, but I thought she was just worried about pleasing her rather demanding employer. "Tell me about the son."

"Nicky Dargos. Not every mother's dream," Noah said. "He's been in and out of juvie since he was fifteen and just did his fourth stint in rehab. A known druggie and possibly a dealer. His age saved him from doing hard time as a teen-ager, but now that he's older, he'll probably face a long jail sentence the next time he screws up."

"Wow, I had no idea," Ali said softly. "Poor Lucy. She seems so nice."

"There's more," Noah went on. "Abigail made an unofficial complaint to the police that things were missing from the mansion. Small items that someone could pocket—an antique snuffbox, a cigarette lighter, a silver bracelet. This was a few months ago." He paused while the server placed the dishes in front of us. "The investigation never went anywhere. The police offered to alert local pawnshops, but Abigail didn't even have photos of the items. All they could do was recommend that she have someone do an inventory of the mansion and take photographs and document everything."

"That must be why she hired Angus," I said. "Angus Morton," I went on when Sara raised her eyebrows. "He's a university student spending the summer working for Abigail. Rose mentioned that he's cataloging everything at Beaux Reves. She didn't know many of the details, but I thought perhaps Abigail was doing it for insurance purposes. If someone's been stealing from her, that puts a whole new slant on things."

"Shall we divide up the work?" Ali suggested. "If we need any legal help, we can ask Persia. She knows all the lawyers in Savannah. The 'good, the bad, and the ugly,' as she says."

"Persia is one of our Dream Club members," I explained to Noah. "She's been working as a paralegal here for over thirty years. I bet she could check out this Norman Osteroff you mentioned."

Noah nodded. "That would be a good starting point. Ask her to get a general feel for how other lawyers regard him, and see if she can find out anything about his relationship with Abigail. If he's been the family lawyer for decades, there's probably nothing there, but you never know."

"I can check out the son, Nicky Dargos," Sara volunteered. "If he's had a string of arrests, there must be some newspaper articles about his crimes. I can run his name through the system and see what pops up."

"I can find out more about this grad student, Angus," I volunteered. "I'd like to know how he got the job. Why didn't Abigail just go to one of the respected appraisers here in town? There's something odd about him spending the summer at Beaux Reves."

"I wish we could have met him the other day," Ali said. "Trying to get inside the mansion was like trying to storm Fort Knox."

"It always makes me feel like someone's hiding something when they're that secretive," Sara said. She gave a little shrug. "Although maybe I'm being unfair. Perhaps Abigail was just a very private person."

"That she was," I agreed. On that note, the talk turned to more casual topics and Noah caught my eye a few times, giving me a sexy half smile. It was hard to concentrate on the conversation with Noah just sitting right across the table from me, but I gave myself a mental shake and told myself to be professional. After all, like it or not, we were in the middle of a murder investigation. Again.

4

It was a somber group that gathered in our upstairs apartment that night. We decided we needed to call an emergency meeting to deal with the shocking news about the murder. Abigail's death was the lead story on the local television stations and everyone except Dorien Myers had heard the sad news. Dorien had been in Charleston all day, hoping to get a catering job, and hadn't had time to read the evening paper or switch on the television.

"I just can't believe it," Rose Harper said, dabbing at her eyes. "When Lucy called to tell me the news this morning, I just burst into tears. I couldn't stop crying, I felt weak as a kitten."

"Lucy called you?" I exchanged a look with Ali. "I didn't think Lucy was close to any of Abigail's friends."

"Well, we're not close, my dear," Minerva said. "Abigail and Lucy come from a generation where that would be impossible. There was always a certain formality at Beaux

Reves, and class lines were never crossed. Even after thirty years, Lucy always called Abigail 'Mrs. Marchand.'"

I nodded. I'd noticed that. So both Abigail and Lucy were old-school.

"What did Lucy tell you exactly?" Ali asked.

"Why, just that Abigail had died during the night. It came as a terrible shock, of course."

"Died during the night?" Dorien said in her braying voice. "That makes it sound like she died in her sleep. Do you think she was she trying to pull the wool over your eyes?"

Rose looked shocked, her mouth tightening. "Good heavens no, Dorien. That's not what she meant at all. When I asked how Abigail had died, she was quite forthcoming. She said that her mistress had tripped and fallen down a flight of stairs. That grand marble stairway in the foyer."

"Poor thing." Rose went on, "She didn't find Abigail until she got up to fix breakfast. I suppose she's a heavy sleeper because she said she never heard a thing during the night."

Well, that much was true, I reasoned. It was possible that Lucy hadn't heard anything. But I would hardly call Lucy's comments "forthcoming." No mention of the ME turning up or the fact that Beaux Reves was now a crime scene.

"Did she mention that the police came to the house and interviewed her?" Persia asked. She was perched on the edge of her chair, listening intently. I'd pulled some brownies and apple tartlets from the downstairs refrigerator and arranged them on a pretty blue-and-yellow hand-painted platter, a gift from the Harper sisters. The apple tartlet recipe was new and it called for wonton wrappers to form the tartlet shells. The tartlets and brownies would have to do instead of our usual, more elaborate spread.

"Well, she was a bit vague on that." Rose hesitated, looking slightly uncomfortable. It was clear she didn't want to say anything that suggested Lucy was responsible for Abigail's death, and I wondered if she was withholding information.

"And she said the doctor came to the house, of course, even though it was obvious that Abigail was dead. Any resuscitation efforts would have been in vain."

"You mean Abigail's personal physician?" Ali asked. "Not the coroner."

"Yes, of course." Rose gave a little sniff and Minerva reached over and patted her hand. "This is the last thing I expected."

"How sad it all is," Sybil chimed in. She reached for a brownie, hesitated, and then grabbed one. Ali and I exchanged a look. Sybil is very fond of sweets, and every time she has tried to give up sugar she has failed miserably. "You know, I had a really complicated dream about Abigail Marchand last night."

"Tell us about it," Ali prompted, passing a pitcher of iced tea. Usually we take turns recounting our dreams. It made sense for Sybil to go first tonight. Everyone seemed to be in shock over Abigail's death—except Dorien, who was taking it in stride—and I was eager to hear Sybil's dream.

"It was nighttime, and the grounds of the estate were shrouded in shadows," she began. She closed her eyes for a moment, as if she was visualizing the scene. When she opened her eyes, her voice was low and hypnotic. "The white stucco mansion was dark, all the shutters were closed. The massive wrought iron gate suddenly swung open, and I could feel myself drifting toward the front portico."

Etta Mae frowned. "You were *drifting*?"

She's one of our newer members and probably doesn't know that Sybil often describes herself as "drifting" or even "flying" over a scene in her dreams. It's an image that many of our members can relate to; they often dream that they are floating near the ceiling, looking down on a scene. And this is also a commonly reported image in near-death experiences.

"Maybe 'floating' would be a better word," Sybil said. "Moonlight was slanting over the beautiful carved door, and I could smell honeysuckle in the air. Everything was still."

"As still as death," Minerva said, dabbing her eyes.

"The honeysuckle," Ali said quietly. "There was a big honeysuckle bush next to the stone lion in the front of the mansion." She turned to face me. "Do you remember we commented on it?"

I nodded. So far, Sybil's description was spot-on. Still, all of this information could have come from a guide book, I reminded myself.

"I recognized the estate as Beaux Reves, of course," Sybil continued. "I've never been there, but it's been photographed so many times, I feel like I know it. I saw a woman in a filmy white dress standing on a veranda surrounded by big stone planters. They were filled with the most beautiful flowers I've ever seen: New Guinea impatiens, petunias, tea roses, and daylilies. The vases looked old and vaguely Egyptian to me. They reminded me of a fresco, with images of women etched into the stone."

"We saw those vases!" Ali said, excited. "There was a pair of giant stone urns with figures in bas-relief. The women had their arms folded in front of them, and they were carrying baskets on their heads. Sybil, this is amazing—you were really at Beaux Reves in your dream. I have no doubt about that." Sybil smiled and bowed her head in acknowledgment.

Ali sank back, awed.

I could picture the vases from our lunch at Beaux Reves; Sybil had described them perfectly. I glanced over at Dorien, whose mouth was twisted in a sneer. It was clear that she wasn't enthralled with Sybil's dream. Sybil has a dramatic conversational style, and some people find it a bit over-the-top. She adds a wealth of detail to her dreams and I always find her to be an engaging raconteur. Does she embellish the truth and spice it up a bit? I have no way of knowing. I do know that she has been helpful in solving previous murders, though, so I have no doubt that she has an unusual gift. We are all grateful to have her in the club.

"Was it Abigail you saw—the woman in the white dress?"

Sybil took a deep breath. "No, it wasn't Abigail," she said after a moment. "At first I thought it was, because there was a strong family resemblance. This woman had bright auburn hair streaming down her back; she wasn't blond like Abigail. She could have been a relative, I suppose."

"Desiree," Minerva and Rose chorused.

"Desiree?" I asked.

"Abigail's younger sister," Minerva explained. "Her life ended tragically, too." Everyone grew quiet and even Dorien looked up, interested. "Desiree was the opposite of Abigail, who was quite prim and proper, as you know."

"Desiree was something of a wild child," Rose interjected. "Ready to do anything on a dare, had loads of suitors, traveled the world. Sometimes I found it hard to believe she and Abigail were even related. Their interests were so different. Desiree was out for a good time, and Abigail devoted her life to good works."

"What happened to Desiree?" Ali asked.

"No one is quite sure. She drowned a few years ago," she said simply. "The whole thing was very strange because Desiree had a lifelong fear of the water. She attended a ball that evening, and later, someone spotted her walking down by the docks. I think she was a little"—she gave an apologetic smile—"tipsy, because she was singing and swinging her high heels in her hand. She was seen walking along the embankment, and I guess she was pretty wobbly."

"How very odd," Sybil said. "The woman in my dream was standing by a pool of water, looking into it. She was wearing a silky white dress—I thought it was a nightgown, but I suppose it could have been an evening dress. It looked like a slip."

"That's it!" Minerva said, clutching her sister's hand. "That's what Desiree was wearing when they found her. A white slip dress. They were all the rage at the time. I remember thinking that only very young, very thin women could get away with wearing dresses like that. Of course, on Desiree it looked beautiful." She paused. "You know, I probably have a photo of her in that dress, somewhere. I remember her picture appeared in the society column; they did a big write-up on her. She was the belle of ball that night, as always. No one else in Savannah looked like Desiree," she added. "She was a stunner."

"The woman in my dream was a stunner, too. She was beautiful," Sybil said softly. "She was standing so still, just peering into a dark pool of water, and then suddenly a hand came out of nowhere and gave her a shove. She tumbled into the pool, and the water closed over her."

"How horrible," Persia said. "Could you see who pushed her?"

"No, I don't have a clue. I have a sense it was a man, but I'm not sure why I think that. All I saw was a gloved hand coming out of the dark. One hard push and the lovely woman in white was gone. There was a splash, I remember, and then there wasn't a sound." She gave a little shudder.

"That could have been exactly what happened to Desiree," Minerva said, her face pale. "You know, they always suspected foul play, but there was never any proof. The police investigated, of course, but the death was ruled inconclusive. I remember a lot of people in Savannah at the time suspected foul play."

"What did Abigail think happened to her sister?" It occurred to me that Abigail Marchand had the money and connections to launch a full-scale inquiry. Surely she would have done everything she could to find out what happened to her sister?

"Abigail did what she could," Rose said slowly, as if sensing my thoughts. Her hesitant tone made me think there was more to the story. "I don't know," she said, shaking her head. "I guess sometimes you just don't get answers in these cases."

"You do if you look hard enough," Dorien said brusquely. "Were they close, the two sisters?"

This time Minerva and Rose turned to look at each other. The unspoken thought was *not like we are.* "Well, it's hard to say," Minerva said slowly. "They were so different, you see. I had the feeling Abigail never really approved of her sister. Did you feel that way, Rose?"

"I certainly did," Rose said emphatically. "As different as chalk and cheese. Still, Abigail seemed devastated by her death. Even if Desiree was a flighty, silly girl, blood is thicker than water, you know."

"That it is," Minerva murmured, bobbing her head. "But I know Abigail made every effort to bring her sister's killer to justice, if there really was foul play in her death," she said, rising to Abigail's defense.

"Was Abigail a recluse, back when her sister died?" I asked.

"Oh my, yes; nothing has changed in that regard," Rose said. "In fact, I think she was worse in those days. I remember her saying she wanted to hire a private detective to look into Desiree's death, but she had no idea how to go about it. She finally turned the whole matter over to her lawyer, and she let him do his best to get to the bottom of it. I don't know what he uncovered, but nothing more was ever said about it. I didn't want to bring it up for fear of upsetting her. I suppose in the end, Abigail had to accept that her sister's death would remain a mystery."

"A hard thing to accept," Ali murmured.

For a long moment, no one spoke. The only sound in the cozy living room was the whirring noise of the Casablanca fan. Barney jumped into Ali's lap, and she picked him up and hugged him. Whenever she's upset, she finds it very comforting to snuggle the cats close to her and speak softly to them. Scout sashayed in front of the sofa, tail swaying, like a queen reviewing her loyal subjects. Lucinda and Sybil, who are big-time cat lovers, bent down to pet her.

I was beginning to wonder if we should call the meeting to a close. Abigail's death had seemed to shatter the calm of the group, and no one was too interested in venturing into other topics. And then Lucinda Macavy spoke up. "I have a dream to report." She went on to describe a dream about her teeth falling out. "I woke up in the morning, looked in the mirror, and saw that all my teeth had fallen out. I was horrified." Her hand instinctively went to cover her mouth. "It seemed so real! I gasped out loud and ran downstairs to call someone for help." She paused, looking a little sheepish. "Has anyone had a dream like this? I feel a little silly mentioning it, but it really bothered me. I haven't been able to get it out of my head."

"You're not being silly," Sybil cut in. "If it's important to you, it's important to us."

"My uncle Bubba had a dream like that," Etta Mae said. "He dreamt that all his teeth fell out. When he got up in the morning and looked in the mirror, he had no teeth."

"Surely you're not saying his teeth really *did* fall out in the night." Dorien said. She has a sharp, almost ferret-like face. It's a shame, but her choppy haircut seems to emphasize her worst features.

"Well, no," Etta Mae said, backpedaling swiftly. Dorien has the power to intimidate almost everyone. "He had all his teeth pulled out years ago. He forgot to put his dentures in when he went to bed the night before. That's why he nearly had a conniption when he looked in the mirror."

"Oh, well, that explains it," Dorien said mockingly. "Now it makes perfect sense to us." She gave a little eye roll to the group, and I knew it would be a long time before Etta Mae spoke up again. Dorien's sarcasm is a real turnoff, but Ali and I have never come up with a workable solution.

"Going back to Lucinda's dream," I said, hoping to ease the tension I sensed gathering in the room. "Persia, what do you make of it?"

Persia immediately jumped in to tell Lucinda that "missing teeth" is a classic anxiety dream and it probably meant that she was experiencing some unusual stress in her life. "Is there something special going on right now, dear?" Persia asked.

Lucinda nodded. She went on to say that one of her cousins was coming to Savannah for a visit and she was in a tizzy trying to get everything ready for her arrival. "My house is such a disaster," she wailed. "My kitchen cupboards are a mess, and the hosta has completely overtaken the garden. It's like a jungle out there."

Ali and I exchanged a look. We've been to Lucinda's adorable little house, and she keeps it in perfect condition. Even Martha Stewart would approve.

I bit back a smile at the notion that things were "out of order" at Lucinda's and reminded myself that everyone has different standards. Ali and I are not neat freaks by any means. We tend to be casual, with loads of books, newspapers, and overflowing tables in our comfy apartment above the shop, but not ready for a photo op.

Our vintage candy shop downstairs is a different story. Thanks to our capable assistant, Dana Garrett, things at Oldies But Goodies are always shipshape. The candy bins are well stocked with the "classic" candies we're known for, the glass cabinets are sparkling, and the whole place has a festive air, due to Dana's flair for decorating.

The evening ended on a positive note, and I noticed Sybil and Persia stopped to say a few sympathetic words to Rose and Minerva, who were the last to leave. I packed up some brownies and apple tartlets for the two Harper sisters to take home and watched as they made their way slowly down the stairs. Their hearts were heavy over the loss of their friend, and they looked older and less spry than ever. Even though they saw Abigail only occasionally, they had been friends with the reclusive heiress for over fifty years. Her death must certainly have been a shock to them.

5

Ali and I rose early the next day, ready to go downstairs and get back to work at our vintage candy shop. We'd left everything to Dana as we tackled the issue of Abigail's death, but now it was time to get back to business.

Ali had been struggling to keep the shop going when I'd arrived in Savannah a few months earlier to help her. I'd loved the place from the moment I walked in the front door. The name, Oldies But Goodies, is written in an old-timey script on etched glass and matches the vintage theme. With its bleached oak floors, tin ceiling, and bins of retro candies, entering the shop is like taking a trip down memory lane. In an earlier life, the shop had been a jam factory, a community newspaper, and briefly served as a day care center. I don't know how Ali got the idea of turning the place into a vintage candy shop, but I'm glad she did.

Sunlight streamed in the front window from Clark Street, then zigzagged its way past the bins and counters of goodies.

I could smell fresh croissants, and I smiled at Dana, who was pulling a heavy tray out of the oven. She placed it on the counter, along with a jar of homemade blueberry jam and a clay pot of sweet cream butter. It was Dana who came up with the idea of selling jams and chutneys, and they've become popular items.

"Breakfast of champions," Ali said, grabbing a croissant and slathering it with butter and jam. Dana had already brewed a pot of fresh coffee—hazelnut, my favorite—and a pot of Yorkshire Gold tea for Ali.

"What a way to start the day," I said appreciatively, sinking onto a bar stool and eyeing the freshly baked pastries. Dana had also defrosted a homemade coffee cake from the freezer. It's a recipe that Ali has been tinkering with, and the final version has a rich poppy seed filling and a buttery crumb topping. I think it's going to be a keeper. *Poppy seed cake or croissant? Which do I want?* They both looked delicious. Dana must have read my mind, because she cut a small wedge of coffee cake, added a hot croissant, and passed the plate to me.

"I'm so sorry about your friend," Dana said softly. "It's just awful."

"Thanks," Ali said. "We only met Abigail once, and I don't know why I'm taking this so hard," she commented. "We both are," she added quickly.

"It was such a shock," I murmured.

"Is there anything new on the case?" Dana asked tentatively.

"No, I'm afraid not," I told her. I paused for a moment and then decided to turn the conversation to cheerier topics. Ali is a sensitive soul, and I knew if we talked about Abigail any longer, she would be sad and depressed for hours. "What's the plan for today?" I asked Dana.

One thing I love about Dana is her initiative. Give her a project and she runs with it; she's one of the most creative people I've ever met. Ali and I were astounded when she told us that her parents insisted she major in criminal justice. They felt that majoring in marketing would limit her job opportunities. I think it was very shortsighted of them because she's a genius at promotion and would be a valuable asset to any company.

"The front window," she said promptly. "Want to see what I've done so far?"

I grabbed my coffee and tagged along after her. The shop wasn't open for business yet, and I was happy that the three of us had this time together to plan and strategize. I made a mental note that we should meet at least once a week before the store opens and toss around ideas.

Dana does a wonderful job with the window display— which she rotates—and this month she's featuring vintage candy posters for Jujubes, Good and Plenty, Jawbreakers, and Necco Wafers. She found the lovely old posters on eBay and mounted them on wooden easels. I made a mental note to reimburse her. Dana will buy supplies out of her own money if I'm not careful.

"Where did you get the mannequin?" I asked in amazement. I knew I wasn't imagining things. A tall female mannequin with a frizzy blond ponytail was standing in the middle of the shop window, looking off to the side. She had a saucy smile and one eye was half-closed as if she were winking at passersby. The mannequin hadn't been there last night when we closed up, so Dana must have brought it in this morning.

"Someone tossed it in the Dumpster in front of Harold's, that department store that closed down on Market Street. Can you believe it? A perfectly good mannequin. These things are pricey. I don't know what they were thinking. I jumped right in and got it." She brushed a speck of dirt off her sleeve. "Luckily no one had thrown anything on top of it. It must only have been there for a few minutes. I'm so happy I spotted it."

I had to chuckle at the thought of Dana Dumpster-diving for us. She will always go the extra mile to do her job.

"Very clever," Ali said. "And the outfit?" The mannequin was dressed in a turtleneck sweater, a poodle skirt, ankle socks, and saddle shoes. Circa 1955, I'd guess. She had short, straight bangs and reminded me of Kathleen Turner's character in *Peggy Sue Got Married*.

Dana laughed. "The outfit was left over from a fifties party at Kappa Kappa Gamma. My roommate gave it to me, but she wants it back when we change the display."

"Tell her thank you, I love it!" I never fail to be amazed at Dana's creativity. The mannequin was holding an aqua blue "princess phone" to her ear with one hand and a Butterfingers bar in her other. "Definitely something that will stop traffic," I told her.

"I think it turned out well," Dana said modestly. She took a step back to appraise her work. Next month, Dana will do something completely different; she never seems to run out of ideas. Tourists stop to admire her displays, and then they wander inside to check us out. And they usually end up not only buying a nice selection of candy, but settling down for a light lunch or coffee and pastries.

Ali and I had decided to expand the shop's offerings last year, and it was quite a hassle, but worth it. We thought it would be fun and good for business. We were right on both counts. The experiment paid off big-time.

The backyard is small but charming, with coral and white impatiens lining an oyster shell pathway. We found a few wrought iron tables and chairs at a tag sale, and Ali made seat cushions and tablecloths. The Harper sisters keep us supplied with fresh pink carnations in mason jars for each table.

The customers love sitting under the beautiful live oaks, lingering over coffee and pastries, and we have some regulars who show up every day. Sometimes there's an overflow crowd, but the breakfast bar inside the shop will accommodate half a dozen more people. Right now, we're only open in the daytime, but we're thinking of stringing Japanese lanterns in the trees and staying open one or two evenings a week. With a business, you're always planning, always wondering how to make a splash in a competitive market.

Plus we're running a thriving takeout business. Ali passed out flyers and discount coupons to the businesses in the Historic District, and now a lot of office workers order their lunches ahead of time and come dashing in to pick them up.

"What do you think of the candy buttons?" Dana asked. She was holding rolls of white paper with tiny candy buttons on them, a favorite "back in the day."

"What do you plan on doing with them?" I have no design sense and love to watch Dana work her magic with these displays.

"Well, first I thought of just hanging them from the ceiling, but then I decided they might look like flypaper," she said with a giggle.

"I see your point." Ali laughed. "I think you're right. They can't hang straight down. How about draping them from the ceiling, sort of like Roman shades? You could arrange them in graceful arcs and fasten them with thumbtacks. And you could give a twist to them, like you do with crepe paper."

"I like that idea," Dana said. "It would add a nice touch. You've solved the problem."

We left Dana to finish the window display and went back

to our breakfast. The shop would be opening in another half hour, and there were a lot of things I wanted to discuss with Ali. She pulled out some covered containers from the refrigerator and started working on the lunch specials.

We always offer homemade salads, soups, and sandwiches. Lately, we've added paninis and a flatbread menu, but those items are made fresh for each customer. The soups, salads, and desserts are all labor-intensive, but customers appreciate the fact that we use all fresh ingredients with no preservatives.

One time, a whole family insisted on having their sandwiches made with soft white sliced bread. We make our own sandwiches on delicious whole-grain bread delivered fresh each day from a local bakery. Instead of telling the family that we didn't have any of their favorite bread on hand, Ali dashed to a nearby supermarket and bought some. The first rule of business is to give the customers what they want.

"What's on the agenda for today?" she asked, deftly mincing a cooked chicken breast and adding celery and spices. Ali is a vegetarian, but she makes the best chicken salad sandwich in town, and the secret is cream cheese. Our friend, the restaurateur Caroline LaCroix, taught her how to make it. And Caroline insists that it should be served only on a fresh croissant.

"I think we need to pay a few visits in town," I told her. "I want to see Noah and I'd like to drop by and see that lawyer, Norman Osteroff. I think it would be worth it to have a quick chat with Lucy, the housekeeper. She could certainly tell me a little about Desiree, Abigail's sister." It occurred to me that the two deaths could be related, although at the moment, I didn't see how.

"It sounds like you've got a full day planned," Ali said, wrinkling her brow in concentration.

"Do you want to divide up or shall we go together?"

She opened the refrigerator and took a long look. "There's an awful lot to do here. I need to make chicken salad, tuna salad, and egg salad," she said. "I'm not sure when I can get away. Dana can handle the candy sales and the cash register"—she gave a little helpless shrug—"but I need to get the salads going right now, and then I have to defrost a couple of soups from the freezer."

She pushed a lock of blond hair out of her eyes, looking a bit frazzled. Adding the café to the shop has meant a lot more work for both of us, but I think it will pay off in the end. When I first arrived, the shop was operating in the red, and Ali had to tuck into her savings to meet her monthly bills. Now we're finally turning a profit, and I think things are on the upswing. We have a lot of repeat business, which tells me we're doing something right.

"Ali, don't worry about it. I can handle things myself this morning," I told her. "Let's touch base after lunch. I think I'd like to have you with me when we call on Norman Oster-off. I have the feeling he's not going to be thrilled to see us."

My first stop was Beaux Reves and Lucy Dargos. The imposing house looked empty, with its shutters closed against the Savannah sun and the grounds deserted. I announced myself at the entrance and the massive wrought iron gates swung open. As I drove up the winding road lined with live oaks and magnolia trees, I thought of all the family secrets that might be unveiled with Abigail's death.

Sudden death always seems to leave a few loose ends, and I hoped that my chat with Lucy might be fruitful. Had she discovered any of Abigail's correspondence, anything that might have a bearing on her death?

I knew that Abigail was a great letter writer, and came from a generation that believed in the power of handwritten notes. But the Harper sisters said they'd communicated by e-mail with Abigail over Magnolia Society business. I wondered if there was a laptop tucked away somewhere inside the mansion. Had the police seized it as evidence? Or was it squirreled away somewhere out of sight?

"I thought you might pay me a visit," Lucy said with a sad smile. She wiped her hands on her apron and led me into the kitchen. The front hall was dazzling. Every surface was polished, and a faint lemony smell drifted in the air.

"That wonderful smell," I began.

"Fresh lemon juice. It's a homemade wood polish I make myself," she said proudly. "I've been taking care of this furniture for over thirty years now," she said, running her hand over a beautiful mahogany table. "Not a scratch mark on it."

I paused to admire the finely crafted round table and the huge vase of violet and blue hydrangeas arranged in the center. The vase looked like a Chinese blue-and-white porcelain flower vase. *Probably worth a small fortune.* "It looks like you're keeping up the place exactly as if Abigail were still here," I told her.

"Of course." She brushed back a tear and smiled. I noticed she was wearing a St. Christopher medal. "This house is so full of memories," she added, ushering me into the kitchen. I was glad she invited me into the kitchen instead of the formal living room. The kitchen is always the heart of the house, and I hoped that a less formal atmosphere might lead to some confidences. I knew that Lucy was fiercely loyal to Abigail, and I would have to tread softly if I wanted to get any information out of her.

"So," I began, when I was settled at a breakfast bar with a glass of sweet tea, "how are you doing? I know this is a very tough time for you." Lucy pushed a plate of homemade blueberry muffins toward me. The delicious scent almost made me swoon, but I shook my head. There are times when one simply has to restrain oneself. I felt virtuous, but I was salivating.

I took another peek at the blueberry muffins. *Streusel topping!* "Well, maybe just a small one," I said. She grinned and passed me a plate and a porcelain dish of butter. Was I really that obvious?

"I'm doing okay," she said slowly. "I miss Mrs. Marchand a lot, but I try to focus on what she would have wanted. She would have expected me to take care of the house just like I've always done. People think she was demanding, but she wasn't, not really. She just knew what she wanted. These are beautiful things, and she wanted them cared for properly."

She let her gaze slide over the spotless kitchen with its white cabinets and black granite countertops. Clearly these were expensive renovations. The appliances were all high-end, and I recognized a gleaming burgundy La Cornue Grand Palais range, which looked like it was straight out of the Orient Express, and a wine cooler disguised as an antique cabinet. I doubt Abigail ever entertained and wondered who had selected the items.

I noticed a collection of colorful porcelain wall plaques; sunflowers, poppies, and an especially pretty one with a fish. They had a Latin feel to them. "These are beautiful. Are they hand-painted?" I asked.

Lucy smiled. "I brought them from my village in Mexico. Mrs. Marchand let me hang them here to remind me of home. I don't usually get homesick, but some days, I long to see my relatives."

"I suppose it's hard raising Nicky on your own," I ventured. I had to tread carefully; I didn't want to risk offending her, or she'd clam up. "Without family around to guide him, I mean."

"I do my best to lead him on the right path," she said softly. "He's a good boy. Don't believe what you might have heard about him. He wants to be an electrician. Next year, he's going to take classes and get a two-year degree, and that will start him on his way. As an electrician, he can always find work."

"Yes, he can," I agreed. It was oddly quiet and peaceful in the kitchen with the sun streaming in the large windows over the sink. They looked like a recent renovation with double-paned glass.

"Did you know they haven't released her body yet?" Lucy asked suddenly. For the first time, a flash of anger crept into her dark eyes. "We can't even plan a proper funeral."

"I know," I said, nodding. "It's very sad. It might take a few days." I paused; the house seemed unnaturally still, and I wondered if Lucy was the only person living here. But hadn't someone mentioned a summer student? And where was Jeb Arnold, the estate manager?

As if she had read my thoughts, she said, "It's quiet here today. Angus is doing some research at an art museum in Charleston, and Jeb has gone to visit his sister for a few days."

"Angus . . . ?" I said innocently.

"Angus Morton. Mrs. Marchand invited him here for the summer to catalog the paintings and antiques." She raised her eyebrows and her mouth twisted in a little grimace. "Mrs. Marchand was, how do you say it? Generous to a fault."

I nodded, and I wondered what she was hinting at. It was obvious she didn't like this Angus fellow, and I wondered why. "Is he working for free?' I said, hoping I could keep her talking. "Or is this connected to his studies?"

"She pays him a small salary and he gets to live here for

free." She made a sweeping motion with her arm that encompassed the kitchen and the sun-dappled garden I could see from the bay window. "And yes, you're right. He gets some sort of college credit for it. I suppose it's a trade-off, you could say." She sniffed. I knew I was on to something. Lucy really didn't like Angus or didn't trust him. But why?

"If he's coming home later today, I'd love to meet him," I ventured.

Immediately, her eyes were shuttered. She had a nervous tic I'd never noticed before, a strange little twitch to her mouth. "Why would you want to do that?" she said bluntly. There was definitely a frostiness in her tone.

"Well," I said, thinking quickly, "Ali and I found some old pieces of china in the basement of our candy shop. A few dishes and serving pieces. I think they were left there by a previous tenant at the turn of the century." I forced myself to smile. "Who knows, they might be valuable. Maybe Angus could tell me."

"Maybe," she said grudgingly. "But trust me, he doesn't know as much as he pretends to. Mr. Big Shot." She snorted. She got up and reached for some ice cubes from the freezer and tossed them into the pitcher of sweet tea on the table. Even with the Casablanca fan whirring, it seemed warm in the kitchen, and I lifted my hair up off my neck for a moment.

I wondered why she didn't like Angus. Did she resent having extra work to do and one more person to cook for? I wondered what the terms of the arrangement were and if he would be staying on for the rest of the summer, even though Abigail had passed away. I took a good look at Lucy. She had a small but muscular frame, and it occurred to me that she could easily push a frail old lady down the stairs. But what would be her motive?

"He acts like a big shot? In what way?" I asked pleasantly.

She let out a little puff of air before sitting down again. She placed her hands on the table in front of her, almost as if she were reaching out to me, a clear sign that she wanted me to believe whatever came next.

"Angus says things are missing from Beaux Reves," she said sullenly. "And he thinks my son took them. I've been working here for thirty years. I know this place like the back of my hand. I know what's here and what isn't here."

I sucked in a little breath. I never thought she would be this forthcoming about Nicky. I remembered what Noah had said about the kid's record in juvie, and it was certainly possible that he was up to his old tricks. Lucy's lips had thinned when she mentioned Angus. She was clearly defensive about her son, but was she also in denial? How far would she go to protect him? Would she kill?

"Why in the world would Angus suspect your son of theft?" I tried to inject a note of surprise into my voice. "I'm sure your son is a wonderful young man," I said as sincerely as I could.

Lucy shrugged and gave a dismissive wave with her hand. "He's a good boy," she said, not making eye contact. "He had a little trouble in the past, that's all. It was nothing. He had some friends I wasn't too crazy over, and I think they set him up." She was still staring at the breakfast bar as though she had never seen it before. If Noah were here, he would surely take this as evidence she was lying. She wouldn't make eye contact with me.

She finally looked up, but I stayed silent, hoping she would say more. "You know I would never let anything happen to Mrs. Marchand's belongings," she said in a wheedling tone. "I take care of them like they're my own."

I tried not to raise my eyebrows at that last statement. With millions of dollars coming her way, maybe she really did think of Beaux Reves as her own private paradise. I wanted to find a way to poke around upstairs to see if I could find any evidence of a diary or at least a date book, but Lucy glanced pointedly at her watch and stood up. Teatime was over.

I thanked her and drove back the long winding drive, more puzzled than ever. The sun was high in the sky, making interesting patterns through the live oak leaves lining the road. I squinted against the bright sunlight and hummed along with the radio that was tuned to an oldies rock station. Bobby McFerrin was urging everyone not to worry and to be happy. I sang along with him, so happy that I'd deliberately "forgotten" my sunglasses on the hall table.

6

"So you didn't find out anything?" Ali asked later that afternoon. She'd met me at the Riverwalk, and we planned to stroll for a bit and then head over to the lawyer's office. I'd had quite a time trying to convince Norman Osteroff's secretary to grant us a quick appointment. It was a Sunday and Osteroff had ordered his secretary to meet him there for a few hours to take a deposition. I had to fib and say that one of our friends—Sara Rutledge—was planning to write a feature on Beaux Reves for the *Savannah Herald*, and we were helping her with her research.

Whether or not he would believe my story was up for grabs. I'd heard that Osteroff had the reputation of being one of Savannah's shrewdest lawyers, and I was afraid he'd see right through my plan, but I was out of ideas. I hoped he wouldn't call the newspaper and ask to speak to Sara's editor. I'm sure he has the money and clout to be put right through to the publisher, if he wanted to. This was worst-case scenario, of course. One phone call from Osteroff to the newspaper, and Ali and I would be toast.

"Nothing really useful," I answered Ali. I told her about Angus, the graduate student, and Jeb, the estate manager who was out of town. "Lucy was just rattling around in that big house all by herself. She seems to be taking Abigail's death very hard, but it's difficult to know. And she admitted that her son has had some problems in the past. She made a big deal out of defending him. Blamed it all on bad companions." I remembered how Lucy's eyes had darkened when I questioned her about the thefts Angus had reported. How far would a mother go to protect her son?

Ali stopped dead in her tracks, and I nearly crashed into her. "We might be standing right on the spot where Desiree tumbled into the water," Ali said solemnly, glancing down into dark blue water. The river was sparkling in the bright Savannah sunlight, but the beauty of the scene was wasted on Ali.

Ali's voice was low and soft, her eyes filled with shadows. "She could have been walking right about here. I can just imagine her, young and beautiful with everything to live for . . ." Her voice trailed off and she stared at a tanker that was docked nearby. Ali's thoughts can take a melancholy turn from time to time, and I tucked my arm through hers to hurry her along the walkway. "No more dark thoughts, okay?" I said, patting her hand. She gave me a tremulous smile and nodded.

It was the perfect day to lunch outdoors, and the umbrella tables at the riverfront restaurants were packed with tourists. But Ali wasn't watching the tourists eating ice-cream cones in the bright Georgia sunlight or taking in the sweet scent of magnolias. Her mind was reaching back to a lovely young girl in a white slip dress who died before her time.

"It's sad, isn't it?" She blinked and looked at me. "First Desiree and now Abigail."

"Yes, it is. But, Ali, the best thing we can do right now is focus on finding Abigail's killer," I said briskly. "And who knows, maybe we'll finally know what happened to Desiree, too. We can't lose sight of our goal."

"I know you're right," she said, falling into step with me. "Let's give old Norman a run for his money. He certainly can't stonewall two of us, can he?"

Stonewall us? He could and he did. Norman Osteroff is a world-class stonewaller. It was obvious from the get-go that he wasn't buying the notion that Ali and I were visiting him on a "fact-finding" mission.

He waved us to a seat in his luxurious office and his geriatric, blue-haired receptionist—who was as frosty as he was—offered us a cold drink. I declined, only because he looked so annoyed and clearly wanted us out of there as soon as possible. Ali asked for an iced tea, and the receptionist allowed herself a brief eye roll, and then quietly left to get one.

I settled into a comfortable red leather chair with brass tacks and admired the fine furnishings—a huge mahogany desk, Oriental rugs in muted shades of Wedgwood blue and pale yellow, a Queen Anne sideboard piled high with manila files. Osteroff reminded me of a character from another century, and I wondered if he insisted on using paper files. Certainly legal offices had all gone to computers, hadn't they? *How can they research case law without access to LexisNexis?* But there wasn't a computer in sight. *Odd.*

The walls were dotted with lovely oil paintings, Impressionist landscapes and street scenes from the Historic District. There was a charming watercolor of Waving Girl, the statue of Florence Martus that graces the Savannah Harbor; it was hanging right next to a small watercolor of Beaux Reves.

I wondered if it was a gift from Abigail. The painting depicted the mansion and gardens on a sun-dappled day with puffs of white clouds dotting a turquoise sky. The shutters were thrown open and a profusion of yellow and white roses spilled out of sandstone vases next to the front door. Osteroff saw me glancing at the paintings and cleared his throat.

"We promise not to take up much of your time," I said apologetically as he looked at his watch and scowled. Mr. Congeniality, he wasn't. I wondered how Abigail had put up with him all these years and then reminded myself that he must have treated her very differently from the way he was treating us. After all, she was his star client, and I was sure she'd provided a handsome income for him over the years.

"Just a few quick questions," Ali promised. Her friendly grin was lost on the straitlaced lawyer, who looked like he hadn't cracked a smile in thirty years. In his stiff white collar and black suit, he reminded me of a cross between Ebenezer Scrooge and an undertaker. Not a good visual. Rose Harper always says that Ali could "charm the pants off a honeybee," but this time she had her work cut out for her.

"I have a two o'clock," he said petulantly. "So if you can be brief . . ." He was tapping a fountain pen on a datebook, and I noticed he checked his watch and jotted down the time of our arrival. By reading upside down, I managed to learn that his daily calendar was divided into ten-minute increments. I wondered what it would be like to track your activities every ten minutes, all day long. *Crazy-making, that's what it would be like.*

When I was doing my MBA, I had a professor who

recommended this strategy as a great way to track your productivity, but I could never handle it. And Ali, free spirit that she is, would never manage it, either. Measuring out our lives in ten-minute spoonfuls would drive us both insane. We'd probably already squandered two or three minutes of our allotted time with the stone-faced lawyer, so I figured we'd better get straight to the point.

"You told my secretary you're here about an article," he said, jumping in ahead of me. He had remained standing, which was a little disconcerting. Either it was some sort of power play or he hoped he could nudge us out the door more quickly this way.

"Yes," I said brightly. "Our good friend Sara Rutledge is a reporter, and she's doing a piece on Beaux Reves. Now that Abigail has passed away"—I paused and bowed my head for a second—"we thought you might be able to fill in some details."

"Why in the world would you think that?" he asked churlishly. He glanced out the window for a moment—his office was on the tenth floor, and he had an excellent view of the Historic District—and then sank into his desk chair. He picked up the old-timey fountain pen again, thought better of it, and put it back down on the leather-topped desk.

I noticed it had faint nibble marks on the tip and wondered if this was his secret vice—nibbling on pen tips. Maybe this was his version of squeezing a stress ball. He looked so rigid and controlled, it was hard to imagine him ever suffering from stress or anxiety.

"Well, you've probably known her longer than most people," I ventured. "So that gives you a unique perspective on her and on Beaux Reves."

"That may be true," he said curtly. "But all the more reason to protect her legacy and honor her wishes." He shook his head from side to side in a quick, nervous gesture. "If Abigail were with us today, she never would have granted an interview to your friend. She refused all media requests, and in her later years, she rarely left the estate. And one thing she made clear—she loathed reporters."

He gave a little snort of satisfaction and then leaned forward, shooting me a keen look. "I'm surprised you're not aware of this, Ms. Blake. It makes me wonder how well the two of you really knew Abigail."

I exchanged a look with Ali. I was fairly certain that Norman had Googled us, discovered we owned a vintage candy shop on Clark Street, and probably knew our net worth down to the last dollar. We obviously weren't part of his social scene. He probably thought of us as carpetbaggers. We were newcomers to Savannah, didn't have a fancy pedigree, and certainly weren't old money. I bet not much got by those glacial blue eyes. I remember the shrewd look he shot at us the day of the luncheon; his eyes had been cold and unblinking. I bet he didn't miss a trick.

The receptionist returned with Ali's iced tea. Ali took a tiny, delicate sip and then put the glass on a coaster. I glanced at Osteroff and nearly laughed. It was all he could do to restrain himself. He began drumming his fingers on the tabletop, frowning.

"What is it you want to know?" He gave a strangely feral smile that was probably intended to be gracious but missed the mark. He had obviously decided it was smarter to throw us a few crumbs to get out us out of his office. "Something about Beaux Reves, you said?" He looked ancient in the harsh sunlight streaming in the window, and his voice was querulous, an old man's voice. It suddenly occurred to me that he might be older than I'd originally thought, and might even be a contemporary of Abigail.

"Yes, anything you can tell us would be helpful," I said, reaching into my tote bag and pulling out a notebook. "Anything about the mansion itself, or perhaps the Marchand family."

He sat back, plunked his elbow on the desk, and stroked his chin. "Well, you can find out anything you need to about the history and the décor of the mansion in Savannah guide books," he said swiftly. "You don't need me to rehash all that." Ali looked at me and raised her eyebrows. *Uh-oh.* This was going to be harder than I'd thought.

"No, we don't," I said agreeably. "But as for the Marchand family—" I began, and he cut me off.

"I have a question for you, Ms. Blake," he said, pointing his pen at me as if it were a lethal weapon. "Why did Abigail invite you for lunch with her? She mentioned that you were new in town, but that's all she said. The woman could be damn secretive when she wanted to be," he added peevishly.

Ali quickly explained about the Harper sisters, their long friendship with Abigail, and the desire for "new blood" in the Magnolia Society.

Osteroff allowed himself a small chuckle. "So she tried to rope you into volunteer work?" he asked. "She was always good at getting people to do things for her. Then she'd take the credit." He'd broken off eye contact, and seemed lost in thought, staring out the window again.

"So you know about the Magnolia Society?" I asked, hoping he would reveal more details.

"Yes, of course I do. I did the legal work to get them recognized as a legitimate charity. We wanted to make sure all the donations were tax-deductible. That was years ago." He turned back to face us. He'd obviously forgotten about his packed schedule because he crossed his legs and settled back as if he was ready for a chat. "I figured it was just another one of Abigail's impulsive decisions, but she was dead set on establishing the group and keeping it going."

"It's a philanthropic society, right?"

"That's what she liked to think." He cackled. "Actually, it's a bunch of old dears with too much time on their hands. And more money than they know how to spend."

Ali sneaked a look at me and I could read her thoughts. Neither one of us had expected this snarkiness from the old-timey lawyer. I wondered if they could have had a falling-out shortly before her death or if there was some long-standing resentment on his part.

"Did she ask you for a donation?"

I shook my head. "Not money, just our time. And she even backed off on that once she realized . . ." I stopped, wishing I could take back the words.

"Once she realized what?" Osteroff leaned forward so quickly in his chair, he nearly catapulted himself onto the desktop.

Ali bit her lip. "Once she realized she'd be around long enough to handle the Society's business herself."

Osteroff was either a good actor or he was genuinely surprised. "Why wouldn't she be around? Her parents lived well into their nineties. She came from good stock. I don't think the woman was ever sick a day in her life."

"She never mentioned any premonitions to you?"

"Premonitions? Like what?"

"Abigail was having nightmares," I explained. "She was dreaming about her own death. She was sure she was going to die sometime soon and she wanted to make sure the Magnolia Society would continue on without her."

"This is news to me," Osteroff said. "Dreaming of her own death? Abigail was a sensible woman." He snorted. "At least more sensible than those silly friends of hers in their orthopedic shoes. Those sisters with the flower shop." I knew he was referring to the Harper sisters, and I bristled. "I never figured Abigail would be the type to get caught up in such nonsense." This time he stood up and looked pointedly at his watch.

"Do you know anything about a distant relative suddenly turning up?" Ali asked. "Someone she hadn't seen in years?"

"No." His voice was tense, clipped. "Now, if there's nothing else . . ."

"How well did you know Desiree Marchand?" I asked him. It was a shot in the dark, but it found its mark.

"Desiree was the younger sister of Abigail," he said curtly. "She was a lovely young woman, and she drowned several years ago." His tone was as flat as the Savannah River on a calm day, not a ripple anywhere. Another pointed glance at his watch. "There's no mystery there, if that's what you're thinking." No mystery? Interesting that he would choose that word. I hadn't said a word about a mystery.

"No, of course not," I said. "I just thought Sara—our friend—might like to add something about Desiree to the article. Abigail never mentioned her to us."

"I'm sure it was a painful topic for her," he said shortly. "I don't think she ever fully recovered from her sister's death. And now if you'll excuse me—"

Right on cue, the elderly assistant knocked once and poked her head in the door. "Your two o'clock is here, Mr. Osteroff." She stood in the doorway, holding the door open, clearly ready to usher us out.

"Thank you for your time." I stood up while Ali took a last gulp of her iced tea. I picked up my purse and then paused when I spotted a set of framed photographs of horses on the far wall. The horses were sleek, with gleaming coats, grazing in a lush green pasture. They looked like Arabians, but I'm no expert. "You raise horses?" I asked, surprised. I hadn't figured Osteroff for an animal lover.

"My wife's expensive hobby," he said with a wry smile. "I've never owned a pet in my life, but I have to admit, these horses have grown on me. They're beautiful animals, aren't they?" He looked fondly at a picture of an attractive forty-something blonde holding the reins of a large chestnut horse. *Trophy wife?* "That's Elyse with Thunderbolt," he said proudly. "She's teaching me how to groom him. Maybe raising horses will be my retirement hobby some day."

I smiled. It was hard to picture Norman Osteroff in jeans and a work shirt, wielding a currycomb. Would the high-powered lawyer, with his tony office and well-heeled clientele, slip off into retirement at a horse farm? I seriously doubted it. And with that, our meeting was over.

T

"So it was definitely murder?" Ali and I were grabbing a late lunch with Noah. Since it was a picture-postcard Savannah day, and we couldn't bear to go inside, Noah bought muffalettas for us to eat in Forsythe Square. The tasty treats, with their distinctive layer of marinated olives, originated in New Orleans but have become popular in Savannah. I dashed to an outdoor vendor and bought three large fresh lemonades for us before we settled on a wrought iron bench near the famous fountain.

"I'm afraid so."

He handed us our sandwiches, and Ali opened the wax paper to peer at hers suspiciously. "Mine is vegetarian, I hope."

"Always." Noah grinned at her. Noah is almost as close to Ali as I am and plays the role of protective big brother with her. "I know the drill. No salami, no ham, and they doubled up on the provolone and the mozzarella for you."

"Perfect," she said. "This is heaven." She smiled, tucking into her sandwich.

"Now, time to get down to business," Noah said. He took a big drink of lemonade. "And a sad business it is. According to the ME, there's no doubt that Abigail was pushed." He glanced at me.

"You're sure?" I suppose I still found it hard to believe anyone would kill Abigail.

"The coroner is sure," Noah replied. "And the police chief agrees. That's good enough for me."

"I wonder how they decide something like that," Ali said, her brow furrowed.

Noah hesitated for a moment. "Taylor, I'll send you the crime scene photos and you'll see why they came to that conclusion. There are certain details . . ." He nodded his head toward Ali, who was busily breaking off crumbs of bread and tossing them to a robin that was hopping in front of us. This wasn't the time or place for gory descriptions. "How did you do with Osteroff?" he asked, changing the subject.

"We didn't get anywhere, I'm afraid. He clammed up when we asked about Desiree and couldn't wait to get us out of his office. You might have done better." I like to give credit where credit is due.

Noah is a first-rate interviewer, and I am always amazed at what he picks up on—the slightest hint of a frown on a suspect's face, a nuance in the voice, or even an obvious "tell." Noah taught me be to be aware of body language and facial expressions. A suspect who's lying might unconsciously send a mixed message to an interviewer. Sometimes people say no, but unconsciously nod their heads up and down in a *yes* gesture. It's a strange phenomenon, and I've noticed it several times since Noah first mentioned it. Now I watch for it all the time.

"Not necessarily. He's one of the best lawyers in town, and he has the reputation of holding his cards close to his vest. People may not like him, but they respect him."

"Osteroff isn't all bad," Ali piped up. "He likes horses."

Noah laughed. "Well, then he does have some redeeming features. How did he happen to mention horses?" I explained that his trophy wife raised what looked like Arabian horses and Osteroff seemed to have a soft spot for them. "Any leads on the mystery houseguest?"

"Not a word. All the Harper sisters could tell us was she's called Sophie Stanton and she popped up out of nowhere. I'm not even sure what the relationship is to Abigail. Abigail did tell Minerva once about a long-standing family feud and it seems the European relatives were estranged from the Americans for quite some time. Maybe even decades."

"Don't you think it's odd that she suddenly turned up now?" Noah asked.

"Very," I replied. "I'm not really sure what to make of it. We asked Osteroff about her, but he denied even knowing her. He pretended he didn't know what we were talking about. Now that Abigail is gone, I don't think anyone in town would even recognize her. Is there any way you could check her out for us?"

"I could run her name through a couple of databases," Noah offered, "but unless she has a driver's license or something to connect her to Savannah, I don't know what I'll find. She may not even be using her real name. Sophie Stanton, you said?"

"Yes. I'll double-check with the Harper sisters tonight. I wonder if Stanton is her maiden name or her married name. I guess we could start there."

"And she came over from Europe?"

"South of France, I believe." I closed my eyes for a moment

and leaned back, enjoying the warm sunshine on my face. It was so calm and peaceful with the gurgling fountain and the songbirds in the magnolia trees. If I'd been sitting here alone, I think I would have dozed off. Instead I sat up, blinked a couple of times, and blew out a little puff of air, determined to shake off my fatigue. We were smack in the middle of a murder investigation, and I had to stay focused.

"Then she must have a passport," Noah said. "I've got some friends over at the State Department. I can ask someone in the Bureau of Consular Affairs to check it out for us." Noah has a strong network of friends in high places, and I'm always impressed by his ability to access information so swiftly.

"Let's recap," he continued. "Did anyone ever meet Nicky Dargos, Lucy's son?"

I shook my head. "He was out when I called at Beaux Reves, and he wasn't around the day we had lunch there. I can ask the Harper sisters if they've met him, but I doubt it. I think they would have mentioned it."

"And no one's met this Angus fellow, the grad student."

"No, and I'm really eager to talk to him." I thought fast, remembering I'd asked Lucy if he might like to take a look at some of our basement "finds." "Lucy wasn't too keen on my meeting him even when I told her I'd pay him to appraise some china we'd found in the basement of the shop."

"What china?" Ali said, feeding the last of the bread to the robin.

"There isn't any. I just said that to get my foot in the door with him."

"That's not a bad idea," Noah said, and there was a look of admiration on his face. "Good thinking, Taylor. I'd do it sooner rather than later, if you can swing it. Don't wait for Lucy to set up a meeting; do it yourself."

"I don't have any contact information," I said doubtfully.

"He must have a cell phone," Noah said, pulling out a tablet. "Angus Morton?" I nodded and his fingers raced over the screen. "Got it," he said a moment later and turned to me. "I texted it to you."

"What if he asks me how I got his phone number?"

"You'll think of something; you're creative." He stood up, finished up the last of his lemonade. "So do we have a plan?"

"We do," I agreed. "I need some face time with Nicky Dargos and Angus Morton."

"And I'm going to find out some more about this mysterious relative, Sophie Stanton," Noah said. "Is she really a long-lost relative, or is she a scam artist?"

"She's out of town at the moment, according to the housekeeper, but I suppose she'll have to come back eventually." I paused. "I wonder why she didn't come rushing back the moment she realized Abigail had died. It makes me think they weren't that close, after all. The whole situation is strange."

"She'll have to return to Savannah at some point. We'll probably meet her at Abigail's funeral," Ali said. "If she's really a relative and she's staying at Beaux Reves, it would look pretty odd if she didn't show up."

"It would definitely raise some eyebrows. I can't wait to have a chat with her," Noah said, his eyes darkening.

"My dream was very strange. I felt like I was trapped in an Agatha Christie novel." Minerva paused to take a tiny bite of an éclair. Chocolate éclairs are a new item on the café menu, and I wondered how they would hold up in the refrigerator overnight. The pastry was so thin and flaky that we might have to make them fresh each day.

I turned my attention back to Minerva. The Dream Club

was in session, again; we needed to meet daily to keep up with all the new developments in the case. Minerva had asked to go first that evening. The summer heat was still bearing down on us, even though the sun had set, and I'd made extra pitchers of sweet tea to serve with the brownies and éclairs.

"An Agatha Christie novel? It sounds like fun. Which one was it?" Persia jumped in. Persia is a great Agatha Christie fan and is something of an expert on the famous mystery writer.

"And Then There Were None," Minerva replied. "Her most popular book, I believe."

"I read that book. She said it was the most difficult book of her career," Ali said softly. "Interesting that you would think of that, Minerva. I wonder what the significance could be?"

"Yes, but what's the connection with the dream?" Dorien asked. "Do you mean someone mentioned the book in your dream, or—"

"No, no one mentioned it," Minerva said firmly. "But the name of the book just flew through my mind. In my dream, I was saying it over and over to myself, under my breath, like a mantra."

"It sounds odd and a little sinister," Sybil offered. "What was the mood of the dream? Did you have a sense of fore-boding?" I'd learned from Ali that it's best to focus on the emotional content of the dream. It's more reliable than the actual details. When someone in the Dream Club recounts a dream, I listen very carefully for any underlying emotions—desire, fear, anxiety, or happiness.

"Yes, a very strong sense of foreboding," Minerva con-tinued. Her voice wobbled a little, and she gave a nervous laugh, touching her throat. "It's odd, but the feeling is still with me. I felt that something dreadful was going to happen from the moment I pulled open these giant oak doors. They looked almost medieval, with black hardware, the kind of door you would see in a castle with a moat. I stepped inside and found myself standing in a great hall with dark wood paneling and high ceilings. A very fancy floor, some sort of mosaic tile."

"It sounds like a museum," Lucinda said under her breath. I glanced at her and wondered if she was thinking of a particular building in Savannah.

"I was surrounded by a circle of women, and there was a lively conversation going on. I didn't recognize anyone in the group, and I was wondering how I should introduce myself"—she paused dramatically—"when it happened."

"When *what* happened?" Sybil asked.

"The women started disappearing," Minerva said breathlessly. "One by one."

"What do you mean 'disappearing'?" Dorien's tone was brusque. She picked up an éclair with her napkin, scrutinized it as though she were examining a counterfeit bill, and then replaced it on the serving tray. Dorien is persnickety about everything, especially food. She's struggling to make a living from her catering business, and I sometimes wonder if she's jealous of our success with our little café downstairs.

"I can't explain it," Minerva said, "but I knew the women were dying off. One by one, their images would grow fainter; each woman would turn into a shadow and then she would disappear completely."

"Did the women speak to you?" Persia asked. "Did any of them reach out to you for help?"

"Not a word. And no one made a move toward me. I'm not even sure they realized I was there." Minerva hesitated. "I had the sense that all this had taken place a long time ago. There was nothing I could do in the present to help them. It seemed sad but inevitable." She turned to Ali. "Does this make sense to you?"

"Yes, it does," Ali said in a gentle voice. "Time and space have no meaning in dreams, so we can easily visit a scene from the past. Somehow we know it's the past even though no one spells it out for us. There's a sense of distance, as if what we're seeing and experiencing took place in another time."

"These women," Ali asked, "how were they dressed?"

"Oh, they were very well dressed, in bright colors and heels. They looked like socialites."

"Socialites?" Dorien snorted. She has had a hardscrabble life, and she often makes jabs at anyone she considers to be in a higher social class. "You mean a bunch of stuck-up snobs?"

Minerva shook her head. "No, that's not what I mean at all. They were dressed the way people used to dress for cocktail parties."

"No one really dresses up much anymore," her sister Rose chimed in. "Just last month, I saw someone wearing jeans to a concert at the Savannah Philharmonic. Can you imagine? And the jeans looked like they were spray-painted on her. She was wearing a blazer over them, but still, in my day, we were taught to dress for the occasion. My mother would have had a conniption if I'd gone to a symphony dressed like that. I would have been grounded for weeks."

"We were raised in a different time, my dear," Minerva said, reaching over to pat her hand.

"Who has an interpretation for Minerva?" Ali asked brightly. I wondered who would speak up; this was one of the most difficult dreams we'd been called on to analyze. I was completely stumped and didn't have anything to contribute.

"Are you sure you're not leaving something out?" Dorien

asked bluntly. I wished she hadn't worded it quite that way, but Dorien is not known for her tact. Minerva is forgetful, and we all knew she may have omitted a key element, but I would have said it more gently.

"Just one other thing," Minerva said. "There was a little gold box in the dream. It looked like it might be something you keep jewelry in. It was sitting on a pedestal table. From time to time, the women would glance over at it, and I wondered what it contained."

"Minerva," I said suddenly. "You said that you kept thinking of the title of the Agatha Christie novel, *And Then There Were None*. That must be related to the dream in some way. Did all the women really disappear?"

Minerva smiled. "Not quite. At the end of the dream, there was one woman left in the circle. She walked right past me as if I was invisible and picked up the gold box. She smiled as she lifted the lid . . ."

"Yes," Lucinda said breathlessly. "And then . . ."

"And then I woke up." Minerva gave an apologetic smile. "So now I'll never know what would have happened next."

"And neither will we." Dorien snorted.

"You might be able to return to the dream some night, if you concentrate hard enough," Sybil suggested.

Minerva shook her head. "I know some people can do that, but I've never been able to." She made a little fluttery motion with her hands. "I wish I could give you more to go on, but that's all I have."

We were all silent for a moment, and Ali pulled Barney onto her lap. The gray tabby had been circling the coffee table even though he knows he's not allowed to sample—or even sniff—the goodies. He immediately started purring and pushed himself against her. His calico companion, Scout, was snoozing on the windowsill.

"I have to admit, I'm stumped," Etta Mae said. "I'm new to this whole dream interpretation thing, and I'm just not getting anything from this one. Were the women real or were they supposed to be ghosts? Maybe they were murdered," she said uncertainly. "But I guess that doesn't make sense, either."

"I'm not sure," Minerva said, giving a little shrug. "I just know that I felt helpless standing there, as if I were watching a scene from the past. It had this awful sense of inevitability, and I knew there was nothing I could do to change the outcome." She paused and the room was very still. "I think all the women were dead."

"You mean all except the very last one, holding the gold box," Rose offered.

Minerva nodded. "Yes, you're right, my dear. All except one."

8

A few people asked Minerva more questions about the dream, but after a little while, it was obvious that we weren't going to come up with any useful interpretations. Minerva couldn't think of anything in her everyday life that would prompt such a dream, and her sister Rose couldn't add anything to the discussion. Everyone was baffled.

We decided to move on and tackle Lucinda Macavy's dream. "I was standing at the Savannah port," she began, "and I met a woman carrying a suitcase. It was an old-fashioned suitcase, not like the modern ones with wheels. This was a beat-up tan leather suitcase, and it had decals stuck all over it. It looked like the handle was half off and she was struggling to carry it."

"Decals?" Persia asked. "What do you mean?"

"Travel decals. I guess they were all places the woman had traveled to." She shrugged. "I think people used to do that. In the old days, travel was a big thing. It wasn't as commonplace as it is today."

"I remember that from my grandmother's day," Sybil offered. "Was the dream set in the past?"

"Oh no, it was in the present day," Lucinda said. "I'm sure of that because I was standing outside the Riverfront Café. I recognized the umbrella tables." She paused as Ali passed the éclairs. "The woman greeted me, said she was new to Savannah. She added that she could really use a friend."

"A stranger comes up to you on the docks and says she really needs a friend?" Dorien gave a harsh laugh. "That would be enough to make me suspicious right off the bat. I bet she wanted to steal something or involve you in some scam."

"Not necessarily," Etta Mae jumped in. "Lots of Southern folks are friendly, you know. My aunt Tillie was like that. She liked to say that she never met a stranger. If you stopped by her house, you were invited in for sweet tea and cookies, whether she knew you or not."

"My grandmother was the same way," Persia exclaimed. "She invited perfect strangers for Thanksgiving dinner with her because she couldn't stand the thought of them eating alone."

I exchanged a look with Ali. Things were getting off track, but I knew Ali could rein the discussion back in. When you have a small group of friends meeting every week in a Dream Club, it's very tempting to slide off topic and just chat. It's Ali's job to make sure that doesn't happen.

"But getting back to your dream, Lucinda," Ali said gently.

"Oh yes, the dream." Lucinda reached for a coaster and carefully set her sweet tea on it. "I didn't really know what to make of it. After she said she needed a friend, she just stared out into the water. She was talking under her breath, but her words weren't really directed at me. It was as though she was talking to herself."

"Did you recognize anything she was saying?" Rose Harper asked.

"I think they were Bible verses," Lucinda replied. "One was 'The last shall be first and the first, last.'"

"What in the world does that mean?" Etta Mae asked.

Lucinda shook her head. "I have no idea. And she said something else, 'Many are called but few are chosen.'" She looked around the group. "Does anyone have any ideas?"

"Tell us a bit more. What did she look like and how old was she?" Persia asked.

"Youngish, I'd say midthirties. Quite attractive with blue eyes and strawberry blond hair. I suppose you'd say she was a 'looker.' She certainly attracted some male attention as she strolled along with her suitcase."

"I'm afraid I'm drawing a blank," I said after a couple of minutes. "I can't come up with anything."

The woman in the dream didn't resemble Desiree, who was spotted in a white silk slip dress, swinging her high heels with one hand. And I had no idea what the suitcase signified. It sounded like something from years gone by. I was interested in the quote about a few being "chosen." What were they chosen for? A political office? A club? None of it made sense to me.

After a few more desultory comments, Sybil offered one of her dream-hopping episodes. She had traveled back in history and found herself in a gorgeous early nineteenth–century mansion, Château Malmaison in Paris. "It was fascinating," she began. "You probably remember that Josephine built the place for herself and Napoleon. She assumed he would be delighted, but at first he was quite angry with her. He was outraged at the expense."

"Just like a man," Dorien sniped.

Sybil ignored her and went on, her eyes sparkling. "Josephine was sleeping in this enormous bed with an elaborate headboard, dreaming about the improvements she was going to make to the mansion. It was quite run-down when she bought it. She was going to add formal gardens and a greenhouse with hundreds of pineapple plants. Pineapples were practically unknown in Europe at that time and were considered exotic. Wealthy people used to serve them for dessert."

"I've been to Malmaison; the gardens are beautiful," Lucinda offered. "We took our seniors to Paris a few years ago." Lucinda looked wistful, as though she missed her position as headmistress at the academy. "Oh, I didn't mean to interrupt," she said, fluttering her hands. "Please go on, Sybil."

Sybil nodded and continued. "Josephine planned on doing a lot of entertaining and she wanted Malmaison to be a showplace for the whole country. Her mind was full of wonderful images and exciting plans. It was one of the most vivid, colorful dreams I've ever had." She sat back and rested her hands in her lap, a look of contentment on her face.

"I still can't get over the fact that you can jump into another person's dreams," Etta Mae said. "I don't think I'll ever get to that stage."

"Not many people do," Persia said enviously. "Sybil has a special talent, a gift."

"Can you tell me how you do it?" Etta Mae went on, her tone full of admiration.

"I can't explain it. I've done it since I was a child," Sybil said simply. "When I was nine, I caused quite a scandal because I found myself in Ms. Sharpton's dream—she was my homeroom teacher—and she was dreaming about Mr. Robertson, the math teacher. I was foolish enough to tell a couple of my friends. And you can imagine how fast word got around. I should have kept my big mouth shut."

"Oh my, what happened?" Lucinda asked. As the former headmistress of a girls' school, she was keenly interested in the outcome. "I hope you weren't punished."

"Not really," Sybil said with a smile. "Everyone thought I'd made it up, of course, and no one believed I had this talent. I was told to stop spreading gossip, and the principal threatened to put a written reprimand in my chart if it happened again." She chuckled. "The funny thing is that Ms. Sharpton and Mr. Robertson got married a year later. They each divorced their spouses, and no one suspected they'd been having an affair."

Ali glanced at her watch. "Unless someone has another dream . . ." she began.

"Oh, I think we'll call it a night," Minerva said, rising slowly. "We still have to do some wreaths for the Cooper funeral tomorrow morning."

"That we do," Rose said, joining her. "We should have done it this morning, but somehow the day just slipped away." The Harper sisters own Petals, a flower shop that has been in business for almost fifty years. They never advertise and seem to rely on word of mouth to attract new customers.

When I first moved to Savannah, I thought maybe Ali and I could run some joint promotions with them, but I quickly realized they seem to do only funerals. A few wreaths and a potted plant here and there for the dearly departed and their loved ones. The sisters managed to eke out a living but watched their pennies carefully.

"Don't forget this," Ali said, handing them a package of baked goods from our shop wrapped in tinfoil. The Harpers don't cook anymore, and I think they appreciate having some homemade items in the house. Ali saw Rose looking at the leftover brownies and quickly wrapped them up to add to the bag. "Enjoy," Ali said softly as Rose smiled her thanks.

The Dream Club meeting was over, and I mulled over what we had learned. The disappearing women, the mysterious gold box, and the strange woman at the docks carrying an old-fashioned suitcase. Was any of this related to Abigail's death? Or Desiree's? Ali would say it all was related, if only we knew how to put the clues together.

9

The next day dawned bright and clear and I woke to the enticing smell of hazelnut coffee. Ali always brews a pot just for me, even though she's a tea drinker. We took our mugs downstairs to touch base with Dana, our amazing assistant. Dana was dreaming up plans for yet another window display. The fifties display had gone over well and she was toying with the idea of hiring live models the next time.

"Live models?" I said, astonished. I pulled up a stool at the counter, enjoying the way the shop looked in the early morning hours. The display bins were gleaming, everything was polished to perfection, and the sunlight was slanting across the oak floor. "Do you mean they'll pretend to be mannequins?"

"Yes, exactly! I spent a summer in Atlanta and one of my friends did a department store window display with students from the local college. They didn't charge much, and all they had to do was hold a pose for twenty minutes."

"Twenty minutes?" Ali said doubtfully. "I don't know, that sounds like a long time to me."

"It's not like they have to hold their *breath*," Dana teased. "They just have to stand still. Look, it's easy." She struck a saucy pose, with one hip out, her head thrown back, her hand touching her glossy black ponytail. I was amazed that she was absolutely motionless.

"Very eye-catching," I told her. "But are you sure they can do it?"

"I like it. Very cute. It will draw in the tourists," Ali added.

Dana ignored both of us, kept her pose, standing as still as a statue. She didn't even blink. I had to admire her ability to focus.

Barney strolled over and stared at her curiously, probably marveling at the strange antics of his human guardians. He rubbed his whiskery face against Dana's bare leg and tried to nuzzle her shoe, but she still didn't move a muscle. Barney looked up at her, puzzled, his brow furrowed. I glanced at the clock; she'd been motionless for a full minute. *How in the world does she do this?*

"Okay, Dana, you've convinced me." I clapped my hands, startling Barney, who dashed under one of the candy bins. Both Barney and Scout are rescues, and although they're socialized, they still retain some feral ways. Loud noises and shouting tend to freak them out, and they run for cover. Life on the streets must have been challenging for them, and I think they have flashbacks from time to time.

"Sorry, Barney." He stuck his head out from under the bin and I reached down to let him sniff my hand. When he cautiously emerged, I scooped him into my lap for a quick cuddle. "It's okay; everything's fine," I reassured him as he began to purr.

Dana relaxed her pose and grinned. "See? It's easy. Anyone can do it."

"I think you're amazing." Ali reached for a batch of poppy seed muffins we'd made the day before. "I guess these weren't big sellers," she said, peering at them. She lifted out a muffin and tapped it with her finger. "Are these stale?"

"They're not stale," Dana said. "I had one for breakfast. They're better if you put them in the broiler oven for a couple of minutes, though. And go heavy with the butter and jam."

"What do you honestly think of them?" I asked. "Why didn't they move?"

"They're a little dry, that's all." Dana poured herself a cup of coffee and joined us at the counter. "Did you use sour cream in the recipe, Ali?"

Ali flushed. Guilty as charged. Whenever she tries to lighten up a recipe, it's a gamble. I remembered her wheat germ–soy cookies from a few months ago. They were studded with currants and looked like ants on cardboard. I didn't dare serve them to the Dream Club, and we finally fed them to the birds in the back garden. "I tried to do a healthy version with fat-free yogurt. I'm not sure what happened. I wonder what I did wrong."

Dana and I exchanged a look. "I think the substitutions are the problem. You know how folks are down here in Savannah," Dana said apologetically. "You can tweak their recipes, but only up to a point. When you start making too many changes, it doesn't taste like the original. You're bound to get some pushback."

"Dana's right: we're selling nostalgia." I kept my tone soft. I grabbed a muffin and took a bite. Not bad, but not great. Certainly not up to our usual standards. Blueberry, apple streusel, and donut muffins are huge bestsellers for us, and there was no point in offering something that wasn't up to par. "Maybe shelve this recipe for a while," I said, and Dana nodded.

After a quick breakfast and some instructions for Dana, Ali and I set out to track down our leads. When I told Ali we were making a return trip to Beaux Reves, she asked if we should call ahead. I assured her it was better to stage an impromptu visit. The last thing I wanted to do was give Lucy Dargos an excuse not to see us. With any luck, we might also meet Nicky, her son, and Jeb, the estate manager. And who knew, maybe Sophie Stanton had returned from her trip. It was a little early to call on people, but that was all part of my plan.

To say Lucy Dargos, the housekeeper, was unhappy to see us would be an understatement. She was scowling as she answered the door and immediately grabbed my sunglasses from the hall table.

"I found them," she said in a peremptory tone, handing them to me. "I should have called you; I'm so sorry. There was no need for you to come back." She kept her squat frame blocking the doorway. She obviously had no intention of inviting us in, and I could hear noises in the kitchen. And a woman's voice. Perhaps Sophie Stanton was back from her travels?

The smell of freshly brewed coffee wafted down the hall, and I could feel myself salivating. I'm a caffeine addict, no doubt about it, and I hadn't had my quota for the day. Without four cups of coffee, I have brain fog, even though Ali says that's impossible.

"I hope we're not disturbing you," I said, flashing a bright smile.

"Well, I was just serving breakfast . . ." She hesitated,

and I could see she was wrestling with her conscience. Southerners are trained to be hospitable, and not asking us in for coffee would go against the grain.

"Breakfast!" Ali said delightedly. "I was just saying to Taylor that I needed something to eat. I have low blood sugar, you see. When it plummets, I can just faint away with no warning." She raised the back of her hand to her forehead, and I was afraid she was going to swoon right on the spot.

All those college drama classes had finally come in handy. Ali was so convincing with her low-blood-sugar act, she almost had *me* fooled. I think she was reprising her role as Blanche DuBois in *A Streetcar Named Desire*. Like the fragile, overly dramatic Blanche, she depended "on the kindness of strangers." I could only hope that her act was going over well with the stone-faced housekeeper.

"My aunt Delores has diabetes," Lucy said finally, opening the door a little wider. "So I know exactly what you mean. When she gets low blood sugar she passes out, right on the spot. Maybe you should come in and sit down for a spell. And have something to eat with us."

"Oh, that would be lovely," Ali said, sweeping past Lucy into the hall. I just realized Ali had never seen the inside of Beaux Reves, and I could see she was awestruck, taking it all in. The fifteen-foot ceilings, the stunning Art Deco black-and-white tiled floor, the oil paintings in heavy gilt frames lining the wall. The front hall in Beaux Reves is at least five times bigger than my former Chicago condo.

If only I could explore the whole mansion. According to the guide book put out by the Historical Society, Beaux Reves has a ballroom, a solarium, and a formal dining room that can seat fifty people at round tables. And the upstairs bedrooms are supposed to have fireplaces along with private balconies and sitting rooms. I racked my brain but couldn't think of an excuse to zip up there. I wondered if any part of the mansion was considered a crime scene, but no yellow plastic tape was visible in the front hall. The CSIs must have done their work and left.

I was beginning to wish I hadn't acted so impulsively. I'd thought visiting Lucy on the fly was the way to go, but maybe I should have taken some time and come up with a more detailed action plan. Noah always harps on the fact that trained investigators always know exactly what they want to accomplish *before* they meet with a suspect or take a statement. They have an agenda, and they leave nothing to chance. What did I hope to accomplish here today? I'd already used up the forgotten-sunglasses card, and it was unlikely I'd get back in here for another visit. I'd better make this visit count.

I found myself envying Angus Morton, the young grad student, living in the lap of luxury. Of course, maybe his life at the mansion wasn't as luxurious as I imagined? Maybe he spent his days tucked away in some dusty attic, cataloging antiques? Even so, it would be a small price to pay to enjoy your free time in such luxury. We passed a beautiful yellow-and-purple orchid plant in an Oriental porcelain vase and made our way into the kitchen. I started to reach out and touch it. Was it real? Of course it was real! Ali rapped me sharply on the knuckles and shot me a disapproving look.

"Don't touch it; they're very fragile. It's a lady's slipper," Ali whispered.

"It's an orchid, right?" I kept my voice low. Lucy turned her head slightly as if she was trying to follow the conversation.

"Yes, but a very rare one," she said admiringly. "A single cutting can go for five grand."

I raised my eyebrows. Ali always says I have the soul of an accountant, and maybe I really am too focused on the bottom line. But five thousands dollars for a plant? I shook my head and followed Lucy down the hall, marveling at the habits of the very rich.

To my delight, I saw a young woman and two young men sitting at the kitchen table as Lucy ushered us inside. *Bingo!* I'd lucked out. The young woman with the porcelain skin and strawberry blond hair must have been the mysterious Sophie Stanton. She looked up at me over the rim of her cup, her gaze curious and intent. Her head was tilted to one side, and she had an air of utter confidence. Her chin was lifted upward slightly. She was a beauty with finely chiseled features and that wonderful mane of reddish-blond hair. Hadn't someone mentioned a strawberry blonde lately? Who was it?

I didn't have time to ponder the question because Lucy motioned for us to take a seat, and quickly introduced us to our tablemates. It was just as I suspected. The woman *was* Sophie Stanton, who nodded coolly as she gave me a quick once-over. The sullen-looking young man in a vintage rock T-shirt sitting next to her was Nicky Dargos, Lucy's son, and Angus Morton, the graduate student, was at the head of the table.

All the people I wanted to see, gathered in one place. This had to be a good omen. I locked eyes with Ali for a moment, and she grinned. I bet we both were thinking the same thing. This was like something out of an Agatha Christie novel!

"Make yourselves comfortable," Lucy said, turning her back to us, bustling around the stove. "I'm doing bacon and eggs for Nicky and pancakes for Angus."

"You know, I'm just having fruit and yogurt," Sophie piped up. Her voice was low and cultured, without a trace of an accent. She didn't sound European, but more like

someone who had lived in the states for years. I was sure I
detected a touch of New England in her patrician tone. Boston? Bar Harbor, perhaps? It was almost as though she had
done her best to eliminate all traces of an accent.

"I know; you told me," Lucy said with a hint of irritation.
"You can help yourself. It's on the sideboard. The boys are
hungry. They need a hot breakfast."

"Yeah, I'm starving, Ma," Nicky whined. "Hurry up, will
ya?" Lucy whirled around and pretended to tap him with
the spatula. "All those calories you eat and you never gain
an ounce," she said fondly. "I wish I knew your secret."

The kitchen was a cozy place, and soft Spanish guitar
music played in the background. I was surprised to see a
boom box plugged into an outlet near the sink. The cord was
so short it looked like it might topple into the sink at any
moment.

Lucy caught me staring and said, "I have an iPod, but
my son keeps forgetting to buy a charger for me. This boom
box is twenty years old, but it still works." She pretended to
cuff Nicky playfully on the head as she passed behind his
chair, and he winced.

"Hey, Ma, I got better things to do than buy a charger,
you know? Use the boom box for now." He glanced at me.
"Mama has to have her Latin music playing twenty-four
seven. But if I try to play a little Drake, she goes nuts."

I took a good look at Nicky and Angus. Physically, they
were polar opposites. Nicky was thin and wiry with a
pinched face and a slightly feral look. He reminded me of
a hungry jackal, and it was hard to imagine him doing any
physical harm to anyone. He had narrow shoulders, skinny
arms, and looked like he was barely five seven or five eight.

Angus, on the other hand, was a "big, strapping lad," as
my grandmother used to say. He had pale white skin dotted

with freckles, a shock of reddish hair, and he towered over everyone at the table. He must have been well over six feet tall, I decided, with a broad chest and well-muscled arms. A good push from Angus could easily send a frail old lady like Abigail down the front stairs, but why would he want to? This was the part of the story that was missing.

I decided to tackle Angus first. "I understand you're cataloging the antiques here at the mansion." I deliberately kept my tone soft and low-key, but he immediately went on the defensive.

"How did you know that?" His tone was gruff, unfriendly, but I kept a smile plastered on my face.

"One of the Harper sisters mentioned it," I told him. "They were great friends of Mrs. Marchand. She invited us for lunch the other day, but we didn't get a chance to meet you. You had gone to Charleston to do some research."

He grunted and turned his attention to a giant plate of pancakes that Lucy placed in the center of the table. Both he and Nicky made a grab for the food at the same time, like starving dogs. Nicky was the victor, spearing at least eight pancakes with two forks and laughing at the startled expression on Angus's face. Angus had snared only two.

"Nicky," Lucy said reproachfully. "There's plenty to go around. And I really made those for Angus. Why do you act so greedy? Didn't it occur to you that our guests might like some pancakes?" She looked at Ali, who was eyeing the empty platter. "Don't worry, I have another batch ready to go on the griddle." She paused. "Would anyone like chocolate chips in them?"

"Oh, I would," Ali said with a broad smile. My sister can eat like a longshoreman and still keep her model-thin figure.

"Have there been any surprises in your work?" I asked Angus.

"Surprises?" He barely looked up at me, but his tone was annoyed. "What do you mean?"

"I don't know," I said vaguely. "Sometimes you read about people poking around attics and basements and they come across treasures. Wonderful things that the owners didn't even know were there."

Angus snorted. "I think you've been watching too much *Antiques Roadshow*," he said curtly. "That sort of thing only happens on TV. Mrs. Marchand gave me a very detailed list of what she wanted appraised, and I just go through the items one by one."

"It sounds fascinating," Ali said in her breathy voice.

Angus looked up in surprise, and his features relaxed. Maybe he was taken in by Ali's blond good looks or her sunny smile, but he seemed to instantly relax. After spearing another piece of pancake, he leaned back in his chair to study her.

He obviously liked what he saw. Ali looked particularly cute today in a navy-and-cream striped top with a boat neckline and snowy white capris. Her blond hair was swept back in a high pony-tail, making her look very young and vulnerable. If Angus had a "type," Ali surely fit the bill, I decided. His pale blue eyes flashed with interest, and he was suddenly animated.

"It's a pretty cool job," he admitted. "A lot of students would kill for an opportunity like this."

Kill? Obviously a poor choice of word, under the circumstances, but Ali let it slide.

"How did you ever find it?" Ali gazed up at him with puppy eyes. Ali can turn on the charm when she wants to, and I had the feeling it was going to pay off big-time.

"Mrs. Marchand made a major gift to an art museum where I was interning," he explained. "My supervisor asked me if I'd like to spend the summer at Beaux Reves, and I jumped at the chance. Who wouldn't want to live here for a few months?" he said, waving his hand around the enormous kitchen. "I'm living like a king," he said, obviously pleased with himself. I thought of Lucy's referring to Angus as "Mr. Big Shot."

"Yeah, well, you may be living like a king, but I feel like a janitor," Nicky said in his wheedling voice. "You don't do any of the heavy lifting around here," he said with a snort. "Try spreading two hundred pounds of compost at eight o'clock in the morning and you'll see how the rest of us live."

"Now, Nicky," Lucy said, "you should be willing to help Jeb. He doesn't ask you very often." She put another giant platter of pancakes on the table, after passing them first to Angus. Nicky dug in like he hadn't eaten for days. Lucy slid a plate of fried eggs and bacon across the table to him; the kid was a bottomless pit. "Nicky, Jeb appreciates your help, and so do I." She crossed herself and muttered a few words of prayer. "And if dear Mrs. Marchand were here, she would be grateful; I know she would."

"Whatever," Nicky muttered, pouring a giant helping of maple syrup over his pancakes. "Maybe Jeb should stop betting on the ponies."

Jeb. That had to be Jeb Arnold, the estate manager at Beaux Reves. *So Nicky is jealous of Angus and resents having to do occasional landscaping work for Jeb Arnold. Nicky's mother makes excuses for him and denies he had anything to do with the theft. And maybe Jeb has a gambling problem?*

I had no idea how this was getting me any closer to finding Abigail's killer, but I tucked the information away for later. You never know when a tidbit will come in handy and a connection between two facts will suddenly click. Solving a crime is like putting together a giant jigsaw puzzle. Some of the pieces fit together effortlessly, some you have to work for, but in the end, you have the whole picture.

"You really should stop complaining so much, dude. It's bumming me out," Angus said out of the side of his mouth.

Nicky threw down his knife and fork, ready to spring from his chair. "Do you want to take this outside?"

"Boys!" Lucy said, holding up a spatula. "We have guests. Behave yourselves." She flashed me an apologetic smile and returned to her cooking.

So there was trouble in paradise. Interesting. I wondered about the source of friction between the two young men. Was it a class thing? Was Nicky really being forced to act like a servant and Angus was behaving like the lord of the manor? I needed to find out more about the history between these two. And how did Jeb fit into the picture? But for the moment, I turned my attention to Sophie Stanton.

10

"So how are you enjoying Savannah, Ms. Stanton?" I asked the petite blonde with the heart-shaped face. She was wearing a silky kimono with flowing sleeves, and I couldn't tell if it was an elegant bathrobe or if she was dressed for the day. The rich purple kimono set off the red glints in her hair, and she looked poised and fashionable.

I took a peek at her feet and saw she was wearing a pair of stylish Jimmy Choos, strappy little numbers in black patent leather that would easily have set her back seven or eight hundred dollars. Clearly, she was dressed to go out.

"I love it so far," she purred, flashing me a big movie-star smile. "And please call me Sophie—everyone does." She checked out my pressed khakis and Oldies But Goodies T-shirt, my standard work uniform. She pressed her lips together as if she was trying not to snicker. "Oldies But Goodies, is that a rock band?" she asked. "The name doesn't ring a bell."

"No, it's a vintage candy store over on Clark Street that my sister and I own." I kept my tone pleasant. "Maybe you'd like to stop by someday. We added a little café, so we offer pastries and coffee as well as candy."

She gave a delicate shudder. "I'm afraid I don't eat puddings," she said softly.

Puddings. I know that's what Brits call dessert. Any type of dessert. Was she educated in Great Britain? I had to find out more about this mysterious relative.

"It must have been exciting to reconnect with the American side of the family," I said blandly. She probably felt like I was interrogating her, but I didn't know how else to pry the truth out of her. She certainly wasn't a Chatty Cathy.

"Yes, it was," she said, giving a small smile. She reminded me of a cat delicately toying with a mouse. She tapped a beautifully manicured fingertip against her coffee cup. "Of course, I had no idea that dear Aunt Abigail was living"—she paused delicately to wipe her lips—"in such splendor. I used to visit her place in the south of France. It had gorgeous views, but it was not as grand as this. Sans Souci is a lovely location, in the hills of Cannes overlooking the Bay of Angels." She gave a little sigh. "How I used to love to walk along La Prom." La Prom. I knew that was what jet-setters called La Promenade des Anglais, the boardwalk that runs along the seaside in Nice. "But Beaux Reves is equally charming," she added.

Nicky made a soft grunting sound that could have been a snort of derision or might have just been the sound of him scarfing down his third round of pancakes. Sophie glanced at him and frowned.

"One of our reporter friends is doing a piece for the *Savannah Herald* Lifestyle section on Beaux Reves," I offered, hoping to keep the conversation going.

"Really?" She brightened as if I had finally said something interesting. "I'd like to read it. When will it appear?"

"I'm not sure; she's still doing some research on the gardens. And she might want to add a few paragraphs about the antiques and artwork." I glanced over at Ali, who had her chin in her hand and was deep in conversation with Angus Morton. He was staring at her, obviously smitten. From the snatches of conversation, I could tell that they were talking about furniture restoration. With any luck, Ali might get him to reveal something we could use in the investigation.

I waited until Lucy was busily cleaning the griddle and then said, "Lucy, could you tell me where to find the powder room?"

"It's at the end of the front hall on the right," she said, absorbed in her task. "No, wait," she added, "we're having some plumbing troubles. The pipes, they are so old," she said apologetically. "You'd better use the one at the top of the stairs."

The top of the stairs. Music to my ears. "Thanks so much," I said, pushing back my chair and standing up. I planned on making the most of my foray into the second floor of the mansion and could hardly wait to get started.

I bounded up the stairs and quickly closed the door to the powder room. If anyone glanced up from below, they would assume I was in there. I was grateful for the thick Oriental runners that deadened the sounds as I hurried down the hall.

Which way to turn? I'd assumed Abigail would have a master suite, but after peeking into three bedrooms in a row, it appeared they all were the same size. I really wanted to find Abigail's room but stopped when I glanced into a pale blue bedroom with white area rugs and a four-poster bed with a canopy. It was lovely, and the plantation shutters were open to catch the early morning breeze.

But it wasn't the color scheme or the décor that captured

my attention. It was a large calfskin tote bag sitting on the
bed. It was covered with travel decals, and a guide book was
sticking out. I saw a filmy Japanese-style wrap thrown over
a chair.

I was in *Sophie Stanton's room*! I was sure of it. I darted
inside and closed the door softly behind me. I knew I had
to move quickly. I heard voices and kitchen sounds drifting
up from the heat grates, and in a minute or two, eagle-eyed
Lucy would be hot on my trail. Did I have an excuse for
being in Sophie's room? Nothing came to me, so I figured
I'd better do my snooping and hightail it out of there as fast
as I could.

The tote bag drew me like a magnet. The patches I'd
thought were travel decals turned out to be embossed on the
leather (it was a designer bag, by the way). I quickly riffled
through it, hoping to find some form of ID. If Sophie was
an imposter, she had certainly covered her tracks. I found a
Belgian passport, along with American, French, and Belgian
currency. She had a few British pound notes tucked into a
zipper compartment. But nothing else. Odd.

I peered carefully at the passport photo. Yes, it was definitely Sophie. She was so attractive, she even managed to
look good in harsh fluorescent lighting. There was a guide
book squirreled away in the very bottom of the bag, and it
was earmarked with Post-its.

I pulled it out, expecting a book on Savannah's famous
places. Wrong guess. It turned out to be a guide to Cannes
and the Côte d'Azur. I turned to the first Post-it and saw that
someone had highlighted a paragraph on Sans Souci, Abigail's family home in the south of France.

The description was familiar. *Gorgeous views, a lovely
location perched high in the hillside above the town, overlooking the Bay of Angels.* That was exactly how Sophie

had described it to me in the kitchen, word for word. I sat
down on the bed, thinking. Had she memorized the guide
book, hoping to appear knowledgeable about Sans Souci?
Was it possible she had never even been there? Could she
have learned enough about the south of France to fool Abigail? Abigail may have been way up in her eighties, but she'd
been a shrewd woman and sharp as a tack.

I didn't have long to ponder this because I heard heavy
footsteps tromping up the stairs. *Lucy!* I hurriedly shoved
the guide book back in the bottom of the tote bag, smoothed
the bedspread, and raced down the carpeted hall. I peeked
out over the railing to see Lucy paused on the stairs. She
was calling to someone in the kitchen, "Nicky, I'll be right
back. You don't need any more bacon. Have some fruit. It's
better for you."

Those few seconds were all I needed. I pulled open
the door to the powder room and rushed inside, flushing the
toilet and running the water. I heard a faint knocking on the
door.

"Ms. Blake," Lucy was calling. "Are you all right?"

I smiled and opened the door, holding a small towel in
my hand. "Yes. I had a bit of a stomach problem, I'm afraid."

She looked suspiciously at me but nodded. "If you want,
I can make you some herb tea. That always settles my
stomach."

"Oh, that won't be necessary," I told her. "I'll just walk it
off and I'll be fine. We'd best be on our way. Ali and I have
a full day ahead of us, and I'm sure you do, too."

"There's a lot of work to do in this place," she said grudgingly. "All this furniture to polish." She ran her hand over
the smooth railing. I noticed her hands were surprisingly
large for her short stature, and they looked powerful. She

saw me staring at her hands and thrust them into her apron pocket.

"Well, you do an excellent job," I told her. "Everything is gleaming."

She looked pleased and beamed at me. "It's my lemon wood polish. Mrs. Marchand gave me an antique French bottle to keep it in. You may have seen it on the kitchen counter," she said proudly. "It's too pretty to put away."

I nodded vaguely. "Yes, I did," I told her. I hadn't seen the bottle, but it was easier to let her think I had.

"Everything in here is solid walnut, and it picks up finger-prints," she went on. "I try to go over the furniture and the molding every day, one room at a time. I start at the top of the house and work my way down."

I bobbed my head up and down as if I could sympathize. Actually, taking care of Beaux Reves probably *was* too much work for one person. But hadn't someone said that most of the house was closed off? How many rooms were actually in use and what secrets did they hold?

I was glad I'd seen Sophie's room, but I would have given anything to have had some time alone in Abigail's room and Lucy's private quarters. I remember that Lucy had an apart-ment way up on the top floor and there was probably no way in the world I would ever get up there.

Had the police done a thorough search of the estate when they investigated Abigail's death? I wondered if they'd found anything incriminating in Lucy's apartment or in the guest-house where Jeb Arnold lived. Noah would probably be able to answer that question, and I needed to meet with him fairly soon.

I thought about Sam Stiles, our detective friend with the Savannah PD, and wished she would come back to the Dream

Club meetings so we could chat. She's more levelheaded than most of the members and is somewhat skeptical. Sometimes I think she attends the meetings only because she's friendly with Dorien, who begged her to join.

I realized I was dawdling on the landing and Lucy was giving me a suspicious look. I smiled and walked quickly down the stairs with Lucy right behind me. I caught a faint scent of lemon in the air. Lucy's furniture polish, I decided.

Minutes later, Ali and I were outside the mansion comparing notes. I told her about the tote bag with the travel decals in Sophie's room and she remembered Lucinda's dream about the woman on the docks and her suitcase.

"Don't you see?" she said excitedly. "The woman in Lucinda's dream had to be Sophie Stanton. The reddish-gold hair and the travel decals. It's all so specific, it can't be a coincidence."

"But what does it all mean?" I vaguely remembered that Lucinda said the woman quoted some Bible scriptures to her. Something about only a few being chosen and the last being first and the first being last.

This was baffling to me. Sometimes Ali and her dream interpretations seem so far-out, I can't really see the relevance to the situation. Almost everyone in the club is an avid "believer," and they're willing to stretch the facts in a dream to match their expectations.

I've always taken a more skeptical, utilitarian approach. Ali teases me that she'd have to hit me over the head with a two-by-four to get me to see the symbolism in dreams. I've come a long way since the first meeting, but I'm still not as enthralled with "dream work" as the others. They've been analyzing dreams for a long time and are convinced that dreams can be prophetic.

"I haven't figured that out yet," Ali admitted. "But we

are definitely making progress." She gave a devilish grin. "I'm having coffee with Angus Morton tomorrow."

I stopped dead in my tracks. "You and Angus are an item?" I teased her. "You just met him. And besides, I don't think he's your type."

"It's all part of detective work," she said solemnly. "I'm going to get as much information as I can out of him, and I'm going to start with the thefts at Beaux Reves. We need to find out exactly what has been taken and who's the culprit."

"Even if we find the thief, it doesn't mean he murdered Abigail," I reminded her.

"No, but it's a step in the right direction." She paused and glanced at her watch. "Want to stop by and see Gideon and Andre? I need to borrow some china."

I snapped my fingers. "Got it! You're going to pretend you need an appraisal from Angus. Another way to rope him in."

"Yes, I need to find something that might be high-end or might be a fake, and I bet Gideon can find just the right thing for me."

11

Gideon and Andre are two of Ali's closest friends in Savannah, and they took me under their wing when I first moved here. They own Chablis, a high-end shop in the Historic District, specializing in European antiques.

Every time I see the outside of their shop, I'm struck by its beauty. The Victorian-era frame building is painted a pale lemon yellow and the shutters are cobalt blue. As we climbed the front steps, I admired the fiery bougainvillea on a trellis made of twisted branches arching over the doorway. The front stoop is crowded with overflowing pots of ferns, dusty-rose hibiscus, and pale pink begonias. Chablis reminds me of an enchanted cottage. Two giant porcelain umbrella stands filled with pampas grass flank the front door, which is a vivid shade of purple.

Gideon enveloped me in a bear hug as soon as we stepped inside. Ali had called to say we'd be stopping by and had told him a little about our mission.

"So," he said with a wide grin, "do you need a little help with your latest caper?" Gideon is a wickedly handsome man in his midthirties and a former soap opera actor. He still has some of his theatrical ways, and his voice is deep and commanding.

"Gideon played a detective on *Secret Passions*, so you made the right choice," Andre offered. Andre, Gideon's partner, is a former set designer from Hollywood who moved to Savannah to make his home with Gideon. They're a good match and have been wonderful friends to both of us.

"I promise not to take up too much of your time," Ali said as Gideon guided us to a little sunporch at the back of the shop. It was cool and leafy, and he'd already arranged sweet tea and éclairs for us.

"Don't worry, we have all the time in the world. The antique business is slow this month," Gideon said. "The days are hot and the tourists are browsing instead of buying. Andre and I were just going over the inventory and planning some road trips." He pushed some maps and guide books off the table and I realized I'd forgotten to tell Ali about Sophie and the travel book I'd found stashed in her tote bag.

"We're off to Bar Harbor and Cape Cod in two weeks," Andre said. "So your timing is perfect." I knew that Gideon and Andre often drove up and down the East Coast, scouting out antique fairs and estate sales, hoping to make a killing.

"Tell me what you need," Gideon said. "You want something that looks like it could be expensive, but isn't?"

"Yes, that would work perfectly," Ali told him. "Such a good imitation that even a trained eye might be taken in at first glance. Do you remember that casserole dish with the rabbit on top—the one you kept Lucinda Macavy from buying? It looked like an original but was a fake. You showed me how to spot the tiny details that make all the difference."

"I remember that day at the tag sale." Andre nodded. "I still think we should have let your friend buy the rabbit. It was kitschy, but she liked it, and at the end of the day, that's all that counts. If something brings a smile to your face, you should take it home with you. You were meant to have it. That's my motto."

"And Andre practices what he preaches," Gideon said ruefully. "You wouldn't believe how many times some old dear falls in love with a tea set or a porcelain vase and doesn't have the money to pay us for it. Andre practically gives the item away, because it makes him happy to brighten someone's day."

"Guilty as charged," Andre said, pouring tea for us. "I can't stand to see people disappointed, so I tell them it's been marked down and we forgot to change the ticket. That way they can afford it and their pride is still intact. Southerners are very proud, you know. Gideon is the number-cruncher and I'm the creative guy. Hey, it works, so don't knock it," he added with a grin.

Interesting. That's a little like Ali and me. Ali always has grandiose plans for the candy store (her favorite saying is "Go big or go home") and I have to rein in her flights of fancy and remind her not to be so extravagant. Now that we have Dana as our assistant, it's a little easier to make Ali focus on the bottom line, but some days I really have my work cut out for me.

The store is finally operating in the black, but I don't take anything for granted, and I keep a keen eye on the receipts. Ali had never heard of ROI (return on investment) until I pointed it out to her. I guess to a creative type, ROI is a difficult concept.

"I think I have just the thing for you," Gideon said, handing me a cardboard box. "I picked it out from the storeroom after you called me. Take a look and tell me what you think."

I peered inside and lifted out a miniature tea set sitting on a tray. "Why, it's charming," I told him. "Is it intended for a child's room?" It was porcelain with delicate blue, pink, and yellow flowers. There was a tiny teapot, along with two teacups and two saucers, a sugar bowl, and a cream pitcher.

"It could be for a doll's house or a collector's item. This particular one is a dead ringer for a Meissen tea set that was auctioned off at Sotheby's for six figures," he said. "I remember you said once that your building used to house a day care center, so you could pretend you found it in a closet. It's possible someone could have donated a child's tea set and not recognized its true value. At least that's the story you can use."

"But it's not really valuable, is it?" I turned the teapot upside down to see the mark. It was navy blue but blurry and hard to decipher.

"No, it's an imitation. A rather nice one, but not the real thing." Gideon passed the éclairs, and after a moment's hesitation, I took one. Savannah is a dangerous place to be a foodie—fantastic treats can be found everywhere.

"Will it fool Angus?" Ali asked.

"Only for a moment, if he's any good," Andre answered. "In fact, it will be a good test of his skills. I'll be interested to see what he comes up with."

We tucked into our éclairs and greeted Bibelot, a large black cat, who wandered onto the sunporch and headed straight for an oval bed on a sunny patch of tile floor.

"There's no news on the case?" Andre said tentatively. "There hasn't been much newspaper coverage on it. I think they're keeping it deliberately quiet."

"I suppose so," I said. "Sad that she's gone; it seems like the end of an era."

Gideon nodded. "And then there were none," he murmured.

I nearly dropped my fork in surprise. "What did you just say?"

"And then there were none," he repeated, shooting me a puzzled look. "Of course, that isn't accurate. I should have said, 'And then there was *one*.' I was referring to Laura Howard and the tontine, of course."

"What's a tontine?" Ali and I chorused.

"And who's Laura Howard?" I asked.

Gideon gave me a level gaze. "Well, now that Abigail is gone, rumor has it that Laura Howard is the last surviving founder of the Magnolia Society. With Abigail's death, it's winner take all. I'm sure Laura will have some years left to enjoy the prize, the tontine."

"Tell me about the tontine," I said, trying to ignore Bibelot, who had left his cat bed and was sitting next to my chair, looking up at me imploringly with his brilliant green eyes. Bibelot seemed to sense there was some delicious food on the table, and even though cats can't have chocolate, he probably would have enjoyed the cream filling inside the éclair. Not that I had any intention of sharing!

"The tontine is a prize that goes to the last surviving member of a group. You have to contribute to it, of course. Everyone contributes an equal amount, and if you outlive the others"—he raised his eyebrows and splayed his hands out in front of him—"you've got quite a nice windfall."

"You mean everyone contributes money every year," Ali asked. "And then the winner gets the pot of gold?"

"Not quite." Gideon bent down to scoop Bibelot onto his lap; the cat had been making the rounds, hoping someone would invite him to the party. The cat perched comfortably on Gideon's knees and placed his two front paws on the table, watching me. "It wasn't money, in this case. It was land.

Everyone tossed in a lot of hard cash to buy a pretty parcel of land. It was a steal back then; now it's worth a fortune."

"All the women in the tontine already had their own fortunes," Andre pointed out. "They didn't really need the money; I think it was more of a game to them. Money attracts money."

"It only rains where it's already wet," Gideon said with a chuckle. "My great-aunt told me that a long time ago."

"And the land," Ali said softly, "is it right here in Savannah?"

"Yes, a pricey parcel of land indeed. Prime real estate that some developer would give his eyeteeth to acquire." He turned to Andre. "You know that nice piece of land east of Forsythe Square? The one that's never been developed? That's it."

"I know the one you mean. It's right at the end of a cul-de-sac, and I can't even guess how much it's worth. But the whole idea of a tontine seems rather odd to me. There's something strange about winning a prize just for outliving your friends," Andre said thoughtfully.

I smiled. Sometimes Andre's insights are memorable.

"I know what you mean," Ali offered. "It's not like winning the Nobel Peace Prize or coming up with a cure for cancer."

"How do you know about the tontine?" I asked Gideon. Gideon reminds me of the Harper sisters in that he always seems *au courant* with the latest gossip, and he can reel off the past history of anyone who's noteworthy in Savannah. He has a wide circle of friends from all walks of life, from politicians to playboys, and he throws lavish parties. That may be partly responsible for his knowledge of Savannah society, but I also think he's a good listener, and he stashes away every tidbit he hears.

"It's supposed to be a closely guarded secret," he said, "but my great-aunt Thelma went to church with one of the ladies who was involved with the tontine. Regina Porter. One day they went out for breakfast after church. Mrs. Porter was getting up in age and for some reason, she decided to confide in Aunt Thelma that day. A couple of years later, Ms. Porter died, and then, as I recall, there were just three women left in the group. And then two, and now just Laura Howard."

"It's a fascinating story," I said.

"Do you think it has any bearing on Abigail's murder?" Andre asked.

"I don't know," I said slowly. "I suppose it could."

"Taylor, of course it does! Don't you remember? The tontine appeared in Lucinda's dream!" Ali was so excited the words came out in a rush, tumbling over one another. She grabbed my arm. "Lucinda described a group of women standing in a circle. And they all had their eyes on a gold box. It was some sort of prize."

"I do remember," I said, blinking. "The women kept disappearing one by one . . ."

"And the last one standing walked over to the gold box and opened it. That was the prize, the tontine!"

Andre looked baffled. "A friend of yours dreamt about the tontine?"

"A member of the Dream Club," I said hastily. "It could mean anything—"

"No, it couldn't," Ali interrupted me. "Honestly, Taylor, the truth has to come up and smack you in the face before you recognize it. It was the tontine; I know it was. That was the prize in the gold box." She turned to Gideon and Andre and gave a small eye roll. "Didn't I tell you my sister is a skeptic? The dream symbolism is so *obvious*, and yet she hates to admit it."

"All right, I give up." I held up both hands, palms out, in

a gesture of surrender. "I agree. Lucinda might have been dreaming about the tontine, I suppose. There are some similarities."

"And . . ." Ali prompted.

"And this could put a whole new spin on the investigation," I said. *This could be a game changer.* Noah always said to follow the money. If someone stood to profit—bigtime—from Abigail's death, this was a lead we had to pursue. Now we had a new suspect in our sights. Laura Howard. I hoped we'd meet her soon, because I had a lot of questions to ask her.

12

"I should have known Abigail would plan a party instead of a funeral," Minerva said two days later, dabbing her eyes with a tissue. "She always wanted people to be happy and enjoy themselves."

"She certainly did," Rose chimed in. "I would have liked to attend the burial, but her lawyer insisted it has to be private. She left strict instructions; he'll be standing there alone when she's laid to rest in the mausoleum. That's the way she wanted it."

It was a bright sunny day and we were "celebrating Abigail's life" with a lovely garden party at Beaux Reves instead of a dreary funeral procession. Somehow it seemed fitting that the mansion—which had been closed to the public for so much of Abigail's life—was finally open after her death.

Not the whole mansion, of course. We were restricted to the gardens and the downstairs powder room. Lucy had placed a red velvet rope in the front hallway, discreetly

barring visitors from exploring the house. The Harper sisters
said a few people had zipped into the house to use the
powder room and peered longingly down the hall. No one
dared to venture past the rope.

"I wish they'd allowed pictures," Sara Rutledge said. Sara
was holding a large tote bag with her camera and lenses, but
Norman Osteroff had made it clear that photos were strictly
forbidden. "This would have been a great photo op. I bet half
of Savannah is here."

"Which half?" Andre asked, coming up behind us.

"Well, the interesting half, of course," Gideon said. "Take
a look around. I bet you'll see some familiar faces from the
society pages."

"Savannah's movers and shakers," Sara agreed. "They
all turned out for Abigail. You did an amazing job with the
table settings," she added.

I was surprised to learn that Gideon and Andre had provided the lovely china and serving dishes for the food. Apparently Abigail had approved all the party plans in her will and
ordered her lawyer to carry out her wishes. She'd left nothing
to chance.

There was an elegant selection of tea sandwiches, fruit-
filled pastries, and lavish cheese platters. Trays filled with
tiny buttered biscuits and thin slices of smoked ham were
arranged on round tables scattered over the lawn. Someone
had ordered several pounds of homemade cheese straws from
our friend and restaurateur Caroline LaCroix. I recognized
the *C* logo pressed on each one. Servers in white shirts and
black trousers circulated with chilled glasses of wine, iced
tea, and mimosas, Abigail's favorite drinks.

Each round table held a crystal vase filled with tea roses,
lily of the valley, and baby's breath, straight from the Beaux

Reves gardens. The tablecloths were antique lace layered over bleached muslin, and the soft fabrics were ruffling slightly in the breeze.

"Abigail thought of everything, down to the last detail," Gideon said. "She even wrote down which serving pieces she wanted us to use." He looked around at the people chatting on the sun-dappled lawn of the estate. "This is a great send-off for her. She wanted to make this a memorable occasion for her guests."

"The round tables were a clever idea," Ali said.

"Abigail hated long buffet lines," Gideon explained. "She said it always reminded her of a soup kitchen. She wanted the food be to be arranged on several round tables. That way you're only a few feet away from cakes and hors d'oeuvres, no matter where you're standing."

"Very elegant," Sara offered.

I was sipping a mimosa when I heard raised voices a few feet away. I turned to see Norman Osteroff and Lucy Dargos in what looked like a heated argument at the punch bowl. Lucy was standing with her hands on her hips, leaning in to the white-haired lawyer, her voice tight with rage.

"Mrs. Marchand should have a Christian burial," she said between gritted teeth. "You have no right to deprive her of that. I already spoke to the priest at St. Cecilia's and he will do a requiem for her. There is still time to arrange it. What you're doing is *wrong*," she hissed.

Norman saw me watching them and deliberately turned away, taking Lucy by the arm. He nudged her closer to the house, and I had to strain to hear them. "Stay out of this, Lucy. You don't know what she wanted. You only worked for her. You're the hired help. You were never a confidante."

A low blow, but then I never figured Norman Osteroff to be a nice guy. His face was flushed, and I don't think it was from the large glass of white wine he was holding. I took a chance and edged a little closer, pretending to fill my plate with goodies from the cheese platter. I deliberately ducked my head down as if I were blind, deaf, and dumb.

"She's going into unconsecrated ground—" Lucy's voice was shrill with rage.

"She's not going into *any* ground," Norman corrected her with a heavy sigh. "I've already explained this to you. She's going into a mausoleum."

"Even worse!" Lucy's voice was tight with anger. "She's going into a concrete box. An unholy resting place."

"Honestly, Lucy—" Their voices trailed off as Norman took her more firmly by the arm and guided her back toward the mansion.

"What was all that about?" Ali said, coming up next to me. Lucinda Macavy, Dorien Myers, and Persia Walker were trailing after her. Abigail had left instructions that all the members of the Dream Club should be included at the memorial. She wanted to thank us for offering to hear her dream.

"Some disagreement about Abigail's burial. Lucy, the housekeeper, and Norman, the family lawyer, seem to be at odds."

"Wouldn't the housekeeper know what Abigail wanted?" Dorien asked. "Someone said she's been working here for thirty years."

"She has," Ali replied. "But according to the lawyer, Abigail left very specific instructions about what she wanted. She didn't want anything to do with a church or having any type of religious service. She wanted a completely secular burial."

"Well, I wouldn't put a lot of stock in what the lawyer says," Dorien said. "You can't trust the lot of them, that's what I think. I need something cold to drink. It must be ninety degrees out here; I feel like I'm melting. I'd rather be inside that nice air-conditioned house. If they'd had any sense, that's where they should have held this party." She immediately took off toward a waiter circulating with a tray of mimosas.

Ali raised her eyebrows and Sara muttered, "That's Dorien, charming as ever."

Moments later, I found myself standing next to a tall, slender woman with striking white-blond hair. She must have been in her late seventies or early eighties, but she had the classic good looks that survive the test of time.

"An amazing affair, isn't it," she said lightly, looking over the selection of pastries. She finally chose a couple of mushroom puffs and added them to her plate.

"Yes, it certainly is." The woman was wearing a chic black-and-white dress with stylish high heels. "Did you know Abigail well?"

Her eyebrows lifted in surprise. "Very well indeed. We went to grade school together, and I hate to tell you how long ago *that* was. We've remained friends ever since." She offered her hand and I noticed she was wearing an emerald ring the size of a walnut. "I'm Laura Howard."

Laura Howard! I could hardly restrain my excitement. The one person I wanted to talk to had just magically appeared. I felt like I'd summoned a genie in a bottle. I looked around for Ali and Sara, but they'd drifted over to the far edge of the lawn and were admiring the rose garden.

"Taylor Blake," I said, shaking her hand.

"Are you related to Abigail?" she said, her brow furrowed. I knew she was trying to place me. She probably knew everyone in Abigail's circle and she was trying to figure out how I fit in.

"No, I only met her once. She invited me here for a small luncheon party last week." I gestured vaguely to the outdoor table where we'd sat.

"You must have been a very special guest," Laura said in her soft, musical voice. "She rarely had anyone over to Beaux Reves. You can't imagine how many times over the years I've begged her to host a charity event, and the answer was always no." She paused for a moment, and her eyes welled up. "I didn't mind, because that's just the way she was. She guarded her privacy right up to the end."

"And yet it sounds like her sister Desiree was just the opposite."

If I'd wanted to shock her, I succeeded. Laura Howard made a startled noise as if an electric current had just passed through her. "Yes, Desiree was quite different," she said slowly. "She marched to a different drummer, as they say."

"So I heard." Laura Howard ducked her head and sipped her glass of white wine. A tiny muscle was jumping around her lips, and I had the feeling she was uncomfortable at the sudden turn the conversation was taking.

"What was your connection with Abigail?" she said, not unkindly. "I know all Abigail's friends, and you say you're not a relative, so . . ." She let her voice trail off and gave me an appraising look. I had the feeling that underneath that mask of gentility she was as tough as nails.

"I run a vintage candy shop over on Clark Street with my sister Ali," I told her. "We're good friends with Rose and Minerva Harper—"

"Oh yes, I know them," she said, looking relieved. "Two of the sweetest women in the world. They know everything about Savannah—the history, the culture, the art. But I still don't understand—"

"Abigail invited the Harper sisters for lunch and she asked us to come along. My sister Ali is into dream interpretation . . ."

"Dream interpretation," she said wryly. She gave a ladylike

snort of derision. She'd obviously written me off as loony tunes, but I kept my voice calm. There was no point in acting offended or she'd clam up. As Noah says, never let the suspect know what you're thinking.

"Yes," I said, trying not to sound defensive. "Some people call it dream analysis. We share our dreams and try to figure out what they really mean. We look for common themes and symbolism in them." Naturally, I didn't mention the Dream Club had been successful in uncovering clues to solve murders. At this point, the less Laura Howard knew about our involvement with the police, the better.

"You look for *symbolism*," she said, drawing the word out. She was clearly mocking me. "Is this sort of thing popular? I always think that people who believe in dreams are the same folks who believe in UFOs and psychics." Her mouth twitched in a smirk. The claws were out.

"I was a skeptic, too," I told her, "in the beginning. And in some ways, I still am. But I've heard some interpretations that were spot-on and I've seen parallels between dreams and events in the real world. Things that defy a rational explanation. I look at everything differently since I joined the Dream Club."

"A *dream club*? Oh, good heavens!" It was obvious she thought the idea preposterous. She gave a delicate cough. "I just can't picture Abigail getting caught up in something like that. That wasn't her style."

"She wasn't a member of the club," I said quickly. "But the Harper sisters are devoted members. They come to every meeting. Abigail invited us over because she was having some disturbing dreams and hoped we could shed some light on them."

"What sort of disturbing dreams?" Laura stared at me, her icy blue eyes intent. "Do you mean nightmares?"

"Yes," I said flatly. "She dreamt she was going to die."

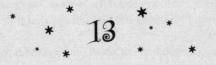

13

"You wouldn't believe the conversation I just had with Laura Howard," Sara Rutledge told me a few minutes later. "She seemed really shaken up, and I think I must have caught her at a vulnerable moment."

"She *was* shaken up," I agreed. "I'd just told her that Abigail had a premonition she was going to die." I quickly filled Sara in on the details. Once Laura had heard my pronouncement, she'd quickly excused herself and walked away. Was she genuinely upset or was it a sign of a guilty conscience? I couldn't be sure.

"Then she got hit by a double whammy," Sara said, leaning close as we crossed the lawn. "No wonder she looked shattered after I dropped my bombshell on her." We were heading for a pale blue canopy where folding chairs had been arranged for the guests. According to the program, there was going to be a brief "sharing time" for friends to comment on how Abigail had impacted their lives.

"What kind of bombshell did you drop?" I watched as Lucy Dargos, sniffling into a handkerchief, slipped into a seat in the first row and pulled her sullen son, Nicky, into the seat next to her. She reached over and rapped him on the fingers when she saw him fiddling with his cell phone.

"I told her I knew about the tontine," Sara said, her eyes twinkling. "I thought she was going to faint dead away on the spot."

"How did you find out about the tontine? It was supposed to be a deep, dark secret!"

"Shh, not so loud—people may be listening." Sara put her fingers to my lips. "One of the judges was a little tipsy from the champagne, and he told me the whole story. It seems that people in legal circles know all about it. They've known about it for years, ever since it was set up."

"And so do people in society circles." I told her about Gideon and Andre's revelation to me. "It sounds like the worst-kept secret in Savannah."

We were lingering at the back of the tent, scanning the guests, trying to find a good place to sit. The Harper sisters were in the second row, flanked by Persia Walker, Dorien Myers, and Sybil Powers. Etta Mae Beasley was sitting right behind them. Lucinda Macavy spotted us and gestured to a couple of empty chairs on her left. My sister Ali was sitting to the right of her.

As we headed down the aisle, Sara continued. "We should have figured that people in legal circles would know about the tontine. After all, it was a legal document, and there's quite a bit of money involved. It's impossible to keep this kind of thing a secret. Especially in Savannah. And can you guess who drew up the papers?" She waited until I sat down before telling me. "Norman Osteroff."

"The plot thickens," Ali said, leaning forward in her seat.

She'd obviously overheard the last part of the conversation. "I knew there was something going on with that guy. He never said a word about it."

"And I bet if you asked him today, he'd still deny it," Lucinda said complacently. "That man plays his cards close to his chest."

"But wouldn't he have to reveal the tontine to the police? This is certainly information they'd want to have as part of their investigation."

"It probably wouldn't occur to the police to ask him," Lucinda replied. "They don't move in the same circles he does. I bet he thinks he can keep mum about the whole thing."

"Well, yes, but now that *we* know," Sara said, "it changes everything. I plan on writing a piece about it for the *Savannah Herald*. I've already texted my editor and she said to go ahead."

"Then the cat will be out of the bag," Lucinda agreed. "I bet you didn't get a word from Laura Howard about it."

"I didn't," Sara said ruefully. "She put her handkerchief to her lips, muttered, 'No comment,' and stumbled away. I think she was genuinely shocked that I'd discovered it."

People were filling up the seats and I knew we'd only have a few minutes before the "remembrance" started.

"But, Lucinda, if you knew about the tontine, why didn't you say something at the last Dream Club meeting?" I asked.

Lucinda smiled. "Well, I only heard about the tontine today. I overheard Judge Parker talking about it to Sara." She turned to Sara. "No one should drink as much champagne as the judge did. And in this heat. Why, did you see how red his face was? He's on his way to another heart attack, I'd put money on it. He's no spring chicken, you know."

"But getting back to the tontine . . ." I whispered.

"I *did* tell you about it at the last meeting," Lucinda replied.

"But it came out as dream material, remember? The women and the gold box. The women all disappeared one by one? I didn't put it all together until just now. That had to be the tontine."

Laura made her way slowly to the podium. Any trace of emotional distress was gone. She looked calm and composed. "As one of Abigail's oldest friends," she began, "I want to welcome you here today to celebrate her life." She paused to look around at us sitting under the large blue tent. Even with a small breeze, the temperature inside the tent was stifling. "As you know, she didn't want a funeral," she went on. "Instead, she wanted us all to celebrate her at her beautiful home."

I tuned out the rest of her remarks and looked at the program. Norman Osteroff, the family lawyer, was going to speak next, and then there would be a brief reading of Abigail's favorite poem, "Ozymandias," by Percy Bysshe Shelley. An odd choice, I decided, and I wondered about the significance. The poem depicts the inevitable decline of great empires and leaders with pretensions to grandeur. In the end, all that remains is a desolate landscape of bare sand.

Was Abigail trying to send a message with this poem? Ali knows more about literature and poetry than I do, and I made a mental note to ask her about it later.

Norman Osteroff's remarks were barely audible. There was some problem with the microphone, and his words seemed to drift in and out in the tent. People began fanning themselves with their programs and he finished quickly and returned to his seat.

Laura Howard returned to the podium and asked if anyone would like to share special remembrances of Abigail. Minerva Harper stood up and said in a quivery voice, "She was one of the kindest, most thoughtful women I've ever met. She was a wonderful friend to us for over sixty years, and we will miss her so much."

"Anyone else?" Laura said after Minerva had sat down and a minute had passed.

"Mrs. Marchand, she was a real lady," Lucy Dargos said, standing up. "I've worked here for more than thirty years. You learn a lot about someone when you live with them every day"—she cast a baleful eye on Norman Osteroff—"and it wasn't just a business relationship. I know that she had a good heart. And I was her *friend*." Norman stared straight ahead, oblivious to Lucy's glare and her pointed remarks. I'm sure Lucy was stung by Norman's callous reminder that she was just the "hired help" and wasn't important to Abigail.

"Wow, that's telling him," I said softly to Ali, who shot me a puzzled look. "I'll explain later," I said in a low voice.

A few of Savannah's socialites stood up to say a few words about Abigail. I didn't know who they were, but Sara kept up a running commentary. "That woman in pearls runs the Junior League," Sara whispered, "and the woman in the lime green Lilly Pulitzer is married to a guy who owns half the Riverwalk."

Abigail certainly counted the rich and famous as her friends, but that wasn't surprising. She owned one of the most magnificent estates in Savannah, and her family was one of the most prominent dynasties the city has ever known. So many people had warm remembrances of Abigail, but somehow their words seemed flat and impersonal as though they were scripted. I didn't hear any personal vignettes that revealed the real Abigail, her generous nature, or her wicked sense of humor.

Except for one. Sophie Stanton.

I'd been wondering if Sophie was present at the ceremony.

I hadn't seen her in the crowd milling around outside while drinks and hors d'oeuvres were being served. And suddenly here she was. She walked dramatically up the main aisle in the tent, wearing a bright lemon shift dress and a straw hat. With her spectacular figure and her rich reddish-blond hair, she made quite an entrance, and I heard someone behind me mutter, "Who *is* that?"

"Sophie?" Lucinda asked me. I'd just realized she'd never met Sophie Stanton, except in her dream sequence. I nodded and she smiled. "I knew that was Sophie Stanton," she said with a ring of certainty in her voice. "She looks exactly as she did in my dream. All that's missing is the suitcase with the travel decals." *But that part of the dream was true, too. She has a tote bag with travel decals plastered all over it,* I nearly blurted out. The coincidences—or symbols, as Ali prefers to call them—were piling up fast.

"What do you know about her?" Sara whispered. "Is this the relative who appeared out of nowhere?"

I nodded. "And she may be inheriting Beaux Reves," I said.

"You're kidding!" Sara's eyes widened. "How did she manage that?"

"She's Abigail's only living relative," Ali said. "At least, that's what she wants people to believe."

"Is Noah checking her out for us?"

"I certainly hope so," I said grimly. It suddenly occurred to me that I hadn't touched base with Noah since our lunch with Sara and Ali the other day. So much had happened, and I felt as though things were spinning out of control. We all needed to sit down together as a group, go over our notes, and see what progress we'd made on the case.

My mind raced over what Ali and I had accomplished in the last couple of days. Our meeting with Norman Osteroff at his office, my visit to Beaux Reves, and my chat with Lucy, the housekeeper.

And what had I learned? I'd discovered an apparent rivalry between Lucy's slacker son, Nicky, and Angus Morton, the grad student who was appraising the artwork at Beaux Reves. Nicky was accused of stealing items from Abigail. Was it true? Naturally, his mother, Lucy Dargos, defended him. But Nicky had had some scrapes with the law before, and it was possible he was picking up a few items at the mansion to fuel a drug habit.

Lucy referred to Angus as "Mr. Big Shot" and clearly didn't like him. Did she really suspect him of something, or was she just taking her son's side? I had the feeling both Nicky Dargos and Angus Morton were hiding something.

Could Angus be helping himself to a few antiques as he "cataloged" them? I remembered the child's china tea set that Gideon and Andre had loaned to us. Ali needed to meet with Angus to appraise the item. Since he was clearly attracted to Ali, that shouldn't be a problem. With any luck, he'd tell her some inside details about his job at Beaux Reves, and whether he suspected some items were missing. If anyone could gain his trust, it was Ali, with her sunny smile and blond good looks.

I thought about my quick trip upstairs to snoop in Sophie Stanton's room and the French travel guide I'd found stashed in her purse. And the impeccably dressed Laura Howard and the tontine! What a surprise that had been, and it certainly put Lucinda's dream into perspective.

How does all this fit together? As soon as Abigail's memorial service was finished, I needed to touch base with Noah. But first I had to hear what Sophie Stanton had to say.

Sophie gave a wide smile to the assembled guests. "Abigail would be so happy to see everyone here," she said in her low, musical voice. "She may not be with us in person, but I'm sure she's with us in spirit." She turned her eyes heavenward. "She's probably looking down and hoping we all had enough to eat and drink. She loved taking care of people."

There was a polite chuckle from the audience. Sophie's voice and mannerisms made me think she might have had some acting training. The gestures, the shadings, and the nuances in her voice seemed planned, not spontaneous. Was she putting on an act? Or was I just overly suspicious?

I saw Laura Howard's mouth twist into a frown. She caught me staring and quickly rearranged her features into a look of polite interest. She seemed irritated at Sophie's remarks, and I wondered why. Did she feel that Sophie was acting like the "lady of the manor," when she was really only a distant relative in town for a short visit? Of course, if Abigail really *had* changed her will, all bets were off, and Sophie would inherit Beaux Reves. It was hard to believe that this magnificent estate could go to a stranger, someone who might be an imposter.

"I only reconnected with dear Abigail recently," Sophie went on. Sunlight was slanting through a gap in the navy tent, glinting off her thick strawberry blond hair. She rambled on for quite a while, speaking fondly about Abigail's influence on her, how Abigail had taught her to appreciate art, music, and traveling.

She said Abigail had introduced her to the pleasures of crossing the Atlantic on grand old ships like the *Queen Elizabeth* and the *Queen Mary*. I thought of how Lucinda had described the beautiful mystery woman in her dream, "She was standing at the dock, holding a suitcase." The implication was that she had just disembarked from a ship. Ali would say it was a slam dunk. The woman in Lucinda's dream was Sophie. Only one question remained: who was Sophie Stanton and what did she really want?

"If Sophie was so close to Abigail, then why has she stayed out of sight all this time?" Sara muttered. "That's what I'd like to know."

"So would I." I lifted my hair off the back of my neck for a moment. It really was dreadfully hot inside the tent. "I never understood how she suddenly reconnected with Abigail after all these years. We need to talk to Lucy Dargos again."

After a few more minutes, Sophie nodded her head in a little bow—almost like a benediction—and left the podium. Laura stepped back up and waited a moment to see if anyone wanted to add anything. No one did. I was gasping for air and longing for a cold drink before we headed home.

I accepted a glass of lemonade from a passing server when a dark-haired man accidentally nudged me. The lemonade sloshed over the rim of the glass onto my hand.

"Sorry," he said sheepishly. He was tall and well built but had dark shadows under his eyes and a haggard appearance. He was wearing chinos and a white golf shirt. I couldn't decide if he was part of the catering crew or he worked at the mansion. He certainly wasn't dressed for a "memorial" cocktail party. I had the sneaking suspicion that he might be hungover, and I thought I detected a trace of alcohol on his breath.

Lucy Dargos called out to him. "Hey, Jeb, could you give us a hand? I want to pack up these dishes from Chablis so Gideon can take them back to the shop." Her tone was brusque, impatient.

Jeb? It had to be Jeb Arnold, the estate manager. The one player in the drama I hadn't met. I was eager to talk to him, hoping he might have some information that could unlock the mystery of Abigail's death. I knew he claimed to have been out of town when she'd died, and I hoped Noah had checked out his alibi. I remembered Lucy's son, Nicky, had made some crack about Jeb playing the ponies. Did he have a gambling problem?

"Are you Jeb Arnold?" I said quickly. I flashed a smile and rested my hand lightly on his arm as he tried to move away.

He hesitated for just a second, and I thought I saw a flicker of fear dance across his face. One of those micro expressions that are so fast they're almost subliminal. He swiftly recovered, gave me a broad smile, and we shook hands. "Yes, that's right. I'm the estate manager here. Do we know each other?"

"No, but I was a friend of Abigail's. She mentioned how helpful you were to her," I said, improvising quickly. "She told me she never could have kept this place going without you."

"Really? She said that?" He rubbed the back of his neck with his hand. "I'll miss the old girl. She wasn't the easiest person to work for, and we butted heads a few times, but her heart was in the right place. It won't be the same without her."

I wanted to ask him why they had "butted heads" and what his plans were. With Abigail's death, he was out of a job, wasn't he? Or did he plan on staying around, hoping the new owner—whoever it was—would hire him?

I couldn't get anything more out of him because Lucy Dargos called to him again, this time in an even more peremptory voice. She was standing with her hands on her hips, frowning at him. I wondered if Lucy had taken on more responsibility now that Abigail was gone and was single-handedly running Beaux Reves. She seemed to be in command, and I had the feeling Jeb wasn't going to defy her.

"Sorry, duty calls," he said with a sheepish smile as he hurried away.

14

"You could have invited Noah to the extra meeting of the Dream Club tonight," Ali said later that evening.

"I thought we had a rule about guests," I reminded her.

"Noah isn't exactly a guest. I wish we could persuade him to join. This club could use a little testosterone."

We'd come home from Abigail's memorial service a couple of hours earlier, changed into shorts and tank tops, and gone over our notes on the case. So far, we had more questions than answers.

Ali had just set out pitchers of sweet tea and snacks for the club members. I'd kept the food simple again. I was sure everyone had stuffed themselves with the delicious hors d'oeuvres at Beaux Reves and wouldn't be hungry.

Lucy had pressed a large package of leftover cheese straws on me as we left, insisting they would go to waste at the mansion. Ali arranged a simple cheese-and-cracker tray on the coffee table, keeping a sharp eye out for Barney and

Scout, who are great fans of cheese in any form. Since we have a couple of chocoholics in the group, I pulled a package of Kahlúa brownies out of the downstairs freezer and placed them on a tray.

"I thought we were going to keep this simple." Ali glanced at the brownies and raised her eyebrows.

"You can never have too much chocolate," I told her.

Ali looked like a teenager in a white tank top, khaki shorts, and Crocs. She flopped down on the sofa, pulled Barney into her lap, and tucked her legs under her. He immediately walked in circles several times before finally settling down. I'm always intrigued when cats do that, and a vet once told me it goes back centuries, to a time when cats were wild and lived in the forest. They would walk in circles to flatten down the leaves before settling down, and this habit stayed with them. I have no idea if this story is apocryphal, but it's the only explanation I've heard. "Where are we with this case?" she asked.

I was sitting in an armchair flipping through my notes. "I wish I knew. There are some huge holes we need to fill," I told her. "Without certain facts, we can't go forward."

"Like what?"

"The crime scene photos, for one thing."

"Crime scene photos," she said in a low voice. She shuddered slightly and bent down to kiss the top of Barney's head. Ali doesn't do well with disturbing images because they tend to haunt her for a long time. I've told her to try to "compartmentalize," but it's just not in her nature. So for the moment, I'm the one who views anything gory or upsetting. I give her a recap of the findings and she offers me her interpretation, so it works out well.

"You don't have to look at them, you know. I'll do that."

I paused as a text message came in from Noah. I read the message, texted back a quick reply, and turned to Ali. "Well, this is interesting. "

"Noah?" she asked.

"How did you know?"

"You always give a little smile when you hear from him. I don't think you know you're doing it."

"I wasn't aware of it," I said crisply. Ali was right. I always feel a warm little glow inside me that starts in my toes when I hear from Noah.

"He says the crime scene photos are ready and there's a big surprise there."

"What kind of surprise?" Scout wandered over, tried to sniff the cheese tray, and Ali gently pushed him away.

"No idea. I think they found something at the crime scene that they're holding back from the media. Whatever it is, it's not going to be in the papers."

"It will if Sara gets her hands on it." Ali gave a rueful smile.

"We'll have to make sure she doesn't, or insist that she not use it," I said. "Sara knows the drill on this."

Sometimes it's difficult having a best friend who's a reporter. It's in Sara's nature to ask questions and to dig for details; that's why she'll be such a great investigative reporter some day. She's "paying her dues" as a freelancer with the *Savannah Herald*, but she has her sights set on a full-time reporting job. The newspaper business is going through some major changes, but Sara is so talented and such a hard worker, I think she'll make it to the top.

"Can we touch base with Noah tomorrow?" Ali asked. We heard the first members of the Dream Club trooping up the stairs, and she sprang up to meet them.

I nodded. "We have to. I'll text him tonight and set up lunch."

*   *   *

"What did you think of Abigail's service?" Sybil Powers asked a few minutes later. The Dream Club members had snared their favorite spots in the living room. Etta Mae, Sybil, and Persia were sharing the sofa, Lucinda was perched on an armchair, and the Harper sisters were sitting on a love seat. Dorien was the last to arrive; she pulled over a kitchen chair after helping herself to some lemonade. Sam Stiles was missing, and I was disappointed. I really wanted to hear her take on the case and decided to catch up with her the next day.

Sara had begged off, saying she needed to spend the evening working on a piece about Abigail's memorial service. It was going to run in the Sunday Lifestyle section of the *Savannah Herald*, and she wanted to give it her best shot. She was disappointed that she wasn't allowed to take photographs at the service, but she managed to dig up some photos of Beaux Reves from the files, and the paper was going to run them along with her article.

The newspaper was playing down the murder aspect of Abigail's death—at least for the moment—and Sara was concentrating on the tributes from high-profile residents of Savannah. She had told me privately that she found the simple words offered by Lucy Dargos to be the most compelling, and I agreed with her.

"I thought it was a lovely service," Etta Mae Beasley piped up. "I had no idea Abigail lived like that. I'd heard about Beaux Reves, but it was better than anything I could have imagined."

"Doesn't it seem odd," Lucinda Macavy said, "for one person to live in such solitary splendor? I think I would be lonely living like that. She rarely left Beaux Reves and hardly ever opened up the place to guests."

"I think that's why it meant so much when she discovered she had a relative from France," Minerva Harper said. "She was at a vulnerable point in her life, I believe." *Very perceptive.* If Abigail was lonely and at loose ends, it would be easier for an imposter to infiltrate her life, posing as a long-lost relative. With her sister Desiree gone and no heirs, Abigail must have longed for a family. Abigail might have been so happy to have found Sophie that she'd put her usual caution and good sense aside and welcomed the woman into the fold. It was certainly something to consider.

"Did she ever tell you how Sophie found her way to Beaux Reves after all these years?" Ali asked Minerva.

"Abigail was a bit vague about the details," Minerva answered.

"Either that, or she was deliberately holding something back. She did that from time to time, you know."

"Yes, she did," Minerva said thoughtfully. "I always wondered if Norman Osteroff had cautioned her about being too trusting."

"Why would trust come into it?" Etta Mae asked.

"Because Sophie Stanton might not be who she says she is," Rose added bluntly. There was a brief silence while we digested this. The problem was, without concrete facts, it was all speculation.

"Well," Persia said briskly, "who wants to go first tonight?"

"I suppose I could," Etta Mae said uncertainly. "I had a dream about a love letter. The details are hazy, but it looked like it was written a long time ago. The paper was yellow and a little wrinkled." I could see a pink flush creeping up her collarbone toward her neck, and I knew she was uncomfortable being the center of attention.

"Anything else?" Dorien said with a touch of impatience. "A wrinkled, yellowed love letter? That's it?"

Dorien's tone was dismissive as usual, and I could see Etta Mae shrinking back into her seat. Ali and I have discussed having a frank conversation with Dorien about the way she talks to people, but we've been putting it off. It's so ingrained and so much a part of Dorien's style that I'm not sure it would do any good. In spite of her brusqueness with others, Dorien is sensitive to criticism. She's easily offended, and it's an ongoing dilemma for us.

"Pretty much, I'm afraid." Etta Mae shrugged. "It was written in navy blue ink, I remember. With beautiful handwriting. But I couldn't make out the words."

"Not too many people have good handwriting these days," Rose said. "All this texting and e-mailing. I think people have forgotten the joys of receiving a lovely handwritten note."

"Can you recall anything else?" Ali prompted. It seemed that Etta Mae was at a loss to describe her dream. When Etta Mae shook her head, Ali said, "Try to remember the emotion you were feeling. Was it a joyful dream, a sad dream? That might help us interpret it."

Etta Mae squeezed her eyes tightly shut as if she was trying to summon up the dream in her mind. "I felt a sense of sadness and loss," she said finally. "I sensed that something had gone terribly wrong, but I don't know what I based that on. That's really all I can remember." She blew out a little breath. "I'm afraid I'm not very good at this."

"That's simply not true, my dear," Rose said kindly. "This is a subjective field, and all of us proceed at our own pace. You will pick up on more and more details as time goes by, I promise you."

"I guess I just don't understand, Etta Mae," Dorien cut in. "Why couldn't you read the words?"

"A few of the words were a little blurry." Etta Mae's tone

was hesitant. "As though water had washed over them. Or maybe it was tears. I just can't say."

"The dream might have been related to an unhappy love affair," Lucinda offered. "Perhaps it was a young couple in love and it ended badly." Lucinda hadn't been lucky in love, and I wondered if her interpretation of the dream was colored by her own experience. Lucinda had been single all her life and not long ago, she signed up for an online dating service.

It was a disaster, and she was embarrassed when it came to light in the course of a murder investigation. All of us reassured her that there was nothing to be ashamed of; it just didn't seem like the right course for a cultured, very private person like herself to take.

Everyone seemed tired and listless, probably from the heat of the day and Abigail's memorial service. We decided to take two more dreams and then break up early. Persia dreamt about being trapped alone at night in a museum. She was smiling as she recounted walking down the hallways, inspecting all the exhibits, and it clearly wasn't an anxiety dream.

"I enjoyed every minute of it," she said with a broad smile.

"I would have been a wreck," Etta Mae said. "I think I have a touch of claustrophobia, and I can't stand being stuck in a place with no way out." I have claustrophobia myself and I could certainly relate to her fears.

"I was happy as a clam," Persia said. "It was like being trapped inside a giant treasure chest. I had the whole place to myself. There were so many beautiful things to look at— paintings, sculptures, antiques." She smiled. "I was like a kid in a candy shop."

"Do you suppose the dream is somehow connected to your anticipation of seeing Beaux Reves today?" I suddenly remembered Persia telling me a couple of days ago how much she was looking forward to being inside the mansion. She hadn't realized the entire memorial service was going to take place outside on the lawn.

"You know, it could have been," she said, her eyes sparkling. "That's a good point. I've been looking forward to seeing the inside of that place for years."

"So it could be as simple as that?" Etta Mae asked. "The dream didn't have any deep significance? Don't all dreams mean something?"

"Not necessarily," Ali told her. "Some dreams just deal with the residue of the day. Everything we see and hear, everything we wish for and desire, is imprinted on our brain during the day. At night, the brain has to make sense of it all, and store all the information, just like a computer does."

"There was another piece to the dream," Persia said excitedly. "I just remembered it. I was walking through the museum with a clipboard, making notes on all the beautiful objects I saw. I had a sense of pride. I knew I had an important job to do and I couldn't make any mistakes."

"But what was your job exactly?" Etta Mae asked. "Were you nervous about it?"

"Oh no, I wasn't nervous at all. It seemed fun and exciting." Persia tilted her head to one side, considering the question. "Was it a job? I'm not sure. I think I was doing some sort of assessment or evaluation, but that part wasn't really clear."

"The clipboard makes it sound official," Minerva noted.

"Yes, it does." Persia reached for a Kahlúa brownie, one of her favorite goodies. "That's really all I have." Unlike Etta Mae, she wasn't the least bit embarrassed by the sketchy details in her dream. Persia has been doing this a long time, and she knows that sometimes all you have to go on are dream fragments, and it's impossible to get a sense of the complete story.

Ali and I exchanged a look, and I wondered if we both were thinking the same thing. *Has Persia been dreaming about Angus Morton?* Sybil is the dream-hopper in the group, not Persia, but Persia's dream could have been called "A Day in the Life of Angus Morton." Persia has never met Angus and I don't know how she tapped into his experience, but it seemed like more than just a coincidence.

I could picture Angus performing the job Persia described in her dream, taking inventory and assessing the value of priceless objects. But no matter how hard I tried, I couldn't see anything beneath the surface. I decided that the dream might not have any deep significance after all.

Ali glanced at her watch. "Time for one more," she said. "Anyone have anything?"

"I wish I did," Lucinda said solemnly. "I tried to dream about that young woman standing on the dock again, but it just didn't happen."

"I had a dream about horses running through a field," Dorien blurted out. "It was one of those dreams you have right before you wake up. I could hear their hooves thundering across the grass."

"Wild horses?" Etta Mae asked, interested. I knew her family had kept horses when she lived in Tennessee.

"No, I'm pretty sure these belonged to someone. I saw a vague image of a ranch house in the background and a corral." She shook her head and spread her hands out in front of her. "That's it."

Ali waited to see if Dorien was going to add anything more and then stood up. "See you all at the next meeting," she said. She wrapped up some brownies for the Harper sisters, who handed her a tote bag.

"This is a book for Sara," Rose Harper said. "We thought she might like to borrow it for her article on Beaux Reves.

It's out of print, but it contains some really lovely photos of the interior of the mansion from years ago. It's interesting to see what was popular in home décor back in the twenties and thirties—all those Tiffany lamps. And there's even a photo of a Valentine's Day ball that was held at the mansion."

"Really? This is wonderful; I know Sara will love it. She'll keep it for a few days and give it back to you," Ali said.

"No hurry," Rose said with a little flutter of her fingers. "She might find something useful, some information you can't really find in guide books."

"Very kind of you," I said, giving Rose a brief hug.

15

"This is a fascinating book," I said to Ali when everyone had left. "It's a shame it went out of print."

"If you really like it, we could try to find a used version and give it to Sara for her birthday. It's coming up next month."

"Good idea. I think I'd like to order one for myself." I flipped through the pages, struck by the beauty of Beaux Reves through the ages. It was not only a gorgeous tribute to a magnificent estate, but doubled as a photo album of the Marchand family.

I spotted a photo of Desiree, looking as beautiful and carefree as I'd expected, standing next to Abigail, who was staring thoughtfully at the camera. It was obvious from Abigail's solemn bearing that she was the "responsible" sister, and her arm was looped protectively around Desiree. The two girls must have been teenagers in the photo, and they were standing in a paddock on the estate, feeding treats to a chestnut horse with a white star on his face.

I suddenly flashed back to Dorien's dream about horses. It couldn't be related to Desiree and Abigail, could it? Dorien mentioned a ranch house and horses running inside a corral, but there wasn't anything like that at Beaux Reves. At least not in the present day.

According to the text, not much had changed at Beaux Reves in the last seventy years. The author claimed that the family liked to keep each piece of furniture and every painting and sculpture exactly where Emil Marchand, the family patriarch, had placed it.

I stared at a photo of the front hall for a long moment and then passed the book to Ali, who was making hot tea for us. "Ali, take a look and tell me what you see," I said.

She peered at the book and said slowly, "It's the front hall at Beaux Reves. I recognize the black-and-white Art Deco floor, the tray ceiling with the carved wood panels, but something's off." She frowned, took the book over to the sofa, turned on the reading light, and sat down.

"I thought so, too." I plunked down next to her. "I wanted to make sure it wasn't my imagination."

"It's not your imagination," she said. "Something's different about the front hall."

"You mean something has been added." I peered at the book again, over her shoulder.

"No, something has been taken away."

Ali has an excellent visual sense, an eye for color and design. "I think I know what it is," she said excitedly. "There's an extra painting here. See this lovely landscape?" She pointed to a large watercolor of daisies in a heavy gilt frame. "This painting wasn't here the day we visited Lucy."

"Are you sure?"

"I'm positive." She studied the picture for a moment. "According to the book, this photograph was taken ten years ago, so it's relatively recent. Look at the two small paintings on either side of it." She pointed to a couple of watercolors of young children playing with sailboats in a pond. The sun-dappled scene with the little boy and girl in sailor suits reminded me of the Luxembourg Gardens in Paris. I had sat on the bank and watched children sail their boats there one sunny afternoon many years ago.

Ali tapped her index finger on the page and continued, "On the day we visited, I remember that the two sailing paintings were squeezed together so tightly the frames were almost touching. Did you notice the same thing?"

"No," I said softly. "You see things that I don't. I just saw a wall of paintings, and the colors and shapes washed right over me. I remember thinking that the paintings in the hall were beautiful, but I didn't pick out any specifics."

I am always in awe of Ali's creative energy. She absorbs colors and forms like a sponge and has the soul of an artist. She always teases me that I have the soul of an accountant because I am much more likely to be intrigued by numbers. In many ways, we complement each other and bring something unique to the table when it comes to running Oldies But Goodies.

"I thought they were charming paintings, but I remember noticing they weren't displayed properly. They would have made more of a statement with some blank wall space in between them." She handed the book back to me. "Do you think this could be significant?"

"I don't know. The paintings might not really be missing. I suppose the Marchand family could have sold the daisy

painting in the past ten years." Even as I said the words, I
knew that was unlikely. Abigail was a stickler for the past and
for keeping the estate exactly as it was when her parents were
alive. Perhaps they'd sent the painting out to be cleaned or
reframed? Gideon or Andre might have some ideas on that.

"I don't think they'd ever sell the painting," Ali retorted.
"It would only increase in value as time went by, and the
Harper sisters said that the family didn't need the money. I
can't imagine Abigail breaking up the collection unless she
was forced to do so."

I thought about the rumored thefts at Beaux Reves and
the possible suspects: the housekeeper's son, Nicky Dargos,
and the grad student, Angus Morton. "I thought the thefts
from the mansion involved small items," I said. "Things that
wouldn't be missed right away. This painting is huge. Abigail would certainly miss it."

"That's the first thing that occurred to me. But it's possible this painting was taken after Abigail's death. Do you
remember how no one was allowed to explore the mansion
at the memorial service? Guests could go inside to use the
powder room, and that was it. The wall with the paintings
wasn't visible unless you stepped over the velvet rope. And
no one would dare do that, although I bet a few people were
tempted." She poured tea for both of us, chamomile for her
and Yorkshire Gold for me. "I wonder whose idea that was—
the velvet rope?"

"It must have been Lucy's idea," I said. "No one else is
involved in running the house now that Abigail is gone. Lucy
has no one to report to anymore. She's the Queen Bee."

"Yes," Ali agreed, "you're right. With her mistress dead,
she's probably running Beaux Reves on her own."

I thought of the peremptory way Lucy had spoken to the
estate manager, Jeb Arnold. She had certainly acted like she

was in command. "Lucy has eyes like a hawk, and I have the feeling she doesn't miss a trick. She told me she cleans one room thoroughly, from top to bottom, every day. If the painting disappeared in the past few days, wouldn't she tell someone?"

"Yes, but who would she tell? She didn't dare say anything. It could have been her own son who pinched it." Ali shook her head. "Are other things missing? We just don't know." She turned the page and gasped. "Taylor, here's another picture of the front hall! And look at this hall table—do you remember it? A lovely mahogany piece with an oval top and claw feet. Probably early nineteenth century."

"I do remember seeing that table." I don't know much about antiques, but I remember that Gideon had shown us a similar table in his shop and pointed out the claw feet, or toe caps as they're sometimes called. They're decorative brass fittings attached to the ends of table legs.

"But it's not the table that's important," Ali went on quickly, "it's what's sitting on it. The resolution isn't very good, but you can see a crystal globe on the table. It could be a crystal ball, like something a fortune teller would use, or maybe it's some kind of a paperweight." She angled the light so it shone directly on the page of the book. "I know that globe wasn't there on the day we visited. I'm absolutely positive. Instead, someone placed that beautiful orchid plant there—the lady's slipper, the one I pointed out to you."

"The five-thousand-dollar orchid," I said. "I remember thinking how extravagant it was."

"Maybe so, but it's not as pricey as the piece of crystal in this picture. I wonder what happened to it. Do you suppose someone has been ransacking the mansion after Abigail's death? If they plan on stripping the place bare, this would be the time to do it. There's no one to stop them."

Barney wound himself around my legs, signaling that it was time for his late-night snack. I don't know if the cats just like the attention or if they are genuinely hungry, but we've gotten into the habit of feeding them a small treat before we all go to bed. I opened a can of sardines and spooned out a small amount into two dishes. The smell made me turn my face and crinkle my nose in disgust, but then I'm not a cat.

"How shall we handle this?" Ali asked. "We need to figure out if the items are really missing or if they were sold off."

"You're seeing Angus tomorrow morning, aren't you?" I put the cat food dishes down on the floor and was immediately rewarded with a chorus of grateful meows. Since both Barney and Scout are rescues, they have what the vet calls "stray cat syndrome." Even though they have plenty to eat, they remember their days of going hungry and tend to wolf down their food if given the opportunity.

"Yes, I'm meeting him very early for coffee, and I'm bringing the children's tea set that Gideon loaned to us. Do you think I should bring the book and show him the photos? If I do, he'll know we're on to him."

"Not if you play it right. You could ask him if the painting and the piece of crystal were sold. You don't have to accuse him of anything." I grinned. "You can pretend you're studying up on the history of Beaux Reves because you're interested. Just turn on the charm, and I bet you'll catch him off guard." I glanced at the clock. Nearly eleven, time to turn in. "Just make sure you meet us at Marcelo's for lunch at noon tomorrow. Noah and Sara will be there, and we can compare notes."

I was surprised at the seven-o'clock phone call from Norman Osteroff the next day. Sara had already left for her early morning meeting with Angus, and both Barney and Scout were curled up snoozing at the foot of the bed. I'd heard Dana putting around down in the shop a few minutes earlier. I remembered she'd said she wanted to get an early start on a new window display, and I planned on lending a hand. I'd just gotten out of bed and padded to the kitchen to turn on the coffeemaker.

I looked at the caller ID screen and blinked in surprise. The pompous lawyer certainly believed in the adage "the early bird catches the worm."

"Ms. Blake," he said formally, "I hope I didn't wake you."

"Of course not," I said blithely, glad that I wasn't on Skype. "I've just returned from my six-mile run and was going to do a few dozen sit-ups." Okay, what I really said was, "No problem," in my early morning croak. "I'm plugging in the coffeepot and planning my day."

"That's why I wanted to catch you early." His voice was crisp, businesslike. "My secretary left on vacation, and I just realized she sent you a letter by mistake. The letter is intended for you, but she should have placed the letter on my desk and I would have shared it with you in person." He made a little wheezing noise that I suppose was irritation. "I'm sorry for the short notice, but you and your sister need to stop by my office this morning. It's very important."

He paused as if he wanted me to say something more, but I didn't give him the satisfaction. It was taking all my powers of concentration to plug in the coffeemaker, measure out the hazelnut super-octane coffee, and fill the canister with filtered water. Barney and Scout were winding themselves around my legs, probably wondering why I was bothering myself with such silly human pursuits when I should be spooning out their breakfast.

"Yes, well," he went on, "I'll expect you both at my office at nine sharp to give you a letter from Mrs. Marchand. It was

Mary Kennedy

delivered by messenger the day after she invited you to Beaux Reves for lunch."

That got my attention, and I dropped the measuring cup onto the counter, which sent Barney running for cover under the sofa.

"A letter from Mrs. Marchand? We never received it." I couldn't get my mind around the idea that I needed to trot over to his office to receive a letter. Couldn't he just tell me the contents over the phone?

"I must give it to you in person," he said flatly. "Both you and your sister will need to be here. I can't say any more at the moment. Please just be at my office at nine sharp. I apologize for any inconvenience. I will certainly reprimand my secretary." *He'll probably dock her a week's wages*, I thought glumly. I doubted Osteroff believed in the adage "To err is human; to forgive, divine."

"My sister has already left for an appointment, but I'll be there," I said. "And please don't worry about—" Before I could say another word, he'd rung off. Norman Osteroff was clearly not a man who cared about social niceties.

I showered quickly, gulped two cups of coffee, and raced downstairs to help Dana. As it turned out, she didn't need my help at all. She had everything under control. The shop was spotless, the counters gleaming, the candy bins neatly stocked. She was standing on a ladder, redecorating the shop window with a selection of white wicker baskets hanging from the ceiling at various heights. Each basket held a selection of candy and a wicker wheel barrow was overflowing with jelly beans.

"I found them on eBay," she said proudly. "The wicker wheelbarrow was really a plant stand but I think it looks great filled with penny candy. What do you think?"

"I think you're a genius. Make sure you reimburse yourself

out of petty cash, and if you need me to write you a check, just let me know."

"It's colorful, isn't it?" she said happily. She stepped down off the ladder to admire her work and I stepped back into the shop.

An enticing aroma of hazelnut coffee wafted through the room, and I detected a whiff of cinnamon. "And it looks like you've already gotten things started for the breakfast and lunch crowd."

She nodded. "All taken care of. I made that recipe for baked French toast last night and popped it in the oven a few minutes ago. It smells good, doesn't it? I added extra cinnamon and some candied pecans to the recipe Ali gave me. I think it's going to be a hit."

She'd already started pots of tea brewing for our early morning visitors and pulled out trays of goodies from the freezer. Cinnamon rolls were thawing on the counter, ready to be slid into the oven, and the soup of the day was already simmering in a stockpot. I lifted the lid to take a peek. Potato and leek, one of my favorites. Fresh croissants and apple cider donuts—a new item—were arranged on trays and covered with clear plastic wrap.

"I need to go out early, and I was so afraid I was leaving you in the lurch. I was feeling a bit guilty."

"No need to feel guilty," she said with a grin. She hopped onto a stool to pour herself a cup of coffee. "Ali has all the sandwich spreads made and labeled in the refrigerator, and she showed me how to use the new panini maker. And we still have some of Caroline's cheese straws left over, so I thought I'd serve them as freebies with soup orders. We should probably think of some signature item we could serve, something with our logo on it."

"Good idea." I nibbled on a croissant and tried the new ginger-peach jam that Ali had made. It was delicious. The candied ginger raised it to a new level. Did I dare have a second croissant? I debated for a moment and then grabbed a small one. After all, I had to keep up my strength for my meeting with the dour lawyer Norman Osteroff.

16

"Good morning," Osteroff said formally, half an hour later, ushering me into his office. He was dressed in a black suit with a gray tie, either in honor of Abigail's passing or as a nod to his own somber personality. "My assistant has taken the *entire* week off, so I'm afraid I can't offer you a beverage." He pursed his lips in disapproval and made a faint rattling noise in his throat, as if she'd committed an unthinkable act.

"That's fine," I said quickly. The last thing I wanted to do was linger over coffee with him. I decided to get straight to the point. "I can only stay a few minutes—you mentioned a letter from Abigail?" I slid into one of the upholstered leather chairs while he settled himself at his massive desk. He looked pale and tired, I noticed, with dark circles under his eyes and hollows in his cheeks. Had he been genuinely fond of Abigail and mourning her death? The man seemed so cold and devoid of emotion, it was hard to tell. As Minerva Harper once said, *The man has about as much warmth as a wet flounder.*

"I discovered that a letter has already been mailed to you," he said slowly, "but I wanted to meet with you and put it in context." I waited while he tapped his fingers on the desktop. I had the feeling he was weighing his words carefully. He picked up an envelope and fingered it as if debating whether to open it. "This is a copy of the letter Abigail wrote, and it contains a most unusual request. In fact, in all my years practicing law, I don't think I've ever seen anything quite like it."

He paused and stared out the window at his view of the Historic District. It was a beautiful day in Savannah, the air soft and balmy, and I wondered why he never opened the windows. The office, with its heavy furniture and dark colors, made me feel claustrophobic. The air was stifling, and I couldn't wait to get back outside into the warm Georgia sunshine.

"The letter?" I prompted him. He passed it silently across the desk to me, and I quickly skimmed the lines. It was a request, all right, and I was taken aback. *Make an inventory of my belongings; I have designated certain items to be donated to specific charities. I am trusting you, my dear friends, to make sure this is done according to my wishes.*

I recognized Abigail's spidery handwriting and the cream-colored stationery from Beaux Reves. I was certain the letter was legitimate. "Well," I said, sitting back in my chair, "this is certainly unexpected. I have no idea why Abigail asked us to do this, but of course Ali and I will honor her wishes."

"You do understand the request?" Osteroff had his elbows on the desk, his fingers steepled under his chin. I think he wondered if I understood the implications of what Abigail had asked of us. Maybe he considered it a slap in the face, a lack of confidence in his abilities? Shouldn't Osteroff be the person Abigail turned to for such an important task? Yet she had chosen us. *Interesting.*

"Yes, of course. It's a little puzzling, though. She invited that young man Angus Morton to catalog the contents of Beaux Reves. Was there a problem with him?"

Osteroff cleared his throat, looking uncomfortable at the question. "I'm, uh, not at liberty to say." He placed his hands flat on the desk. "I can tell you, though, that I have a fiduciary responsibility to make sure her wishes are carried out. I'm not sure why she chose you and your sister to take on this task"—he leaned across the desk, fixing me with his beady eyes—"but she must have had her reasons." Never one to chat, he immediately stood up to escort me to the door.

"Two questions," I said, stopping him in his tracks. "Does Lucy Dargos know that Mrs. Marchand instructed us to go through Beaux Reves? And will Angus Morton continue to live at the mansion?"

"The answer is yes to both questions," he said curtly. "Angus Morton is there"—he hesitated—"for the moment." *For the moment? Not exactly a vote of confidence.* "Angus Morton will not impede your progress. And I will call Lucy Dargos to make sure she understands that you have access to every room in the house. You won't have any problem with her." He opened a file drawer and handed me a folder. "This is an inventory from a few years ago. I'm not entirely sure it's up-to-date, but it's a good place for you to start."

"What do we do with the results of our inventory?" I asked.

"You will bring your findings back to me, and we will take it from there," he said abruptly, and elbowed me into the waiting room. He gave me a ghoul-like grimace—his version of a smile—and that was it.

"I don't get it," Ali said an hour later. "That's all he had to say?" I'd texted her about my surprise meeting with

Osteroff, and we'd decided to meet at Forsythe Square and walk over to Beaux Reves together.

"It was a very brief conversation. He seemed to be scowling at me the whole time. Either he doesn't like me, or his breakfast didn't agree with him," I said wryly.

"I think that's his permanent expression," Ali said. "I bet he wasn't thrilled that she chose us."

"I'm sure he wasn't," I said, remembering those dark eyes and the tightness around his lips. "I can't figure out why Abigail reached out to us. After all, we only met her at lunch that one time. Why entrust us with such an important job? She must have known people who are more qualified."

"Maybe, maybe not," Ali countered. "She trusted us, and in the end that's all that mattered."

I paused to smile at a baby in a stroller holding one of our Oldies But Goodies helium balloons. Dana had come up with that promotional idea a few months ago, and the balloons were popular. As Dana says, the more times we get our name out there, the better.

My thoughts had been churning around Osteroff, and I'd completely forgotten about Ali's meeting with Angus. "How did your coffee date go?" I said teasingly.

Ali flinched at the word "date." "Please don't call it that," she said with a grin. "There's something seriously weird about Angus," she added as we strolled along. The sunshine was filtering through the trees, and I longed to sit on one of the wrought iron benches with a lemon water ice and spend the morning people-watching.

"I think he's definitely interested in me," she began, "but I managed to cool his jets by saying I have a boyfriend back in Atlanta."

"Smart move. Did you get any information out of him?"

"Not much. He looked over the tea set that Gideon gave

us, and he pointed out how he knew it was a fake. He was very specific, and he took his time with it."

"Really?" I raised my eyebrows. "So maybe he's the real deal after all. I guess I always wondered if he was an imposter and had somehow wormed his way into the estate for the summer."

"I made notes on what he said, and I'll run them by Gideon to be sure, but I think Angus knows his antiques." She paused. "But as far as him being an imposter, there's something I don't quite trust about him. I just can't put my finger on it."

"Just a gut feeling?"

"Yes, a feeling that he's up to something." She turned her gaze to me. "Won't this be a bit awkward at the mansion? Angus has been hired to catalog the inventory, and now we've been asked to sort through the same items. It sounds like we're going to get in each other's way."

"It could be awkward. Especially if there's any funny business going on." As soon as I said the words, Abigail's request made sense. I was positive she'd sensed something was amiss and she wanted us to prove it. I was more determined than ever to get to the bottom of what was going on at Beaux Reves.

Lucy Dargos was more welcoming than I'd expected her to be. She offered us cups of coffee, and we sat at the kitchen table for a few minutes, going over the folder that Osteroff had given me. If she felt intimidated by us, she managed to hide it.

"I didn't know about this list," she said. "How will you know if things have been added or sold since this list was written? Maybe there have been changes in the inventory." A fair question, but she sounded a little defensive.

Ali gave her a level glance. "I thought Mrs. Marchand prided herself on keeping things exactly as they were when her parents were alive, Lucy. You've been here thirty years. Can you remember any new acquisitions or any items being sold off during your time here?"

Lucy quickly shook her head, her dark eyes flashing. I think Ali had hit a nerve. "No, nothing that I can think of." She saw Ali glancing toward the front hall, and a shrewd look crept into her eyes. I knew Ali was getting ready to ask her about the large daisy painting we'd seen in the Beaux Reves guide book.

"There was a painting out there once," Ali began, gesturing toward the hall. "A large painting of a field of daisies." Ali kept her voice low, nonthreatening. "It's not here now. Do you have any idea what happened to it?"

"A painting of daisies?" Lucy was stirring her coffee, stalling for time. The nervous twitch around her mouth was back, and I knew she was wondering how much to reveal. "I don't recall—" she began, but Ali cut her off.

"A huge painting," she said in a sharper tone. "You must have seen it. It was hanging right between those two watercolors of the sailboats. The field of daisies was in the foreground, and there was a town in the background."

"Oh yes, *that* painting," Lucy said, licking her lips. She widened her eyes and raised her hands, palms up, in a classic gesture of innocence. "*Sí*, I do remember it. We sent it out to be cleaned." She shrugged and placed her hands back on the kitchen table. Once again, I was struck by how strong her fingers looked. She was used to doing heavy housework around the mansion. She was easily strong enough to overpower a frail old lady like Abigail Marchand.

"I didn't know they cleaned oil paintings," I said.

"Sometimes they do," Lucy told me. She refused to make eye contact with me and was staring fixedly at the tiny violets on the tablecloth. The twitch around her mouth was back. *Interesting.* "You know, no matter how hard I try to keep this place clean, there are little dust particles in the air. They settle on the paintings. And Mrs. Marchand was thinking of having it reframed," she added.

"Really." Ali's tone was incredulous.

"Yes, she was," Lucy went on, speaking so rapidly the words were tumbling over one another. "You know, those very fancy gilt frames have gone out of fashion. People like simpler frames these days. And they are easier to clean." She tilted her chin up, as if daring Ali to disagree with her.

"And the painting is . . ." I let my voice trail off and stared at Lucy until she was forced to look up at me.

"It's with a restorer and will soon be back in place," she said flatly. Her tone had shifted. All traces of fear had vanished, and her tone was hostile as she stood up and started to clear the coffee cups. "And now I must get back to work," she said abruptly. "If you need any help, just ask me. Where are you going to start?"

Ali and I exchanged a look. The last thing we wanted was Lucy Dargos trailing after us as we made our way through the mansion. The less she knew, the better. "I think we'll just start with the front hall and make our way upstairs," I said politely. "I understand that your private apartment is on the top floor, and naturally, we won't go in there."

Lucy swallowed and her eyes widened for a second. She obviously hadn't thought of that possibility. "Thank you," she said, getting herself under control. "I can assure you there is nothing that belongs to the estate in there."

"No, of course not," I said soothingly. Ali and I turned toward the hall, and I could see Lucy had picked up a dishcloth and turned back to the sink. Her shoulders had slumped, probably in relief. "Just one more thing," I called out. "Where was Desiree's room?"

Lucy turned in surprise, wiping her hands on her apron. "It's the fourth room on the left on the second floor. Miss Desiree's room is bright yellow; it was her favorite color. We have kept it exactly as it was when she was alive. Mrs. March-and insisted that nothing be disturbed."

"Then that's where we'll start," I told her. She began to protest, but I waved my hand dismissively. "Don't worry, we're just looking. We won't disturb anything."

"I don't think she's thrilled to have us here," Ali whispered as we made our way up the stairs. We stopped briefly on the landing, and I heard the front door open and close. Heavy footsteps headed toward the kitchen, followed by a husky voice greeting Lucy.

Angus Morton! I looked at Ali and put my finger to my lips. Had Angus already gotten the word from Norman Osteroff that we were free to inspect the mansion? Or would Lucy tell him? I leaned over the banister on the upper landing to listen, but someone had closed the door between the kitchen and the hall.

"I can't hear much," I said in a low voice to Ali, "but they're definitely talking down there." I turned around, but Ali had vanished. "Ali?" I whispered.

She stuck her head out of a bedroom down the hall and motioned for me to come quickly.

"It's Desiree's bedroom," she said, pulling me inside a bright yellow room. "And you can hear perfectly through the heating grate." She grinned and hunkered down on the floor. I squatted next to her, just in time to hear Angus give a gasp of surprise.

"They're here *now*?" he asked. He tone was gruff, annoyed.

It was surprising how unpopular we were. "What do they want?"

Lucy said something I couldn't quite catch, but I heard the name "Osteroff." "No, he didn't tell me a thing," Angus went on. "Why would they be doing an inventory? Something's up, I know it." Again, soft murmuring from Lucy and harsh words from Angus. "I don't want any tea," he said irritably. "I'd better track them down and see what they're up to. And keep your idiot son quiet. If he says anything, there'll be hell to pay."

Ali stood up slowly, her face pale. "I can't believe that Angus could be involved," she said slowly. "I just had coffee with him. He seemed like a nerd, but a nice guy." She shook her head in dismay. "How could I have been so wrong about him? He might be Abigail's killer!"

"Don't get ahead of yourself," I said, pulling her out the door into the hallway. I didn't want Angus to see us poking around Desiree's room. "And pull yourself together. Don't let him think we overheard anything."

We were pretending to inspect a small oil painting in the hall, a rather sentimental scene of lilacs and roses, when Angus bounded up the stairs. I was struck by how tall and powerful he was.

"We meet again," he said cheerfully to Ali.

I could feel her shrinking back from him, so I was overly friendly to compensate. "This is so exciting," I said, babbling on girlishly. "Ali and I have always been curious about the mansion, and I never thought we'd have a chance to see it firsthand. We're taking our own private tour."

His expression hardened, and he shot a curious look at Ali. "It seems that Mrs. Marchand's lawyer asked you to do your own inventory." He raised his eyebrows as if he couldn't understand why anyone would make such a ridiculous request.

"Yes, he did. Well, it was actually Abigail herself who made the request. Mr. Osteroff just passed along the letter from her."

"I see." There was a long silence, and I thought I saw his gaze shift to the landing. Exactly the place where Abigail had been pushed down the stairs. For one crazy moment, I wondered if he was planning on doing away with one of us and then realized that would be too hard to pull off. There were two of us to contend with, and no one would believe our deaths were accidental. That would simply be too much of a coincidence.

"Could you tell us something about this painting?" Ali asked. Her voice was a little shaky, but she no longer looked like a frightened rabbit, and I was relieved.

"A small oil, circa eighteen nineties. Not particularly valuable. The artist was a local one and he was making a stab at Impressionism, but as you can see, he wasn't too successful." His voice was curiously flat, devoid of any enthusiasm. It was hard to believe he was really an art aficionado, but from the amount of detail he offered, he seemed to know his stuff. And Ali had mentioned that he had appeared knowledgeable when she'd shown him the antique tea set.

"He wasn't successful at his attempt at Impressionism? Why's that?" I asked, pretending to be interested.

"The light's all wrong," Angus said impatiently. "See the way it slants across the lilacs, but then it seems to stop dead at the roses? There should be diffused light throughout the whole painting. Impressionism is a lot more complicated than it looks. A lot of artists in that time period simply slapped some blurry flowers on a canvas, added some sunlight dappling through the scenes, and thought they'd nailed it."

"Oh, I see," Ali said, examining the painting. "You know so much about paintings," she said in a slightly gushing tone.

Angus relaxed, falling for the bait. He adjusted the lapels on his linen blazer, preening. "Well, I've studied art for a long time," he said modestly, "and I was bound to pick up a few things here and there."

"All that knowledge," I said wonderingly. "It almost seems wasted at Beaux Reves." I wasn't sure how hard to push. "But I suppose this was never the endgame for you."

"Certainly not. I wanted to beef up my résumé and my advisor suggested spending the summer here. My real goal is to be an appraiser at Sotheby's. A good recommendation from Mrs. Marchand would have meant everything."

A recommendation? I hadn't thought of that angle. And he had said *would have meant*, so it clearly had fallen through because of Abigail's death.

"Of course, that's impossible now," he said churlishly, as if he were reading my mind. "No Mrs. Marchand, no recommendation. I should have asked her for a letter when I first arrived here." *Talk about a narcissist! His employer was murdered, and all he cares about is his own career plan.*

Ali and I exchanged a look. I think our brains were whirring along on the same track. If Angus needed a recommendation from Mrs. Marchand for a job with Sotheby's, why would he murder her? Wouldn't that be killing the goose that laid the golden egg? So maybe the conversation with Lucy in the kitchen had nothing to do with murder. This cast a whole new light on things.

"Maybe Mr. Osteroff could give you a recommendation," I said tentatively.

"That old gas bag?" Angus sneered. "He wouldn't know a Monet from a money market account. I'm afraid I'm screwed."

"Lucy Dargos?" I suggested, wondering what he would say about the longtime housekeeper.

"A scullery maid?" he scoffed. "Pots and pans are all she knows. And that son of hers? Don't get me started."

I was wondering how to get Angus out of the picture so we could continue our sleuthing when his cell phone rang. He checked the readout and frowned. "I've got an appointment in town," he said, "so I've got to leave for a while." He gave us a piercing look, and I could feel Ali tense. "But I'll be back as soon as I can." He paused. "In case you need anything."

Hah! As if. "That's so kind of you. Thank you so much," I said, pouring on the charm.

17

"What will we do?" Ali asked the moment Angus tromped down the stairs. "We're supposed to meet Noah and Sara for lunch."

"We'll just have to work fast," I told her. "And we don't have to do everything today. It's up to us to decide how long we need to spend on the inventory. Text Sara and tell her that we'll be at Marcelo's by two. We'll take a quick look at Desiree's bedroom and maybe do one other room before we leave."

"It seems overwhelming," Ali said, looking down the hall, which seemed to stretch on forever, with endless wings and corridors hinting at endless treasures.

"One thing at a time, Ali," I told her. Sometimes my MBA training comes in handy. I leave the intuitive, subjective elements to Ali, and it works well. My sister is classic "right-brained," and I'm very "left-brained." What does that mean in practical terms? It means I'm logical, analytical, and objective. I approach everything as a task. I don't get emotionally involved and I try to devise the most effective way to do a job. Ali is the opposite. She runs on sheer emotion and instinct. That's why we make a good pair.

Right now, our first priority was Desiree's bedroom. Even though I'm left-brained, I had the gut feeling that the key to Abigail's death was somehow linked to Desiree's murder all those years ago.

The room was "girly," with its sunny yellow walls and charming white pointelle bedspread embroidered with daisies. I ran my hand lightly over the spread, admiring the fine handiwork. There was nothing out of place. Either Desiree was a compulsive neat freak, or Abigail had ordered the room tidied up after her death. It seemed more like a guest room than a bedroom belonging to a family member. There were few personal items in sight. A skirted vanity table held a silver comb-and-brush set, a small jewelry box, and what looked like an antique pedestal mirror.

"Empty," Ali said, pulling open a drawer under the vanity top. "Not even a lipstick. And someone has cleaned out the jewelry box. It's odd, isn't it?" She stood up, placing her hands on her hips. I had the feeling the closet and bureau drawers would also be empty. My optimism was quickly evaporating.

"It's very strange. I thought Lucy said the room was kept exactly as it was when Desiree was alive. Someone has obviously gotten rid of her clothes and all her personal effects." And this could have happened in the past few days, since Abigail's death, but we had no way of knowing.

"Why would Lucy lie about something like this?" Ali asked.

"Who knows? Maybe she never thought we'd check. Or

maybe someone raided the room in the past few days." I paused. "Someone Lucy might be protecting."

"Nicky," Ali said. She raised her eyebrows. "That would explain a lot. And it's not just valuables that are missing. What about photographs and keepsakes?" She lifted down a lovely hand-painted box from a shelf. "This might be promising. It looks like the kind of box you'd use to store letters." She lifted the lid and showed me the contents. "Empty. I'm afraid we've struck out again."

"Try the closet, and I'll check the nightstands," I suggested. Matching walnut nightstands were on either side of the bed. "Not a thing," I muttered a moment later. Could Lucy have removed everything from the room when Norman Osteroff had called to instruct her to give us free access to the house? Or had Nicky cleaned it out after Abigail's death?

Ali frowned as she flung open the closet doors. "Nothing here. At least nothing interesting." She pulled out a silk Japanese-style dressing gown, splashed with pink and magenta on a midnight blue background, and laid it carefully on the bed to inspect it. "Nothing in the pockets."

"What do you suppose has happened to her jewelry?" I asked. "That's what I can't understand. Remember that newspaper clipping Minerva showed us? Desiree was wearing some pretty serious bling when she was photographed for the society section."

I nodded. "I remember. It was probably worth a small fortune. Do you suppose Abigail has the jewelry stashed in a safe somewhere? After all, there are strangers in the house this summer, and maybe she didn't completely trust Angus or Sophie Stanton."

"That's a good point." I sat on the edge of the bed to think. "Abigail could have the jewelry tucked away somewhere, and she could have given Desiree's clothes to charity. And any odds and ends or makeup or perfume"—I glanced at the pristine vanity table—"might have just been thrown out." There was one empty perfume atomizer on the table, and it looked elegant, made of gold filigree in classic Art Deco style.

"So that would account for the clothes and jewelry. That still doesn't explain the lack of personal items. Letters, souvenirs, photographs. Maybe even a diary."

"You're right." I stared at the paintings on the wall. A selection of pastels and watercolors, mostly pastoral scenes and a couple of seascapes. A field of flowers and a small painting of Beaux Reves, with the shutters thrown open to catch the sunlight. It reminded me of the one I'd seen in Osteroff's office. I didn't know enough about art to know if the paintings were valuable, and I snapped a few pictures with my phone. We might be able to check them against the inventory or show them to Gideon and Andre.

"I don't see anything else to look at here," Ali said. She glanced at her watch. "Do you?"

"Probably not." I hesitated. "There's just one thing. That painting on the far wall. It seems out of place, doesn't it?" I pointed to a small painting of an Egyptian pyramid. It was in bold tones of sand and copper, a desert scene. "It doesn't look at all like the other paintings; it's not in the same style and the colors are all wrong."

"Maybe Desiree was sick of flowers and sailboats," Ali said.

"Or maybe it's here for a reason." I thought of the poem, "Ozymandias," that Abigail had included in her memorial service. I remembered thinking at the time that it was an odd choice. Was Abigail trying to tell us something? She obviously had her suspicions or she wouldn't have told Osteroff that she wanted us to check the inventory at the mansion.

It sounded like she didn't trust Lucy. Or Osteroff. Or Angus. And she certainly didn't trust Nicky Dargos.

"'Ozymandias,'" Ali said softly. "That was another name for an Egyptian pharaoh, Ramesses II. And that painting is set in the Egyptian desert, so . . ."

I sprang off the bed and raced to the painting. I tried to lift if off the wall, and nothing happened. "It's stuck to the wall. Something's wrong. It's practically welded in place."

"Wait, I see a tiny medallion on the bottom of the frame. Try pressing that." Ali's eyes were glowing with excitement. I touched the medallion, and the frame swung open, revealing a square niche in the wall. It was about a foot wide, a foot high, and pitch-black inside.

"Bingo," I said. "How did you think of that?"

"The tomb scene from *Raiders of the Lost Ark*." She grinned and then suddenly raised her finger to her lips, her gaze drifting to the open doorway. "Shh!" My hand froze in midair at the sound of footsteps on the stairs. Lucy was trudging up the steps, singing softly in Spanish. "Quick," Ali urged.

I reached inside, my heart thumping so loudly I was sure it could be heard two rooms away. The niche held a collection of papers, and I grabbed the first one I could reach and jammed it into my pocket. I closed the door to the portal just as Lucy passed by in the hallway. She was armed with a hand vacuum and the boom box, and apparently was in the midst of cleaning.

"Everything okay in here?" Her tone was cheerful, and if she was suspicious, she was covering it well.

"It's fine," I said, forcing a smile. "We just finished up, and we're going to meet some friends for lunch. We'll be back tomorrow morning if that's okay."

"Yes, sure," she said. "I know you have a job to do."

She sounded so pleasant I wondered if I'd been wrong to suspect her of anything. She didn't have any motive to murder Abigail, unless her son, Nicky, really *was* helping himself to treasures from Beaux Reves. If Abigail had found out and threatened to go to the police, I could imagine Lucy doing anything in her power to stop her.

And there was that pesky issue of the thirty million dollars' inheritance. Unless Abigail had changed her will— which we wouldn't know until the reading next week—Lucy stood to inherit a fortune. A million dollars for every year she'd spent working at Beaux Reves. Abigail was in good health and could have lived for a long time. Had Lucy become impatient for the big payoff?

Lucy continued down the hall, and Ali let out a deep whoosh of air as if she'd been holding her breath. "Wow, that was close," she said in a breathy voice. "What do you have there?" she said, eyeing my pocket.

"Let's wait till we're outside to look," I told her, making tracks for the stairs. I barely stepped into the bright Savannah sunshine before pulling a creased piece of paper from my pocket. "It's written to Desiree," I said to Ali as we stood on the portico. "It looks like a love letter."

"A love letter?" She peered over my shoulder. "'My darling Desiree, I can hardly wait to see you tonight. You are the light of my life. Sending you a gardenia to wear in your hair. Hoping they'll play our song and I can take you in my arms. Your conquering hero.'"

"I don't know what to make of it, do you?" I folded the letter carefully and placed it in my purse.

"A gardenia," she said slowly. "Wasn't Desiree wearing a white flower in her hair in that clipping from the society column? It could have been a gardenia."

I thought back to the faded clipping that the Harper sisters had given us. "She was wearing a flower, yes. I'd like to look at that picture again—" I stopped talking when I heard a door slam and then voices at the side of the house. Raised voices, and one of them was Lucy's. Lucy must have slipped down the back staircase, because it sounded as though she was standing outside, at the edge of the patio, arguing with someone. Ali and I edged closer.

"You know what you have to do." Lucy's voice was tight with anger. "Don't come whining to me. You got yourself into this mess, and now you'll have to sell it. That's the only thing you *can* do. See how much they'll give you for it. Maybe it's worth big bucks; maybe it's a fake."

"Easy for you to say," a man's voice retorted. "You win either way." He gave a derisive snort. "Come next week, you'll probably be thirty million dollars richer."

"That's if she didn't change her will," Lucy said coldly. "Anything could happen. I gave thirty years of my life to this place, and I could be out in the cold with you."

"What do you mean, out in the cold *with me*? Did she cut me out of the will?"

"Who knows?" She gave a harsh laugh. "Why should you get any money? Maybe she wanted to teach you a lesson. She knew you gambled your paycheck away. She told me one time she didn't want to throw good money after bad."

"Thanks for the vote of confidence," the man said with a snort. "I'm going into town."

"Jeb," she called after him, "get me a charger for my iPod. Nicky never got around to it."

"If I have time," he muttered.

Footsteps were heading toward the end of the portico, and Ali and I flattened ourselves against the stucco wall as a man rushed by. *Jeb Arnold, the estate manager.* We waited until he got into his Jeep and then made our way down the driveway. Lucy had advised him to sell something. But what?

"Jeb Arnold," Ali said thoughtfully. "I wonder how he fits into all this. Did you know he had a gambling problem?"

I nodded. "Nicky Dargos made some crack about him playing the ponies when we were sitting in the kitchen for breakfast." She looked surprised and I added, "You were playing up to Angus and probably didn't hear it."

"I didn't," she admitted. "How does all this fit together?"

"I'm not sure. Let's hope our friends can help us."

We zipped into Marcelo's at two o'clock sharp and spotted Sara and Noah talking animatedly at a booth in the back. Business was bustling at the popular Italian eatery, and delicious smells were wafting in the air. A server hurried by balancing steaming plates of ravioli, and I nearly cried with joy. The rich tomato aroma mingled with the scent of fresh basil, and I could almost taste the crusty Italian herb bread, fresh out of the oven.

"Are we late?" Ali said, slipping into the booth on Sara's side. That left me free to squeeze in next to Noah, and I had to admit, I liked the idea. Noah smiled at me as I settled in, and his eyes skimmed appreciatively over my outfit. I'd dressed carefully in a gauzy peasant top in ocean colors and white linen pants. I'd added espadrilles and silver hoop earrings, casual but a lot dressier than my usual workday attire at the shop.

I have no idea where our relationship is headed, but I always seem to dress up a little when I think I may be seeing him. I wasn't even aware I was doing this, but Ali pointed it out to me. Sisters know all our secrets, even the ones we don't know ourselves.

"Very nice," he murmured under his breath.

"Let's order," Sara said. "I'm starved." The server appeared as if by magic and we all made the same choice— ravioli with marinara sauce and iced tea. Sara looked at me and raised her eyebrows. "You're not going to make her take the bread away, are you?"

"No, I couldn't be that cruel," I teased her, reaching for a piece of the crusty loaf. "I know how much you love home-made bread."

Noah quirked an eyebrow. "I never know when Taylor is going on one of her no-carb kicks," Sara explained. "She'll send the bread basket back to the kitchen unless I watch her like a hawk."

"A no-carb kick?" Noah asked. He looked genuinely puzzled.

"Please, no diet talk," I urged. "We have to get right to work."

"Where do things stand with your inventory at Beaux Reves?" Sara asked. I'd texted her that morning to tell her about Abigail's surprising request and explained that we'd be spending the morning at the mansion.

"We're just scratching the surface," I told her. "We started with Desiree's room, and guess what we found?" I pulled the letter out of my purse and Sara scanned it before passing it to Noah. "It was hidden in a niche in the wall behind a paint-ing." It suddenly occurred to me how lucky we'd been. If I hadn't spotted that Egyptian painting and remembered the poem at Abigail's memorial service, we'd never have come across the letter.

"This is fantastic," Sara said softly. "I bet it was written by her beau, her escort to that fancy ball. He mentions 'our song,' and he wants to take her in his arms." She gave a little sigh. "This is so romantic."

"This needs to go to the police," Noah said with a frown. "Do you want me to drop it off for you? I'm going to the precinct right after lunch."

"Thanks." I passed back the note, and he carefully tucked it into a little evidence bag. "I'll be interested to see what Sam thinks about it. She told me she's coming to the Dream Club meeting."

Noah shot me a level gaze. "The police said they went through the house with a fine-tooth comb, but apparently it wasn't fine enough. You found something the cops missed. If I know Sam, heads will roll. She's not a fan of sloppy police work."

Noah knows our friend Detective Sam Stiles from the Dream Club, and his nephew, Chris, is a rookie officer on the force and reports to her. Sam has the reputation of being a tough, no-nonsense detective who has no patience for slackers and doesn't tolerate mistakes.

She's something of a skeptic about dream interpretation, but attends the meetings when she can. She initially showed up because of her friendship with Dorien Myers, the rather caustic longtime group member who fancies herself a psychic.

"But Beaux Reves is huge and there's a lot to look at," Ali said. I knew Ali would step in to defend the police; she can't stand to see anyone criticized. I'm not as forgiving as she is, but I think this time she was right. Beaux Reves is overwhelming. No police department would have the resources to go over every room. And in the early days, it wasn't even clear if a crime had been committed. The first responders assumed it had been an unfortunate accident and that Abigail had taken a fatal tumble down the stairs.

"It was just sheer luck that Taylor spotted that painting," Ali went on, "and it reminded her of the poem at Abigail's memorial service. The police probably only spent a few minutes in Desiree's room since there was no reason for them to turn the place inside out. No one uses it, and it looks almost like a hotel room. You'd never think there was anything valuable tucked away there."

"What's the significance of the gardenia in the note?" Sara asked.

"Maybe you could help us with that. Can you look in the archives and see if you can find the original photo?" I asked Sara. "The newspaper clipping from the Harper sisters was a bit faded. I'd like to see if Desiree really was wearing a gardenia that night."

"I can try to find the photo—no worries." She whipped out her notepad and scribbled a few words. Even though Sara has every electronic gadget under the sun, she still prefers to take notes the old-fashioned way, with a ballpoint pen and a tiny notepad. "And I have a new lead," she went on. "I came across the byline of a society reporter who retired a few years ago. Harriet Dobbs. She's going to tell me what she recalls about the ball and the guests. She didn't want to discuss it over the phone, so I'm planning to see her later this week." She paused to nibble on a breadstick.

"Why wouldn't she discuss it on the phone?" I asked.

"I don't know," Sara said. "Old-school, I guess. For all I know, she wants to talk off the record."

"Do you think she has information that's important to the case?"

Sara nodded. "I think she may know who Desiree was

with that night. The more we know about Desiree's last hours, the better."

"We still think Desiree's murder is connected with Abigail's, don't we?" Ali asked.

"This might be the break we need to connect the two cases."

"It could be," Noah said. "But we still don't have a motive. I've been following up on Nicky Dargos, the housekeeper's son, and Angus Morton."

"Any surprises with either one of them?" Ali asked. "I had coffee with Angus this morning, and there's something creepy about him."

"No surprises, just what we already knew," Noah offered. "Nicky has a record in juvie, and Angus has the reputation for being odd and a little standoffish."

"Do you mean 'odd' as in dangerous, or just quirky?" Sara asked.

"Just eccentric, not dangerous. A couple of people referred to him as 'lacking social skills.'" Noah paused to signal the server for another bread basket and gave a broad wink to Ali. The two are coconspirators in my battle to resist carbs; they love to tempt me with bread, which is my downfall. As Oscar Wilde said, "I can resist anything except temptation."

"That's a good description." I remembered how brusque Angus had been with me at breakfast the other day, although he'd certainly warmed up to Ali. "He was prowling around the halls when we started our inventory at the mansion this morning. He obviously wasn't thrilled to see us, and he asked Lucy Dargos what we were doing there." I paused as the server placed our salads in front of us. The house salad at Marcelo's is a masterpiece with plump tomatoes, baby Bibb lettuce, artichoke hearts, and Parmesan croutons in a dressing made with olive oil, basil, and balsamic vinegar.

"That must have been awkward," Sara said. "He probably realized Abigail was suspicious of him. Why else would she have you duplicate a job he'd already been hired to do?"

"It doesn't really make sense," I said, "unless Abigail knew that some items were missing. He definitely had his guard up. And I agree with Noah. There's something a little off about Angus; he was sending out weird vibes today."

"Do we know for sure things are missing from Beaux Reves?" Noah asked. "Or is it too early to tell?"

I quickly filled Noah and Sara in on the painting that the Harper sisters had shown us. "The painting appears in this book about the estate," I told Sara. I patted my tote bag. "It's a large landscape, a field of daisies, and it's pictured hanging in the front hall. I brought the book along for you; Minerva and Rose thought you might be able to use it for your article." I passed Sara the bag, and she peeked inside at the cover.

"It looks lovely. Be sure to thank them for me. But what's the significance of the painting?" Sara asked.

"The book says it was hung in the front hall so visitors could admire it as soon as they walked in the door. It had a place of honor, and now it seems to have vanished. I can't imagine Abigail ever selling it," I added. "It was a gift from a great-aunt and had sentimental value, if nothing else."

"Do we have any idea when it disappeared?" Noah asked.

"There's no way to be sure, but Ali noticed it wasn't hanging there when we had coffee in the kitchen the other day." The two sailing paintings were squeezed together as if to fill a blank space on the wall.

"And this was after Abigail's death," Sara said thoughtfully.

"Exactly." I sat back as the server placed a steaming dish of ravioli in front of me. I waited while she grated some Parmesan cheese on top, and then I sampled it. Perfection!

"What does the housekeeper say?" Noah asked.

"That it was sent out for cleaning."

"Cleaning, really?" Noah shook his head. He obviously didn't believe a word of it.

Ali nodded. "That's her story and she's sticking to it."

18

"There's something fishy going on. I've never heard of sending a painting out to be cleaned. An oil painting isn't like a pair of pants." Sara frowned before tucking into her lunch. "There must be some way of checking out her story."

"Gideon," I suggested. "He and Andre would know if paintings are cleaned, and maybe they can even help us find the shop."

"We should have asked Lucy the name," Ali said. "I didn't even think of it, and she certainly wasn't very forthcoming."

"She probably wouldn't have told you," Sara said. "I bet the whole thing is a fabrication."

I was sitting so close to Noah our thighs were practically touching, and he shot me a devilish grin as he inched a little closer. "Am I crowding you?" he said innocently. I'm sure he was enjoying the closeness as much as I was.

"Not at all," I shot back. "I was just wondering what was in that manila envelope lying on the seat next to you."

"Ah," he said, lifting it up. "The crime scene photos. I got them from Sam Stiles last week."

"Please don't open them here," Ali pleaded. "Just tell us what they reveal about her death."

"Don't worry, Ali. I'm going to give them to Taylor, and she can look at them later." Noah paused as if wondering how much to say. He knows that Ali can't bear to see or hear about anything violent. "Without going into detail," he said finally, "I can tell you the photos and autopsy report are pretty conclusive. According to the coroner and the police, Abigail's death was no accident. She was deliberately pushed down the stairs."

"Just as we thought," Ali said softly. Her eyes welled with tears, and I was glad Noah hadn't opened the envelope. I'd look at the photos later today and give Ali a sanitized version of what had happened to poor Abigail.

I felt sad thinking about Abigail's last moments. Had she recognized her attacker? It must have been so shocking to realize that her death would come at the hands of someone she knew and presumably trusted. It seemed certain that she had opened the door to her late-night visitor, so we had to assume it wasn't a random act of violence.

Had she looked into her killer's eyes as she was pushed down the stairs? Had she called out? I gave a little shudder, picturing the awful scene in my head. Wasn't it suspicious that Sophie Stanton was supposed to be away for the night and Lucy Dargos claimed she didn't hear a thing? How could anyone sleep that soundly? Her apartment is on the top floor of the mansion, but it still sounded odd to me.

"But there are a couple of other things," Noah said. "Sam

Stiles spotted something strange lying on the floor in one of the photos."

"Something strange?" I asked.

"An object. It may have been accidentally kicked under a bookcase during the struggle."

"What sort of object?" Ali asked in a tiny voice.

"I'm not sure. Sam asked the CSIs if they could enhance the photograph. It might be a piece of jewelry, I suppose. I had the impression it was a fragment of something."

"Jewelry? Maybe an earring?" I remembered Abigail was wearing jewelry that day at lunch; something simple and tasteful. Probably expensive.

"Maybe. They won't know anything else until it's enhanced. And it may not even be important. It's a shame they missed it when they processed the scene, though."

"Did they go back and try to find it?" Sara asked.

"Yes, but no luck, I'm afraid. All I know is that it was shiny and Sam said she thought it had a fish on it." *A fish?*

Ali frowned. "Well, doesn't that tell us that it really *was* important? The killer must have taken the time to retrieve it and destroy it."

"Not necessarily," Noah pointed out. "It could have been discarded in the normal course of housecleaning. Someone could have swept it up." I thought of Lucy explaining how she cleaned one room at a time from top to bottom. She prided herself on keeping Beaux Reves in excellent condition; every room was spotless. Could she have unknowingly thrown out a clue to Abigail's death? We'd probably never know.

I mentally went down the list of suspects while the server refilled our iced tea glasses. One name drifted to the surface. Sophie Stanton. Sophie was still a wild card who stood to inherit a fortune. I wished I'd had more time to check out her tote bag. The passport had been on top, but where had her wallet been? Her driver's license and credit cards?

There were other suspects, of course. Nicky Dargos and Angus Morton. Either one might have killed Abigail to cover up thefts from the mansion. Even though we'd just started our inventory, I was pretty certain objects were going to come up missing.

And there was the estate manager, Jeb Arnold, who feared he was going to be cut out of the will. Maybe he'd decided to kill Abigail before she changed her mind and scratched him off the list of beneficiaries. But how much money did he expect to inherit? And was it really worth killing over? Both Lucy and her son had accused him of having a gambling problem. Could it be that some people were pressuring him to pay up? He'd seemed disheveled and had smelled faintly of alcohol at Abigail's memorial service. Could it be his life was spinning out of control and he felt murdering Abigail was the only way out?

Another possibility was Laura Howard, who would acquire a prime piece of real estate as the last survivor of the tontine. Was that enough of a motive for murder? Possibly. But she was probably going to get the money eventually anyway since she was a few years younger than Abigail and would outlive her.

And if money was the motive, what about Lucy Dargos, who might have been getting a bit impatient for her promised inheritance? Or maybe she was trying to cover up her son's misdeeds?

But I still kept circling back to Sophie, the woman from nowhere.

"Where do things stand with Sophie Stanton?" I asked. As far as I was concerned, Sophie was the proverbial "mystery woman." She'd appeared out of nowhere, claiming to be a long-lost relative, and Abigail had embraced her as "family." There was talk that Abigail had changed her will, deciding to leave everything to Sophie, even though her lawyer had advised against it.

I wondered if Osteroff had done his own investigation on Sophie. Was it possible that the two of them were working together in some way? And how would we ever pry the truth out of Osteroff? If ever there was a guy who played his cards close to his vest, it was the prominent lawyer.

"I asked a friend at the DOJ to look into Sophie Stanton," Noah said. "She's never been fingerprinted, and she's not listed in any of the international criminal databases. She looks clean to me." He turned to face me. "Do you really think she's the killer?"

"I just don't know." Details were piling up, and we still weren't close to finding the truth. I put my fork down and was lost in thought. After a moment, Noah nudged me. "You're letting some perfectly good ravioli get cold. Why don't we all enjoy our lunch and we'll meet again when we have something else to report."

"Good idea," I agreed.

It was such a beautiful day, Ali and I decided to walk along the Riverwalk on the way home. It was nearly four o'clock; the sun was dipping into the horizon, and the whole scene took on a golden glow. I realized we were only a few blocks from Chablis and decided this would be a good time to drop in on Gideon and Andre.

"We were just going to call you," Gideon said minutes later, sweeping me into a hug. "Let's have lemonade on the porch while we tell you the latest gossip. You'll be surprised what we found out," he said, giving me a devilish smile. No one loves gossip more than Gideon.

"And it's related to the case," Andre offered. "Maybe," he amended.

"Now I *am* interested," I said, dropping onto a wicker settee with Ali. We had to crowd together on one side because Bibelot the cat looked up and gave us a baleful stare. He'd claimed half the settee for himself and had no intention of moving.

Gideon waited until we were settled with lemonade and cheese straws. I waved away the cheese straws, but Ali decided to indulge while I watched enviously. I would love to have her metabolism.

"Two bits of information," Gideon said dramatically.

"And you can decide whether they're helpful to the case," Andre added. "Are you ready?" When we nodded, he went on, "Laura Howard is going through a *very* messy divorce and stands to lose everything." He raised his eyebrows. "That land from the tontine might be the only thing standing between her and a one-bedroom apartment."

"She could be on her way to the poorhouse," Gideon offered.

"The poorhouse! I can't believe it." I gave Bibelot a very gentle push so I'd have a few more inches of space and the black cat glared at me. I decided to cross my legs, scrunch to the side, and let the cat have his way. He stretched out his paws, gave me a sleepy look, and drifted back to dreamland. "She's been married for years, and she lives in a classy part of town. There's no way she could be hurting for money. I don't see why a divorce would change anything."

Andre nodded. "Trust me, it changes everything. She signed a prenup and hubby caught her with an old school friend who moved back to Savannah. She was having a 'dalliance,' as they call it down here. Plus her husband has connections out the wazoo and hired the best divorce lawyer in town. And he has some girlfriend on the side, so he's eager for a divorce. Laura is going to be stuck with some third-rate ambulance chaser from a low-end firm. No high-profile attorney is going to go up against her husband in court. They'd be blacklisted. It's not worth crossing him."

"You said she had a dalliance," Ali said in amazement. "Why, she's a grandmother! How old is she? I thought she was one of Abigail's contemporaries."

"She's younger than Abigail," Gideon offered. "And if you remember her from the memorial service, you must have noticed she's pretty well preserved."

"She's had a lot of work done," Andre said archly. "Her friends say she's gone under the knife a few times. That's how she keeps that youthful glow."

"Wow, I still can't believe it," Ali said. "Breaking up a longtime marriage over someone from her past." She shook her head in disbelief. "What was she thinking? And at her age . . ."

Gideon laughed. "Age doesn't really matter. You know what my aunt Emma always says: *Just because there's snow on the roof doesn't mean there's not a fire blazing in the hearth.*"

"A good quote," I agreed. "And the second bit of gossip?" I prompted. Gideon had soft rock music playing in the background and a gentle breeze was wafting through the screens onto the porch. It was so relaxing I knew I could sit there for hours, but Ali and I had to get back home and prepare for the Dream Club meeting tonight.

"This is another big surprise," Andre said. "Jeb Arnold is trying to sell some arts and antiques to our fellow dealers here in town."

"Jeb Arnold!" My jaw dropped open and Ali nearly choked on her lemonade.

"I told you this would be a surprise," Andre said with a grin. "You didn't have any idea?"

"Well, I suppose we should have." I reached for a cheese straw in spite of my best resolutions and started munching away. I eat when I'm under stress, and this latest news was like a bolt from the blue. *Had we been looking in the wrong direction all the time?* I thought Jeb Arnold was a bit player in the drama, but all of a sudden he was front and center. "He's rumored to have a gambling problem, and maybe someone is pressuring him to pay up or else."

Ali gave a final sputter and composed herself. "We heard Lucy Dargos talking to Jeb this morning," she began, "and she advised him to 'start selling some things.'"

"Gideon, do you know what he was trying to peddle?" I asked. I thought of the missing painting in the front hall that had supposedly been sent out for cleaning. Was that one of the items on his list?

"Paintings, antiques." Gideon fluttered his hands. "Apparently, he brought in some photos of the items he was selling."

"They must be items from Beaux Reves," I said. "Maybe he's been stealing for years. The inventory is so huge, it would be hard to tell if a few things were missing here and there." I wondered how the police would handle this. If it was just hearsay, how would they ever prove it? If only we could get our hands on those photos.

Jeb didn't seem like the kind of guy who would crack under pressure, but I planned on mentioning his antique shop visits to both Detective Sam Stiles and Noah. "I don't suppose he had the items with him?" If there were security cameras in the shop, the police could nail him. Once he was faced with the evidence, he might admit to the thefts and then maybe confess to Abigail's murder. Or was I getting ahead of myself?

"No, he was too smart for that, and he didn't leave the photos with the dealers," Gideon said. "So there's no evidence trail to follow. I guess we can't assume the items were from Abigail's estate, but I think they must be." He gave a little sniff. "I can't really picture Jeb Arnold as a collector, can you?"

"I certainly can't," I said grimly. *Interesting.* All this time, I was sure that Angus or Nicky—or possibly both— were responsible for thefts from the mansion. But maybe I'd been on the wrong track all along. "Do you remember any specifics?"

Andre and Gideon exchanged a look. "There was that crystal ball that he tried to peddle to one of our friends," Andre said excitedly. "It was supposed to be vintage, and I bet it was worth a pretty penny. We didn't see the photo, of course, but Kevin from Forgotten Treasures said it was fabulous. He's actually thinking of making an offer on it."

"The crystal ball is from the mansion," I said. "I'm sure of it. Be sure to tell your friend he'd be buying stolen goods."

"We'll warn him," Andre said soberly. "That's the last thing he wants to get involved in."

I remembered the lady's slipper orchid I'd noticed on the hall table. According to the book from the Harper sisters, a crystal ball once sat there. Was that the crystal ball Jeb Arnold was peddling? How many crystal balls could be floating around Savannah? The estate manager must surely be desperate for money to make such a brazen move. If gambling debts were involved, Jeb Arnold might decide it was a matter of life and death. Namely, his own.

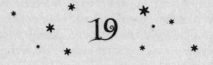

19

"Are you sure you can't stay for the meeting? Everyone will be so disappointed." It was nearly seven in the evening, and Sam Stiles was standing at our kitchen counter, nibbling on a homemade cracker. Ali was experimenting with a recipe for pumpkin crackers with chia seeds that she planned on serving with baked Brie tonight. The baked Brie is always a hit; she tops it with cranberries and almonds before wrapping it in flaky pie crust. We serve it downstairs on toasted baguette rounds and always sell out before the lunch crowd leaves.

But Ali's "Chia Nibblers" were another story. They had an odd taste, and I noticed Sam swallowed the cracker quickly before taking a large swig of coffee. She coughed twice and gave me an apologetic glance. Not all of Ali's culinary adventures are wildly successful, but she enjoys dreaming up new recipes and tweaking old ones.

"I can't stay," she said. "I'm on duty tonight, and I've got to get right back to the precinct house. I just stopped by to give you a photo of something we found in one of the crime scene photos." She opened an envelope and passed me a shot of the upper landing at Abigail's. "It's a little hazy, but my tech guy enlarged it as much as he could. I don't know how the CSIs missed it when they swept the scene, but somehow they did." She shook her head in dismay. Sam runs a tight ship and doesn't tolerate any slipups. "Take a look and see what you think."

Sam was right. The photo was grainy, a poor-quality shot of the second-floor landing at Beaux Reves. A shiny object about the size of a dime was peeking out from under a bookcase, and someone had circled it with a Magic Marker. This was the photo Noah had mentioned at lunch.

"What is it?" I asked. I stared hard at the object but couldn't identify it. Something stirred in my brain. It looked vaguely familiar, but I couldn't quite place it.

"I wish I knew," Sam said wryly. "Everyone seems to have a different idea."

"Did it fall off something? Could it be a button?"

"I don't think so. It's not the right shape; it looks more like a rectangle than a circle. It might be a piece of jewelry. I suppose it could have been pulled off in a struggle," Sam said grimly.

"Does it match anything Abigail was wearing that night?"

"No." Her tone was flat, resigned. "And Lucy Dargos insists that Abigail didn't own anything like that."

"What's your best guess?" I'd learned in the past that Sam's instincts are usually right on target and she has a keen sense of intuition. Her first guess is usually the right one.

"I'm not sure," she said, tilting her head to one side, peering at the photo. "It could be a medallion or a pendant,

I suppose. Maybe it was attached to a chain and when Abigail pulled at her attacker, it broke off." She shook her head and finished her coffee. "It's driving me crazy."

I took a closer look at the shiny object, which seemed to be winking back at me. Was it an earring? Possibly. But Lucy had said it didn't belong to Abigail, so did that mean her attacker was a woman?

"What's *your* best guess?" Sam asked.

I thought for a moment. It looked like an enameled piece of jewelry and appeared to have a fish design etched in black on a tan background. Only half of it was visible, but it struck a chord with me. There was an immediate sense of recognition. "Is that a fish?" I saw two rounded lines intersecting to form a caudal fin, or tail.

Sam nodded. "Yes. You have a good eye. It's a primitive design, a line drawing." She pulled out a sketch. This is what one of our CSIs thinks the whole image would look like." When I glanced at it, I felt a sudden jolt of recognition and gave a little gasp of surprise. "What do you see, Taylor? Do you recognize it?"

"Not exactly," I said slowly, "but I know I've seen that fish design somewhere before." I squinted my eyes and tried to concentrate. Nothing came to mind. *A fish, a fish. Where have I seen a fish?*

"Of course, we have no way of knowing how long it was under the bookcase. And it might not be connected to the case at all. It's just one of those loose ends that nags at me." She paused and lowered her voice. "Noah told me he gave you the crime scene photos. Did you take a look at them?" She leaned down to pet Barney, who was winding himself around her legs. "I know Ali doesn't want to see them."

"No, she doesn't," I agreed. "I looked them over, but I didn't say much to Ali because she gets so upset." I hesitated.

"From what I gather, you think Abigail was pushed because of the position of her body at the bottom of the stairs?"

"Yes, she was splayed out on the floor in the foyer, on her back. That's significant. It looks like there was a struggle on the stairs and she managed to turn to face her attacker on the landing." I nodded, imagining the scene. "So she fell down the stairs backward. She was pushed. If she'd tripped over the hall rug she would have fallen headfirst. In any case, the killer was too strong for her, although she did put up a struggle. The bruises on her arms match stains and tissue samples from the wall." I must have blanched because she said quickly, "Sorry, I shouldn't have been so graphic."

"That's all right," I said. I have a stronger stomach than Ali, but I find these images disturbing, too. "How does the hall rug come into this? I don't remember hearing about it."

Sam gave a short laugh. "The housekeeper, Lucy Dargos, tried to convince us that Abigail must have tripped on a little area rug on the landing. I didn't buy it. The rug was at the top of the stairs, looking a bit rumpled, but something about the scene just didn't seem right."

"You think the area rug was a cover-up?"

Sam shrugged. "I suppose it could be. Or maybe Lucy just couldn't accept the fact that someone murdered Abigail. It might have seemed so shocking that she was grasping for another explanation."

I grabbed the photo. "Is this the rug?" I pointed to a small burgundy Oriental at the top of the stairs. It was rumpled, just as Sam had described. "Because I don't remember ever seeing that rug there before. And I've been upstairs twice in the mansion and walked right past that landing. I think I would have noticed it."

"Interesting," Sam said as we heard the Dream Club members trooping up the stairs. "Another piece of the puzzle," she said softly. "I'd better go; let me know what else you find out tonight."

"I will," I promised. "Wait, just one more thing," I said as she turned to leave. "What did you think of the love letter Desiree had squirreled away in her bedroom? Noah said he'd drop it off at the station house for you."

Sam gave me a thumbs-up. "Excellent detective work." She grinned. "We may have to hire you and Ali as consultants."

"Did you go back and check to see what else was hidden in the wall?" I'd managed to grab the letter and replace the picture before Lucy caught me. I had the feeling there were more papers stashed away inside, but I'd had only seconds to spare. I could still see Lucy standing in the hall with her hand vacuum cleaner and boom box.

Jeb had probably forgotten to buy a charger for her iPod— and Nicky couldn't be bothered—so Lucy had to lug the boom box from room to room and plug it in each time. Apparently she liked to listen to Latin music while she worked. Maybe it made the drudgery of caring for Beaux Reves easier to bear.

"Yes, I sent a couple of detectives back to Beaux Reves an hour ago," Sam went on. "And they made sure Lucy stayed in the kitchen, so she wouldn't know what they were doing." She paused to toss her paper cup in the wastebasket. "That was a great hiding place. You and Ali were clever to spot it. Not much was there, except for a few newspaper clippings and some theater ticket stubs. You found the only valuable item, as far as I can tell."

"And the letter's not really valuable unless we can figure out who wrote it, is it?"

"Afraid not. Let me know if you come up with any hints."

I heard Ali greeting the guests, and my mind was whirring. Had Lucy deliberately tried to mislead the police? Had she placed the rug at the landing after the fact, in a clumsy attempt to cover up a murder?

"There's one other thing," Sam said, "and I don't know what to make of it." She leaned against the counter, and I could see she was tired. "The techs managed to lift a palm print off the hall banister."

"No fingerprints?"

"No, just a palm print, and it was smudged with a greasy residue. But the important thing is the trace elements in the residue. There's no way to tell if they came from someone's palm or from the banister itself."

"What kind of trace elements?" Sam had me intrigued.

"That's what's odd. The sample doesn't match any commercial cleaning product we can find. We ran the ingredients through a database."

"That's because Lucy makes her own furniture polish," I said quickly. "She's very proud of it. I remember her telling me fresh lemon juice was one of the ingredients. She keeps the polish in an antique bottle with a glass stopper on the kitchen counter."

Sam raised her eyebrows. "We found the antique bottle, but the ingredients don't match up with the smudge on the banister. The residue mixed in with the palm print contains lanolin and saddle soap. The lanolin isn't a surprise, but the saddle soap certainly is."

"Saddle soap?" *Saddle soap means horses.* I immediately flashed to Dorien's somewhat hazy dream about horses in a corral. But there were no horses at Beaux Reves, so we hadn't attached much importance to it.

"Yeah, weird, isn't it?" Sam muttered. "We're still working on it."

*   *   *

"What's on the menu tonight?" Persia asked, dropping onto the settee. Persia, who is a great cat lover, scooped up Barney and held him upright on her lap, looking straight into his eyes. Barney is a dignified cat who normally wouldn't stand for this sort of behavior, but Persia has such a winning way with cats, he tolerates it.

"Who's my handsome boy?" she crooned, gazing straight at him. Barney gave her a long, slow blink in return, which is a sign of affection in the feline world. Persia kissed him lightly on the forehead, placed him in her lap, and he immediately curled up nose to tail to take a snooze. People who think cats are standoffish and aloof should meet Barney. He melts into a love bug when he's around a cat lover like Persia.

"I'm still tinkering with that lemon squares recipe," Ali said, placing a platter of delectable pastries on the coffee table. "I used a little more fresh lemon rind in these and just a touch of honey. I think they have a really nice, tart flavor. Tell me what you think."

"Why would you tinker with the recipe, my dear?" Minerva Harper asked. "The last batch you made was sheer perfection. A touch of sweetness and that lemony tang." She sighed happily, spread a napkin on her lap, and reached for one of the pastries.

"They were heavenly," her sister Rose agreed. "In fact, I was going to order some for next month. I'll need enough to feed a crowd; we're planning a going-away party for the pastor. They'd be perfect for the Victorian tea we're hosting. Delicious and elegant."

"I'm so glad you liked them," Ali said, flushing a little. "But you know me, I love to experiment with recipes. I don't like to make the same thing twice."

"Yes, my dear, we certainly *do* know that." Minerva winked at Rose and I tried not to smile. Ali's "wheat germ sandies," studded with chunks of candied tofu, were memorable—and not in a good way. I was relieved when that recipe was finally retired. In spite of Ali's best efforts, there was no way to make those cookies edible. Ali still insists they were one of the "healthiest" things she has ever cooked. I had to remind her that they could hardly be called "healthy" if no one ate them. Even Boris, the dog who lives next door, turned up his nose at them.

"Who's going first?" Ali asked.

"Are we talking dreams or talking about the case?" Lucinda said, leaning forward. She was perched on the edge of her chair, dressed in one of her drab but expensive suits. I remembered her telling me she had a charity board meeting in town earlier today, so I supposed that was why she was dressed up.

"Well, either one," Ali said, surprised. "If anyone has anything new to add to the case, I suppose we should deal with that now, and then turn to dreams."

"I have some news," Lucinda said. She was almost breathless with excitement and waved away the pastry tray when Dorien passed it to her. We had a full house tonight, and I was happy to see that Sara had managed to make the meeting.

"Well, don't keep us in suspense," Sybil said.

20

"It's not a dream," Lucinda said, drawing out the moment, "but it's a clue. At least I think it is. I suppose it falls under the category of *gossip*, now that I think of it." Dorien gave a tiny eye roll, apparently impatient with Lucinda's theatrics. I feel more sympathetic to Lucinda and try to give her some leeway. She's rarely at the center of any gathering, and I could see she was enjoying her moment in the sun.

"Gossip isn't always a bad thing," Minerva said gently. "Sometimes it gives us insights we wouldn't get any other way. We're eager to hear your news, Lucinda." She nodded encouragingly, put down her sweet tea, and gave Lucinda her full attention.

"Some of you may remember that I have a nephew at Tulane," Lucinda began. Her eyes flashed with excitement.

"Yes, we remember, dear; you must be very proud of him," Rose said politely. "But how does this relate to the case?"

"I'm getting to that," Lucinda said quickly. "I happened

to talk to Troy over the weekend, and he'd read about Abigail's death. So we chatted about that for a few minutes and then he dropped a bombshell."

"A bombshell?" Sara asked. She was juggling a plate of pastries on her lap and had her tiny notebook balanced on the arm of an upholstered chair.

She'd brought Remy, who was curled up by the fireplace. Remy is, without a doubt, the world's best-behaved dog. She had stared inquisitively at the cats when she first met them, and then like a proper canine guest, had kept to herself and never looked at them again. She'd been dozing but woke up and gave a low woof when Sara spoke up. "Hush, Remy," Sara said softly. She held her hand out, palm up, and Remy promptly went back to sleep.

"Troy told me he *knew* Angus! How odd is that?" Lucinda went on. "They're not really friends, of course—more like acquaintances; they travel in the same circles. Troy knew all about Angus going to grad school someplace in the northeast and snaring a summer job in Savannah. Apparently Angus is friendly with one of Troy's old fraternity brothers." She paused. "And the fraternity brother gave Troy an earful about Angus."

"An earful? What did he tell him?" Sara said. She quickly scarfed down a brownie and put her plate on the coffee table so she could take notes more easily. Sara is used to eating with one hand and taking notes with the other. When I try it, I end up with lemon meringue in my lap.

"Well, for one thing, Angus is hurting for money."

"That wouldn't be unusual for a graduate student," Rose said gently. "All these young people seem to be burdened with student loans these days. In my time, we never had to deal with debt like that. My heart goes out to them."

"But this is more than just student loans, Rose," Lucinda

said. "Apparently he was in such dire straits that he was going to have to drop out of school completely unless he figured out a way to make money over the summer."

"Maybe he *did* figure out a way to make money," I said wryly. Lucinda looked puzzled. I hadn't mentioned that I suspected both Nicky Dargos and Angus of selling off antiques from Beaux Reves. "Sorry," I said when she stopped talking. "I was just thinking aloud. Please go on."

"Now, this part may be gossip, because I'm not sure he was ever officially charged with anything . . ."

"Charged with something? Good heavens. You mean he has a police record?" Rose said excitedly. Lucinda's comment certainly had caused a stir in the room. Dorien's eyebrows had shot up in surprise, and Sara was scribbling furiously in her notebook.

"Not quite," Lucinda admitted. "It seems there were some items missing from a local museum in Boston, one of the smaller ones. It was poorly staffed, and Angus was assigned to do an inventory."

"An inventory!" Minerva said. She and Rose exchanged a look. "History repeating itself," she said grimly. "Poor Abigail. She prided herself on being a good judge of character. She never would have hired Angus for the summer if she knew there'd been a hint of scandal in his past."

"How did she find Angus?" I asked.

"She answered an employment ad placed in an art magazine," Minerva said. "I remember she checked his references and they seemed fine. He was visiting Savannah this past spring, and she asked him to tea at the mansion. She said he had an impressive résumé, and when she took him on a tour of Beaux Reves, he seemed knowledgeable about the artwork and antiques. The fact that she met him in person is what swayed her, I think. Normally, she would never hire anyone who didn't have a strong recommendation from someone she knew and respected."

"Maybe Angus forged his reference letters," Ali said. "I can't imagine anyone writing him a letter if they knew his history."

"I suppose it's possible," Rose said. "Abigail could be taken in by people, I'm afraid. She said her motto was, *Trust, but verify.* Yet at the same time, she relied heavily on instinct. If Angus turned on the charm during his meeting with her, that could have swayed her. She might not have checked his references too carefully."

I found it hard to imagine Angus turning on the charm for anyone—he'd certainly been unfriendly with me—but maybe he could be personable if there was something to gain. And he'd managed to secure a spot at Beaux Reves, in spite of having been under suspicion at the Boston museum. Was he really innocent or had he talked his way out of it? As Minerva says, where's there's smoke, there's fire. Angus was a cool customer, and I found it hard to get a handle on him.

"There's something I'm puzzled about," Sara said abruptly. "Did Angus have a firm alibi for the evening Abigail was murdered?"

"I think someone in the office said he was in Charleston that day." Persia works as a paralegal, and Abigail's murder was the talk of the law firm.

"That's right," Sara said. She riffled quickly through her notes. "But I thought I remembered there was something a bit off about his alibi? Or maybe I imagined it." Sara is very organized with her note keeping and uses color-coded tabs to indicate direct sources, police reports, interviews, witness

statements, and more. "Wait, here it is!" She held up an index
card triumphantly. "Angus told the police he had a late dinner at the Seven Sisters in downtown Charleston that
evening. He paid by cash, so there's no record of it," she
added with a frown. "This doesn't sound too convincing to
me. That's hardly a solid alibi. Most restaurants close before
ten o'clock."

I found myself wishing that Sam Stiles could have stayed
for the whole meeting tonight. She'd excused herself early
because she was needed back at the station. I would have
liked to have heard her thoughts on Angus.

"Because if Angus had money problems and a shady past
at a museum," Sara went on, "he's looking better and better
for Abigail's murder."

Persia shrugged. "He does have an alibi. As far as being
at the restaurant, I mean. He says he ran into someone from
Beaux Reves who was having dinner at the same restaurant
that night."

"Who?" the Harper sisters chorused.

"Sophie Stanton." *Sophie Stanton?* I was flabbergasted.
What are the odds of that happening?

"Are you sure about this?" I asked.

"Yes, that's what he told the police," Persia said calmly.
"Remember when Sophie Stanton said she was visiting a
friend in Charleston on the night Abigail was killed? Apparently she had dinner at the Seven Sisters."

"So they alibied each other?" I asked. "Didn't that raise
some eyebrows with the Savannah PD?"

"Well, no one has ever discovered a connection between
those two," Sybil pointed out. "So I suppose it was just one
of those odd things that happen in life. Probably the police
didn't think too much of it. And neither Sophie nor Angus
were considered suspects back in the beginning."

"I have the feeling you don't think either one of them committed the murder," I said to Sybil. "Did you have a dream? Or is this just intuition?"

"Just intuition," she said. "And maybe a dream or two," she acknowledged. "I've been having dreams about water ever since Abigail's death." She paused and looked around the group. "And remember how we always believed that Desiree's death is somehow linked with Abigail's?" She sat back and folded her arms over her chest, her gold bangle bracelets clanking together. Sybil's voice was soft, hypnotic, and we waited for her to continue. "Well, I don't know about the rest of you, but I still believe it. Lucinda dreamt about the girl in the white slip dress walking along the riverfront at night, and that's when I started dreaming about dark water. I haven't given up on the idea of solving both murders at once."

"You think they were murdered by the same person?" Dorien asked.

"I do. And I don't think it was Angus or Sophie. I think we're on the wrong track," Sybil said flatly.

"Well, if they both have an alibi," I said slowly, "I guess we could cross them off the list." Yet I felt strangely reluctant to cross them off completely. Sybil might think they were innocent, but I had a gut feeling that something was off about those two. I had the strange sense that they were connected and that there was more to their relationship than met the eye. Did that mean they were murderers? Maybe, maybe not.

Minerva put down her glass of tea and blinked. "Wait a minute, everyone. Persia, did you say they were having dinner at the Seven Sisters in Charleston?"

"Yes, that's what I heard at the office. I know it seems odd that they both had dinner there the same night, but it's not impossible," she added. "They ran into each other just by chance at the Seven Sisters."

"Oh, but I'm afraid it *is* impossible, my dear," Minerva said. "Totally impossible."

"Yes, completely out of the question," Rose echoed. "It never happened. I'm afraid someone is telling a fib." She tut-tutted. "In fact, two people."

"And why is that?" Ali was perched on the edge of the love seat and leaned forward to catch Minerva's reply.

"Why? Because we're friends with the owner, Marilyn Nettles," Minerva said firmly. "Such a dear person. We go way back."

"Yes, we do," Rose agreed. "Why, I remember when Marilyn had her coming-out ball; she was such a sweet young thing. The prettiest girl in Savannah, they said. And there were some lovely contenders that year, as I remember. But Marilyn was the fairest of them all. She used to live right here in Savannah before she moved to Charleston, you see. So that's how we know her and her family." That made sense. The Harper sisters seem to know everyone who has lived in Savannah for the past seventy-five years.

"But the restaurant," I cut in quickly. "The Seven Sisters." I didn't want to be rude, but this was no time for a trip down memory lane and I knew I had to get Rose back on track fast.

"Oh my, yes, the restaurant," Rose said. Her eyes had taken on a faraway look. "Her dear mother started it and Marilyn continued it. She uses all of the original recipes, and you can feel her mother's presence in every dish she prepares."

Dorien was practically vibrating with impatience. "But the restaurant," she said bluntly. "What do her mother and her recipes have to do with Sophie and Angus? Either they ate there that night or they didn't."

"Oh, but I was getting to that," Rose said with a slight re-proach in her voice. "You see, Marilyn's dear mother, Dianne

Nettles, passed away on May eighteenth. So every year, on that date, the restaurant is closed to honor her. It's a family tradition. Abigail died on the evening of the eighteenth. The police had no way of knowing about the memorial day for Dianne Nettles, but I assure you, Sophie and Angus are lying. They couldn't possibly have eaten at the Seven Sisters that night because the restaurant was closed."

There was dead silence in the room, and Rose's words seemed to hang in the air. *The restaurant was closed*. Dorien opened her mouth to say something and then snapped it closed quickly. All of us were trying to make sense of what we'd just heard. Angus and Sophie were lying, and each was protecting the other. I felt vindicated because I'd had the strong suspicion all along that something was going on with those two. Why did they lie about being at the restaurant? This put a new spin on things.

"Up until now," Ali said slowly, "I had no idea there was any connection between Sophie and Angus."

"I don't think any of us did," Persia said. She gave the Harper sisters an admiring glance. "You two always amaze me. I just don't understand how you can know so much about everyone in Savannah."

Rose laughed. "Well, there's no secret, dear." She reached over and patted her sister's hand. "We've just lived here a long time. And we've kept our ears open. It's surprising how much you can learn about people when you listen. Savannah is like a small town in some ways. People love to talk, and everyone knows everyone else's business."

We turned to dream interpretation then, and Etta Mae described another dream about a love letter written in "navy blue ink." My mind shot back to the letter we'd uncovered behind the painting in Desiree's room. Could that be the letter Etta Mae was dreaming about? This was the second time she'd had that identical dream.

"It's always significant when you return to the same dream material," Sybil said. "Usually it means that the issue isn't settled in your mind, or that you didn't quite understand the meaning of the dream."

"Well, I certainly don't claim to understand the meaning," Etta Mae said a little defensively. "It's just a letter. I don't know what to make of it. It's sort of old and wrinkled, like someone wrote it a long time ago."

"And you say it was written on cream-colored paper with navy blue ink," I said softly.

"Yes, that's about the only part that's really clear to me." Etta Mae twisted her hands in her lap. "I had the feeling I was supposed to do something about the letter, but that part's kind of hazy." She shook her head and sighed. "Sometimes I wonder if I'll ever get the hang of this."

"You will, I promise you," Sybil said gently. "Maybe all you were supposed to do was tell us about the dream, and that's exactly what you did. You gave us a reminder tonight about the letter. Sometimes that's enough. You fulfilled the message in the dream." She looked around the group. "Did anyone else have a dream about a letter?"

"No," I spoke up, "but there *is* a letter involved in the case. Or it could be involved; we're not sure. We just discovered it." I quickly filled everyone in on the letter we'd found in Desiree's room.

Persia clapped her hands delightedly. "You see, Etta Mae? That's got to be the letter you saw in your dream. You led Taylor and Ali right to it. Everything is connected, and it all comes out in dream material. This could be a major break in the case, and it's all because of you."

I smiled and kept quiet. The dream about the letter could be sheer coincidence, but Etta Mae looked so pleased I didn't want to burst her balloon. Some people in the group think that every dream has some significance, but I tend to take a more stringent approach. Unless I absolutely can link a dream to a specific detail in the case, I don't pay much attention to it.

"So where do things stand?" Sybil asked, after we'd heard a couple of ho-hum dreams about traveling with pets. Some nights are slow nights for the Dream Club, and this was one of them. No one really had anything inspiring to report, and Minerva said she'd taken some allergy medicine and hadn't dreamt at all.

"Where do things stand with the case? I wish I knew." I poured myself a final glass of sweet tea. I had the feeling Ali was going to wrap things up pretty quickly.

"Have you heard the news about Laura Howard's divorce?" Rose Harper asked. "Such a shame, after all those years. I've always had my suspicions that her husband would pull something like this. Of course, I couldn't say a word to Laura about him; she always defended him. Really a dreadful little man. Laura is much too good for him." She paused and reached for the last lemon square with an apologetic glance at Minerva. "There are times when I really wish I hadn't been right about someone, and this is one of them."

"We just heard the news about Laura's divorce today," I said, giving a quick rundown on what Gideon had told us. "Gideon said Laura couldn't break the prenup, and it looked like she was going to be out in the cold—"

"But thanks to the tontine, she won't be," Minerva said shrewdly. "She could sell off that piece of property to-morrow and make a fortune."

"And make an even bigger fortune if she held on to it," Rose chimed in. "I looked it up online last night and nearly died when I saw how much it was worth."

"You looked it up?" Etta Mae asked.

"City tax records," Rose said crisply. "Once you find out what the taxes are on a particular property, you have a pretty good idea what it's worth."

"Rose, sometimes you amaze me," Sybil said in a tone of wonderment. Rose is full of surprises. She's an octogenarian yet is so computer savvy she researches everyone's genealogy as a hobby.

"I do have a suspect that I'm leaning toward." I hesitated. "But I don't know if the rest of you will agree with me. I'm not even sure Ali and I are on the same page about this."

"Who is it? I thought you were circling back to Sophie Stanton, but you weren't clear on the motive."

"I've moved away from Sophie Stanton as the killer," I said mildly. "For the moment, at least. I've got someone else in my sights right now."

"Even after what you've learned tonight?" Persia asked. "Sophie lied to the police. She covered up for Angus, and that tells me the two of them must be up to something. Doesn't that put her back at the top of the list?"

"Not necessarily. Sophie and Angus may be covering up something, and they do seem like shady characters. But does that make them killers?" I reached down to pat Barney, who was trying to climb up the side of the love seat. "I have someone else in mind. Every time I think about the case, I keep coming back to her."

"Her?" Ali asked.

"Lucy Dargos." Dorien gave a sharp cackle, Lucinda tut-tutted, and Ali looked perplexed.

It was obvious no one in the group agreed with me, but being Southern ladies, they were too polite to say so.

"Am I the only one who thinks she did it?" I asked. "Seriously?" A long beat passed.

Finally Minerva looked over at me and winked. "The cheese stands alone," she said with a smile.

21

If Lucy Dargos suspected that I was harboring such dark thoughts about her, she gave no sign when I arrived at Beaux Reves the following morning. Ali had decided to stay in the shop and help Dana plan a series of tea tastings that we hoped would bring in some business.

I realized we'd been shoving a lot of extra work on Dana lately, expecting her to come up with new marketing campaigns, take charge of decorating the shop window, and generally run the place while we were absent. It was way too much work for one person, even for someone as energetic as Dana. So Ali urged me to go to the mansion by myself and said she'd touch base with me in the afternoon.

"Come in," Lucy said, smiling as she opened the massive front doors to the estate. "Coffee is in the kitchen, and I just took some *ensaimadas* out of the oven."

Lucy's *ensaimadas* are out of this world. I'd sampled them the last time I had coffee in the kitchen and was tempted to ask her for the recipe. They're a Spanish version of sweet rolls and are basically buttery pastry brushed with cinnamon and honey before baking. I could smell the delicious aroma as I stepped into the front hall.

I looked up the beautiful walnut stairs to the second-floor balcony, and she followed my gaze. The coffee was tempting, but I hesitated. *There's so much work ahead of me. Do I really have time to be snacking in the kitchen?* She smiled and shook her head as if she'd read my thoughts. "You can work later," she insisted. "The *ensaimadas* are best when they're hot from the oven."

"You win," I said, caving. Now that I saw Lucy in her work environment, so welcoming and friendly, it was hard to believe I'd pegged her as a killer just last night. There was something so disarming about her wide smile and embroidered apron that I wondered if my initial suspicions about her were off target.

The *ensaimadas* were calling to me with their sugary little voices, and I dutifully trotted after Lucy as she made her way to the kitchen. But then I stopped dead in my tracks. *The painting was still missing.* I gestured to the blank spot on the wall and tried to keep my voice casual. "It's still not back?"

"Oh, the painting," she said dismissively. "I don't know why you trouble yourself with that." She gave a wide smile, waggling her fingers at me. "*No importa, no importa,*" she said in her lilting voice. Was she trying to charm me? Or was I barking up the wrong tree with my missing-painting theory?

"They're still cleaning it?" I asked.

She sidestepped the question. "It will be back soon. Maybe later this week. Come, come," she said, hurrying into the kitchen. "You can have coffee with Miss Sophie."

Miss Sophie? Another chance to talk to the cool mystery guest, and this time I was going to press her harder. I smiled and slipped into a chair directly across from her at the wide kitchen table. She put down her newspaper and frowned, a line appearing between her eyes.

"Hello, Sophie," I said as Lucy slid a cup of coffee toward me. "How nice to see you again. I wasn't sure you would still be living at Beaux Reves."

Sophie paused, probably wondering exactly how rude she dared be. "I'm here for the time being," she said vaguely. "Since Abigail passed away, things are in a bit of disarray."

"Disarray?" I tried to look puzzled. "It looks like Lucy has everything under control," I said, which earned me a deeper frown.

"*My* plans, I mean," she said irritably. "I expected to be here for the entire summer, but now"—her shoulders lifted in an elegant shrug—"things are a bit uncertain."

She looked like a million dollars in a tailored white linen suit with trousers and a black silk blouse, open in a deep V neck, showing off a chunky gold necklace. I could picture her on a yacht in the south of France or maybe lunching outdoors at a ritzy hotel along La Croisette in Cannes. Her open tote bag was perched on the seat next to her, and I could see some papers peeking out of the top. *If only she'd excuse herself for a moment, I'd love to get a look inside that bag. Why is she really staying in Savannah? Is she waiting for the reading of the will?*

Lucy was humming softly to herself, listening to a Latin song on the clunky boom box. Sophie wasn't in a chatty mood, so I helped myself to one of the *ensaimadas* and munched away, planning my explorations for today. I'd brought my inventory list with me and scanned it as I ate. I could feel Sophie's eyes on me, but I refused to look up. She moved restlessly in her chair, and I knew she wanted to ask me something.

"You're going over certain rooms in the house? Both the public rooms and the private rooms?" She didn't hide her curiosity as she tried to read my list upside down from across the table. For once she sounded genuinely interested, not just irritable and unpleasant.

"Yes, I have a few items I need to track down today. I'd like to wind everything up by the end of the week, and I'm making a note of anything that seems to be misplaced." I saw Lucy's back stiffen at the word "misplaced," and her hand stopped in midair as she rinsed out the cups in the sink. I wondered if Nicky had been helping himself to the items I was looking for.

"Exactly what do you think may be misplaced?" Angus said, suddenly appearing in the doorway from the front hall. His face was creased in a scowl; I could see he wasn't thrilled at my choice of words. *He'd like the word* "missing" *even less*, I thought with grim amusement.

"Oh, just a few things here and there," I said, refusing to be intimidated. "Of course, this is really early in the inventory process, so I have no idea what will turn up down the line." I gestured to the list next to me. "Abigail was very precise about what items she wanted me to find. Since the items could be scattered all over the mansion, I suppose I'll have to go into every room." I paused. "Are there storerooms somewhere where I might find some of the larger pieces? The ones that are no longer on display?"

"What larger pieces?" Angus said in the same argumentative tone. I could hardly believe he'd charmed himself into a position at Beaux Reves; he was one of the most unpleasant individuals I'd ever come across. "You'll have to be more specific."

I picked up the list and began reading. "Eighteenth-century Georgian mahogany slant-front desk with original Hepplewhite brass pulls, the writing compartment filled with small drawers and cubbyholes." I glanced at Sophie, who'd stopped eating to listen. "I'd say that's pretty specific, wouldn't you? I didn't see that piece anywhere in the public rooms and I assume it's not in any of the bedrooms. So that made me think there must be a storeroom, maybe in the attic or the basement. And that's where I'll find the larger pieces."

Sophie and Angus exchanged a look, and I was sure I saw a flash of fear in her eyes. Was Angus stealing from the mansion and Sophie was somehow involved? The missing items seemed to be the focal point of a web, drawing in more and more people. First it was just Angus and Nicky. And now I had the feeling that Sophie Stanton and Lucy Dargos might also be involved.

"There are a few pieces up in the attic," he said grudgingly. He looked pointedly at my half-full coffee cup. "I can take you up there before I go out this morning," he offered. "And there are some more in the basement."

"That would be nice," I said vaguely. "Are you going back to Charleston to do some research today?"

He shot a quick look at Sophie. I had definitely touched a nerve. "Why would you ask that?"

"No particular reason, I just wondered." I sipped my coffee, letting him stew for a couple of minutes. Sophie went back to reading the newspaper, but I know she was hanging on our every word. "You had dinner in Charleston the night Abigail died, didn't you? I think I remember reading that somewhere."

"Yes," he said too quickly. "At the Seven Sisters."

"Really?" I put my coffee down and stared at him. "At the Seven Sisters on High Street in Charleston?"

"Yes. Sophie was having dinner there, too," he said, the words tumbling out in a rush. *Pressured speech*, they call it. I knew he was lying. I glanced at Sophie, who was a cooler customer than Angus. She stared right back at me coldly; her features could have been chiseled out of stone. "Tell her, Sophie," he demanded, nodding in my direction.

Sophie gave a tiny catlike smile and placed her hands in front of her on the table. She'd seen this coming a mile away and was ready for it. "Not the *Seven Sisters*, Angus," she said without taking her eyes off me. "It was the *Sisters* on Fairmont Avenue. Don't you remember?" *Score one for Sophie.* Either someone had tipped her off or she had done her research and discovered the Seven Sisters restaurant had been closed that night. *Nice save, Sophie!*

"I thought—" Angus said and then stopped abruptly. He was obviously out of his element. Sophie was what they call a "practiced liar," and he wasn't. Clinging to his clumsy mistake only made things worse. It would have been smarter to follow Sophie's lead.

"It doesn't matter what you thought, Angus," she said icily. "It was the Sisters restaurant. On Fairmont."

Angus nodded, his expression tight. If they were working together, Sophie was clearly the brains of the operation.

"So . . . do you want to see the storerooms?" he asked bluntly, noticing my coffee cup was empty.

"That would be nice." I stood up and tucked my inventory papers under my arm.

"Oh, Taylor," Sophie said suddenly, "I've been meaning to ask you something." I casually moved around the corner of the table, where I had a clear view of her tote bag. I noticed she had one of those narrow little notebooks, the kind Sara had balanced on the arm of the chair last night.

"Is there something I can help you with?" The kitchen was very still, and the only sound was Lucy, who had started humming again to the low music from the boom box.

"I wondered"—for the first time Sophie seemed to falter—"would it be possible for me to attend a Dream Club meeting sometime?"

I hadn't expected this. "I'm sorry, but it's a closed group," I said evenly. "We don't allow visitors." The fact is, we go through a rigorous screening process and are very picky about who we allow in the group. Everyone has to vote on admitting a new member, and they have to have strong recommendations. Last year, we had one gentleman drop out of the group. He was a professor at the local university, and I'd thought he would be a good match. However, after a few sessions, he'd decided he wasn't really interested in dream interpretation and left the group.

"Oh, but I wouldn't expect to say anything," Sophie said, fluttering her hands. "I would just sit there observing, soaking up the atmosphere." She flashed what she probably thought was a winning smile. Like many people, Sophie can be pleasant when she wants something. "I would be as still as a church mouse," she promised.

I shook my head. "I'm sorry, but it's impossible. Having an outsider would be very disruptive to our members. They insist on strict confidentiality, and they wouldn't feel comfortable sharing their dreams if you were sitting there. It's nothing personal; it's just the way we do things."

Her lips formed a thin line, and she sat back in her chair. She blinked and blew out a little puff of air as if she were trying to get her feelings under control. "Oh, I quite understand," she said after a moment. What a transformation. The angry scowl had vanished, and she had morphed her features into what passed for a pleasant expression. "It was just an idea; no worries."

"Are you ready to check out the storerooms?" Angus said curtly. *What a charmer.* He glanced at his watch.

"Of course. Lead on," I told him.

"Angus," Sophie called as we headed down the hall. "Can you give me a lift into town today? My car's acting up."

"Sure." He shrugged. "Be with you in a couple of minutes." He turned to me. "Attic or basement? They both have antiques. But I don't know what's on your list."

I tried not to shudder at the mention of a basement. I have a touch of claustrophobia, and I don't do well in dark, enclosed spaces. When Noah had described the FBI hostage training exercise he'd been subjected to at Quantico, I'd gotten goose bumps. Could I have survived being blindfolded, bound at the hands and feet, and tossed into a storage shed like a bag of potatoes? It's a good thing I never applied to the Bureau, because I know I would have cracked under that kind of pressure.

My claustrophobia is under control but only because I mentally prepare myself for situations and try to take as much control of my environment as I can. I make sure I get an aisle seat on planes, and I avoid elevators whenever I can.

"Let's try the basement," I told him. It was time to "lady up" and not give in to my phobia. I was surprised when Angus made an abrupt right turn and walked into a tiny alcove that led into the library. "This is the way to the basement?"

"It's one way to get there," he said, smirking. I had the feeling I wasn't going to like what was coming. "I hope you're not claustrophobic," he said in a nasty tone.

"Why's that?" I managed to keep my voice level, but just barely.

"Because we have to go through a secret passage in the library, and it's pretty cramped. This is it." I took a quick look around a beautiful library with a magnificent fireplace and a marble mantelpiece. Two ceramic dogs guarded the fireplace, and there was elaborate dark wood paneling with books stashed from the floor to the ceiling.

I would have liked to explore a little more, but Angus pushed against a center panel in a bookcase and a hidden door suddenly swung open. It was pitch-black beyond the doorway, and I could dimly make out what looked like a staircase.

"Will you be okay?" he asked.

"I'll be fine," I assured him. He gave me a strange look as if he knew I was afraid and was enjoying every moment of it.

"After you," he said, his eyes glinting.

I took a deep breath to steel myself against what was coming and started down a narrow set of stairs. It was so tight, my shoulders touched against the walls on both sides. "We need some light," I reminded him. "It's terribly dark in here."

"Sorry," he muttered, not sounding sorry at all. He pressed a switch and the staircase was bathed in a low-level light. It wasn't ideal, but at least I could see where to put my feet. Angus was very close behind me, and I wondered for one horrible moment if he was going to push me down the steps.

When I reached the bottom, I realized we were in a large space with dozens of what I guessed were paintings and antiques stacked against the walls. Some objects were covered with sheets or drop cloths, and the whole place was dank and musty. The air was so foul I coughed, feeling my allergies kicking in. It smelled of earth, soil, and moisture, and I had a sudden image of an open grave.

"When's the last time you've been down here?" I asked him.

He was standing a few feet away from me and seemed reluctant to go any farther. I wondered if he was going to watch me the whole time I inspected the basement, but then I remembered he'd told Sophie he'd give her a lift into town. "I checked out the inventory in the basement when I first arrived," he said, "but I don't spend much time here now. There's so much to do upstairs, cataloging the antiques in the public rooms, that I just haven't had a chance to deal with this."

"The lighting is so dim in here," I said. "How do you get any work done?" I could only see clearly for a few feet in any direction. I could barely make out some flat, rectangular shapes leaning against the wall, and I assumed they were paintings. I saw the edge of a gilt frame peeking out of one. The dark, looming shapes were beginning to creep me out, and I was starting to feel as though I were trapped in a Wes Craven movie. At any moment I'd turn into a terrified, shrieking heroine calling for help.

"It's usually brighter than this," Angus admitted. "A couple of fuses blew the other day. Lucy plugged in too many things at once, and I heard a popping noise. I'm sure that's what did it. I could try to work on it now, but I've got to get to Charleston." He looked at me, gauging my reaction. "Maybe you'd like to do this another day?"

"I'll be fine," I said airily. Actually I wasn't fine at all. But there was no way I was going to give Angus the opportunity to move out any antiques or paintings. My chest was getting tight—either from allergies or nerves—but I wasn't going to let on.

I was convinced the worst thing I could do was show

weakness in front of Angus. Somehow I knew he would laser lock in on my vulnerabilities and use them to his advantage. Now that we were alone in the semidark basement, I was feeling sinister vibes rolling off him. Or was I just stressed out from being in such a claustrophobic environment? I couldn't be sure.

"I can probably switch on another set of lights," he said reluctantly. "At least you'll be able to see what you're doing."

"Thank you," I told him. There was no sense in antagonizing Angus while he was actually offering to help me.

"I'll switch on the lights as I leave," he said and turned toward the direction of the stairs.

I smiled my thanks and moved toward the painting closest to me. I whipped off the drop cloth. "Oh, Angus," I said, pointing to the landscape in the gilt frame. "Is this a new acquisition?" The cloth wasn't covered with dust like the paintings behind it, so I assumed it had been placed there recently.

He hesitated. "Yes, it's very famous—a William Gilbert." I knew that William Gilbert was a prominent landscape painter who'd specialized in painting rural scenes of Savannah and the low country in the early nineteen hundreds. "You can find out more about it on the tag."

"Thanks." I checked the tag and whipped out my notebook. *Bingo. Sunrise over All Saints Church* was one of the items on my inventory. I heard Angus clumping his way up the staircase and in a moment, it was suddenly brighter in the basement. Angus had kept his promise. I breathed a sigh of relief and set to work, first documenting the name and date of the painting, the name of the artist, the gallery where it was purchased, and its location in the mansion.

Then I whipped out my phone and took a quick photo. It

was a lovely landscape with a rolling green pasture, an azure blue sky, and a church steeple in the forehead. I stood back, admiring the craftsmanship and proud that I'd overcome my silly fear of the dark.

And then the lights went out.

22

I gasped aloud. It was as dark as a tomb. Terror slammed into my brain, and I blindly rushed forward, crashing into an end table. I forced myself to stop dead in my tracks, my heart beating in a crazy, accelerated way, while I tried to get my bearings. This was no time to panic. It was taking every ounce of my self-control to stand still.

My heart was drumming a tattoo, and I tried to think of a strategy. Could I turn around and find my way back to the steps that led upstairs? Was that even possible? I did what I hoped was a hundred-eighty-degree turn and immediately tripped over a wooden object on the floor. I reached down and ran my hand over it. A wooden footstool.

I must have moved in the wrong direction, because there wasn't a footstool in my path when I'd been with Angus. The last thing I wanted to do was move deeper into the basement, and I had no way of knowing how to retrace my steps and reach the secret passage.

I felt like full-blown panic was breathing down my neck. It took me a minute to realize I was holding my breath, and I took in a big gulp of air. The air seemed thick, like fog, and I instantly felt light-headed, as if I might pass out. Had the air changed somehow? I lunged forward, trying to ignore my racing pulse, and ran smack into a large veiled painting.

"Help!" I called out feebly. My voice came out as a croak. My throat felt like it was closing up, and I couldn't summon up the energy to scream. I took a few shallow breaths, practically hyperventilating. I'd noticed how thick the stucco walls were, and it was unlikely anyone would hear me.

If I couldn't find my way back to the secret passage, could I find another way out of the basement? Angus had said that this was *one* way to the basement. Was there another? If there was another way in, there must be another way out! My only hope was to find it.

I stood stock-still and forced myself to take three deep breaths. *Think, Taylor, think!* I moved a few feet to the left and thought I spotted a tiny crack of light, a vertical line that was slightly angled. What could it be? I tried to remember what the outside of Beaux Reves looked like from the back.

When we'd had lunch on the patio, I'd noticed two wooden doors lying flat, slightly above ground level. I'd asked Ali about them later, and she said she thought they probably led to a root cellar. Root cellars were common at the time the mansion was built. Could this be my way out?

I stretched my arms straight out in front of me and moved forward toward the light step by step. The light was getting closer, and I saw to my relief there were three short steps leading up to a double wooden door. A tiny burst of fresh air wafted in between the doors. My ticket to freedom!

I nearly cried with relief. I mounted the steps and pushed

against the double doors. The narrow slit of light became larger, but only fractionally. What was wrong? Something was holding the doors closed. Fear was getting the better of me, and I pounded with both fists on the double doors. "Help! Help me!" I shouted. "I'm stuck in here!"

I called out repeatedly, and just when I was ready to sink to my knees in despair, I heard the sound of a board being shifted. In a moment, the double doors opened and a worried-looking gardener peered in at me.

"Are you all right, miss?" He reached down to help me up the last step. The fresh Savannah air had never smelled so good. "What in the world happened to you?"

"I—nothing, I'm fine," I said hurriedly. "I was doing some inventory in the basement, and somehow I couldn't find my way back through the mansion." I glanced down and realized I'd guessed correctly. A board about three feet long was lying on the grass. Had someone slid it through the handles of the wooden doors, deliberately trapping me inside? "Are these doors normally kept barricaded?"

"No, never," he said, shaking his head. He picked up the board and peered curiously at it. "Someone must have taken this from the lumber pile in the garage. And then they threaded it through the handles. Sorry this happened to you, miss. Can't imagine who would do a thing like that."

I have a good idea who would, I thought grimly. I glanced toward the driveway and noticed that it was empty. "Is Angus here?" I asked.

"No, he went into town. Do you need something?" His broad face was kind, and I smiled to reassure him.

"No, everything is fine," I told him. "Are you the only one working here today?"

"Lucy is in the kitchen, and Jeb is somewhere on the grounds," he said. "If you need someone—"

"No worries," I said, forcing a cheery note into my voice. "Thanks for your help." *The quicker I get out of here, the better,* I thought, making tracks toward my car. I pulled open the door, cranked up the AC as high as it would go, and locked the doors and windows. I was surprised to see that my hands were shaking and my legs were trembling. I took a quick peek at myself in the rearview mirror. As pale as a ghost. I grabbed my cell phone and punched in a familiar number. There was one person who could reassure me, and I was relieved when he picked up on the first ring.

"Noah," I said in a quivery voice, "we need to talk. I'm coming right over."

"You never should have been in that house alone," Noah chided me. I was curled up on the leather sofa in his office with my feet tucked under me. He'd called out for sandwiches, and I was sipping a cup of tea he'd made for me on his hot plate. I was thrilled to see his stern-faced secretary had taken the day off. It was nice to be alone with him. More than nice, I thought. It was heaven.

"At least the color's coming back into your face," he went on, brushing a stray strand of hair out of my eyes. "You had me worried there for minute. You looked like you were ready to pass out."

"I was feeling a bit light-headed, that's all," I said defensively. "The combination of the foul air in the basement and my allergies—"

"And having the shock of your life," he said wryly. "I can't imagine you in a locked basement in the pitch dark." I remembered how mortified I'd been when Noah and I had been trapped in an elevator in a high-rise in Atlanta. It had only taken a couple of minutes for him to get the elevator working again, but those minutes had ticked by like hours. I'd been in full panic mode, and had wanted to climb out through the ceiling even though every instinct told me that was a crazy plan.

"It was awful," I said, closing my eyes against the memory.

"We can't ever let it happen again," he said, twining his fingers through mine.

"I just felt I had to go there today. And I had to go alone." I explained about Ali staying behind to help Dana in the shop.

"Was it worth it?" he asked. The phone rang, and he checked the screen before reaching past me to mute the incoming message. I had a sudden pang of jealousy. Was he expecting a call from a girlfriend? Even though Noah and I were "taking things slow" as we'd agreed on, I wasn't dating anyone and I hoped he wasn't, either.

Ali tells me that my fears are unfounded, that Noah will never find anyone else like me and that we are true soul mates. I'd like to believe her, but Ali has a terrible track record with men and is such a hopeless romantic she cries at Lifetime movies.

"Just boring business stuff," he said, as if reading my mind. He nodded toward the phone, and I curled up against him again.

"Are you working on a new case?" Noah is making a name for himself in Savannah circles as a private detective and is working hard to build up a clientele. It's never easy starting a new business, but he's keeping his expenses low by doing most of the investigative work himself and managing with a part-time secretary.

"Industrial espionage," he said with a twinkle in his eye.

"Really? Here in Savannah?"

He grinned and chucked me under the chin. "I'm kidding. It's not really espionage; it's just old-fashioned lust and greed. A CEO thinks his wife is sleeping with his CFO and wants me to check it out."

"Interesting." I nestled into him a little closer. The combination of the hot tea and Noah's sexy presence was making me feel better by the minute.

"He also thinks the CFO is embezzling from the firm. It's going to be tough to untangle the financial issues from the marital ones, and I've got to tread carefully. If the CFO figures out that the boss is on to him, he could open up some offshore accounts, and those are horrendous to trace. And the financials are such a tangled mess, you wouldn't believe it."

"Mmmm," I murmured. "Sounds really complicated."

"Why are we talking about cases when we could be talking about other things? Or *doing* other things?" His voice was low and husky and his eyes darkened in a way that set my heart thumping. Noah brushed his lips against my temple, and I was all set to lean in for a full-throttle kiss when I heard the door to the waiting room open.

"Are you expecting someone?" I said, sitting up abruptly. My pulse immediately went into overdrive. A hair-trigger response, probably brought on by my awful morning at Beaux Reves.

"Relax, Taylor," he said, carefully entangling his arms from around me. "It's the deli sandwiches, that's all." He shot me a rueful smile. "Terrible timing," he said, standing up. "Stay right there," he ordered.

"Don't worry," I said. "I'm not going anywhere."

Noah returned with Swiss cheese on rye heaped with coleslaw, one of my favorite sandwiches. And two bottles of sweet tea. Not as good as homemade, of course, but I appreciated the gesture. After Noah wolfed down half of his sandwich, he pointed to my phone. "Did you get any good pictures today?"

"Just one." I showed him the photo of the painting *Sunrise over All Saints Church* that I'd snapped in the basement. "I took it right before the lights went out," I said with a little grimace. "Angus says it's a new acquisition, and I bet it cost a pretty penny. The artist, William Gilbert, is known for his paintings of the low country."

"It's nice," Noah said and then took a closer look. "You know, I think I've seen a similar painting somewhere. A landscape, done in the same style." He paused and then snapped his fingers. "I remember now—it was in Norman Osteroff's office. It was on the far wall, opposite the windows. Did you happen to see it when you visited him?"

"I don't think so." I tried to picture the lawyer's office with his expensive mahogany furniture and old-timey silver pen set sitting on the desk. "I remember seeing a small painting of Beaux Reves on the wall. I figured it was probably a gift from Abigail. But nothing like this."

"I'm sure that's where I saw it. He and Abigail traveled in the same social circles, so I suppose it's not surprising they bought the same artwork." He paused, looking out the window. Noah's office is right on the edge of a pricey district in the city, but it's on a side street, so he managed to get a good price on the rental. "Norman is dry as dust, isn't he? Impossible to have a real conversation with that guy. I wonder if he ever cracks a smile or enjoys anything in life."

I suddenly remembered the series of framed photographs I'd spotted in his office. "He likes horses, though, so he has one redeeming feature. He told me he helps care for his wife's horses."

"Now, that *is* a surprise," Noah said. "I can't imagine Oster-off throwing down bales of hay in a paddock. He can't be all bad. We have to give the devil his due, don't we?"

"Yes, we certainly do."

Noah turned to me, a devilish grin crossing his handsome features. "Enough talk about lawyers. Now where were we?"

I smiled back. "I think we were just . . ." I began and stopped abruptly when I heard the door to the waiting room open and close again. "Not another delivery?" I asked, my spirits sinking.

Noah pulled his hand through his hair and groaned. "Worse," he said, checking his watch. "I'd totally forgotten. My two o'clock is here."

I stood up, grabbed my purse, and blew him a kiss. "Like they say, timing is everything."

23

"I can't believe this happened to you," Ali said consolingly. "Are you sure you want to go ahead with the Dream Club tonight? We can always reschedule." It was our regular meeting day and I was eager to discuss new developments in the case. The members were scheduled to arrive in a couple of hours.

"I'm fine," I told her. "A hot cup of tea and I'll be as good as new." It was four o'clock, and I'd returned to the candy store after doing some shopping in town. My mind was still reeling after my morning at Beaux Reves, but I knew it was better to get on with business as usual and not dwell on my terrifying experience. I'd downplayed the awful basement scene to Ali. I was afraid she'd have nightmares for weeks if she knew exactly how bad things had been for me. "How's business today?"

"A bit slow," Ali admitted. "The lunch crowd was fairly good, and a few people came in for tea and pastries about an hour ago. I told Dana she could leave early; she's putting in way too many hours with us. It's starting to look like a full-time job instead of a college internship."

Ali was in constant motion as she talked, cleaning finger-prints off the glass cabinets and washing down the white marble prep counter. She'd opened a huge box of jelly beans and was arranging them in colorful swirls on a three-tiered serving plate. "You look like you haven't stopped all day," I told her. Everything was sparkling, and I spotted freshly baked brownies on the counter. They had marshmallow topping and a dusting of chopped nuts. They're one of the most popular menu items and are baked with a touch of Kahlúa.

"I haven't stopped for a minute," she said, brushing a stray lock of blond hair out of her eyes. "I've been working on something new I want to show you." She reached into the refrigerator and pulled out a large tray with a domed lid. "I should have done this ages ago," she said, lifting off the covering. "Voilà!"

I looked at the artfully arranged tray filled with bite-sized portions of lemon squares, tiny wedges of carrot cake with cream cheese frosting, blueberry buckle and apple pie served in cute little jars with gingham tops, and a nice selection of brownies and cookie bars. "It looks delicious, but what is it?"

"It's a tasting tray!" she said proudly. "This way when someone wants to do a big order for a party—like the Harper sisters—they can try samples before they buy." She pushed a tiny cherry pastry toward me. "Here, try one of the cherry tartlets. I came up with the recipe today."

I took a bite and sighed with pleasure. "It's delicious," I said appreciatively. "And the tasting tray is a great idea." I wasn't just being polite. In the past, Ali's ideas have been so over-the-top, we couldn't really implement them. This idea was practical, made sense, and I was sure it would draw in business. I'm proud of Ali; she's becoming a better businesswoman every day.

"Of course, the Harper sisters already know what everything tastes like because they're in the Dream Club, but our other customers don't." She paused and refilled her glass of sweet tea. "I think we really need to expand our party menu. When Rose and Minerva mentioned the event for their pastor, it made me think that we might be missing out on a great opportunity. The tasting tray is the first step."

"I think you're right," I said, reaching for another tartlet. These things were seriously addictive. I was going to ask Ali how she managed to shape the pie pastry into such tiny thumbprint shells when the bell above the shop door jangled. We both looked up as Laura Howard strode in.

Laura Howard! The last person in the world I expected to see at Oldies But Goodies.

"Ladies," she said coolly, slipping into a seat at the counter with us. She glanced quickly around the shop as if checking to make sure we were alone. "I'm simply perishing outside. Do you suppose I could have some of that sweet tea?" She pointed to the icy carafe we always keep on hand for customers.

"Of course you can," Ali said quickly. We exchanged a look as she filled the glass for Laura and added a sprig of mint at the top.

We waited while Laura took a long swig of the tea before speaking. "I was in the neighborhood and remembered you mentioning the shop at Abigail's memorial service." She gave a keen look at the gleaming countertops and spiffy bins of old-fashioned candy, and I was glad that the shop was in tip-top shape. I had the feeling Laura was the kind of woman who wouldn't miss a trick. She was put together like a fashion model today in a pale yellow linen sheath, with a triple strand of pearls and what looked like Louboutins on her feet.

"How are you doing?" Ali said softly. "I know you and Abigail went back a long time."

For a moment, Laura hesitated, and I thought she might cry. "A *very* long time," she said with a wry smile. "It's funny, you don't really think of getting older and time passing, do you?" She was staring past us at a collection of baking utensils and I knew her thoughts were far away. She gave a little flutter with her hands, and I noticed she was still wearing her walnut-sized diamond ring.

"Time slips away from all of us," Ali said sympathetically.

Laura turned back to us as if she knew her thoughts had drifted. She nodded her chin with a sad look in her eyes. "And then life events happen. Your children grow up, a close friend dies, your husband takes up with a younger woman"—she gave a derisive little sniff—"and suddenly you feel old."

Ali and I exchanged a look. Since Laura had mentioned the divorce, I supposed it was common knowledge and we were free to comment on it. I decided not to mention rumors of her own "dalliance."

"Will you be okay?" I said. I meant financially, not emotionally, and wondered how she would answer.

"Can I try one of these?" she asked, pointing to the tray with the goodies. She either was stalling or needed a moment to compose herself before continuing.

"Yes, of course," Ali said, pushing the tasting tray toward her. "Have whatever you want. It's a tasting tray."

Laura took a lemon square and savored it with little cat

bites. "Delicious. I can see why you've made a success of this place." She wiped her hands on a napkin. "To get back to your question, Taylor, I made a mess of things when I signed that prenup. Who knew it would come back to haunt me all these years later? It's going to be impossible to break, and my husband has the best lawyers in town." Her eyes welled up a little and she dabbed at them with the edge of her napkin.

"There's the tontine," Ali said. "That might be your salvation."

"Yes, the tontine," Laura said sarcastically. "Everyone thinks I've made a fortune on it, but I may not see any of that money for years."

This came as a total surprise to me. "Why not? I thought it was a very valuable piece of real estate."

"It is. Or at least it *was.* I'll have to wait years to put it on the market, so it's not going to be a source of ready cash for me. It seems they're opening a very swanky girls' school just half a block away. It will knock the price of my property way down. In fact, it already has."

"Are they allowed to open a girls' school there? I thought they had to maintain the historical integrity of these older buildings."

"Normally it wouldn't be permitted. But the builder is being very clever about it. He's using the same footprint as the original mansion and simply changing the inside. And it's already been approved because it counts as an educational institution. It's not like he's putting up a string of a condos; that would never fly. Plus he has connections with every politician in town."

"What's the problem with having a girls' school close by?" Ali asked.

"Traffic, noise, parking. All negatives. One of my friends is a real estate agent, and she recommended that I hold on to my property for a few years. The value has taken a tumble, but maybe in time, it will come back up. Who knows?" She gave a little shrug. "The girls' school might not be as much of a disaster as people are predicting." She glanced at her watch. "I'd best be on my way." She gave us a warm smile. "Nice place you have here. I'll take a dozen brownies," she said, pointing to the ones that were fresh from the oven. "In fact, I'll take the whole tray. I'm having a few friends over tonight for a wine-and-dessert party. I plan on drowning my sorrows in white wine and chocolate."

"There goes her motive," Ali said to me a couple of hours later as we were setting up for the Dream Club. "She's not going to be making any money off the tontine right away, so there wouldn't be any reason to kill Abigail." Ali arranged some chocolate truffles—homemade, a new recipe—on a hand-painted plate and stood back to admire her handiwork.

"Yes, but she didn't know that," I countered. "She probably knew her husband was on his way out and she was going to be destitute. I'm sure it never occurred to her there would be any problem in selling the land right away."

"She seemed so sad," Ali said softly. "I don't really think she's capable of killing anyone, do you?"

"Probably not." The truth is, Ali doesn't think *anyone* is capable of killing. "Should we be using that plate?" I said, pointing to the truffles. "It's from the Harper sisters and is at least a hundred years old."

"Of course we should," Ali said, placing it gently on the coffee table. "Minerva told me just last week that beautiful things are meant to be used and enjoyed. Her feelings will be hurt if we stash it away someplace."

"Whatever you say." The upstairs looked perfect, and I checked to see that there was hot tea, iced sweet tea, and a small pot of decaf coffee for Lucinda. Barney and Scout were snoozing side by side on the windowsill, and the plantation shutters were open to the soft night air.

"If we take Laura out of the mix," Ali said, sinking into an armchair, "where does that leave us, as far as suspects? Did you come to any conclusions at the mansion today?"

"Not really." I still couldn't think about Beaux Reves without getting a sick feeling in the pit of my stomach. I'd had a horrible shock being trapped in the basement, but did it really change anything? It could have been a mistake— maybe that board had been placed there ages ago—or maybe it was just someone's idea of a joke.

"We have Angus and Sophie," Ali said thoughtfully. "We know they lied about that alibi. The Seven Sisters was closed that night. They couldn't possibly have had dinner there."

"Yes, but they cleared that up today." I quickly told her about Sophie's claim that Angus had gotten the name wrong. "Apparently the Sisters is a real restaurant, and it was open that night. I checked."

"I suppose that might clear them. Their motives were weak."

"Well, Angus needed money; that's not a weak motive," I objected. "And I'm pretty sure he was stealing objects from Beaux Reves."

"Plus you just don't like him, do you?" Ali said with a laugh.

"No," I admitted, "I don't. And as for Sophie, she's still a question mark. There's something a bit off about her, but

I can't put my finger on it. She reminds me of an actress in a play. A bad actress."

"A bad actress? Why's that?" Ali stood up and moved to the landing. Dream Club members had arrived and were tromping up the stairs. We were expecting a small group tonight: the Harper sisters, Persia, Sybil, Lucinda, and Dorien.

"Sophie seems like someone who knows her lines, but she's not believable. And she stands to inherit a fortune if Abigail really did change her will."

"Money. It's always about money," Ali said with a sigh. Sometimes I think she is too good for this world.

"That's the way Noah looks at it," I reminded her. His favorite saying is *Follow the money*.

"Last night I dreamt about a fish on the wall," Dorien Myers said a few minutes later. Ali had agreed to let Dorien go first tonight. Dorien had seemed agitated when she plunked herself into a side chair, and we knew she was dying to tell us about her dream. "I have no idea what it means, but I blame it on my ex-brother-in-law."

"Pardon?" Minerva said, leaning forward. "I didn't quite catch that. You dreamt about a fish and it reminded you of your ex-brother-in-law?"

"I didn't catch it, either," Rose piped up. Minerva and Rose were sitting side by side in nearly identical floral housedresses, their curly white hair framing their faces like halos. They had helped themselves to a hefty selection of pastries and were balancing the plates on their laps.

Dorien sometimes rambles when she's annoyed and goes off topic. "Well, I suppose I should back up a bit," Dorien said.

"Last Christmas, I received the most ridiculous present in my entire life. She paused dramatically. "It was a Big Mouth Billy Bass."

Minerva shot a perplexed look at Rose. It was obvious neither of them had ever heard of the kitschy wall plaque or seen the ads on late-night TV. The fish is a rubberized model of a largemouth bass, stretched over a plaque. It's motorized, and when someone passes by, the fish twitches its tail, turns its head, and bursts into song.

"It's a singing fish, isn't it?" Lucinda ventured. "Someone brought one into school last year and mounted it on the wall outside my office." She put her well-manicured hand to her chest. "They asked me to come out and look at it, and it gave me quite a start. I felt like that silly fish was looking right at me when he sang, 'Don't Worry, Be Happy.' A person could faint right on the spot from a shock like that."

I tried not to smile. The idea of Lucinda, always prim and proper, being confronted by a singing fish was almost comical. She's lucky no one posted a video on YouTube. It would certainly go viral.

"But getting back to your dream," Ali prompted.

"Well, the fish in my dream sang 'Take Me to the River,' and I wondered if it had something to do with the case."

"Oh, I see what you mean," Lucinda said. "You're thinking about Desirée drowning in the river. I don't know," she said. "What does everyone else think?"

"It's an interesting dream," Sybil said. "The metaphor of the song suggesting the river, and the idea that the fish was mounted on the wall."

"Yes, like the plaque," Dorien said, excited.

"So you have imagery from your subconscious—the water—merging with the residue of the day," Persia said. "It's interesting how your mind combined the two and created a dream out of it." She turned to me. "What do you think, Taylor?"

"I don't know, I'm still trying to get my mind around the fish on the wall," I said with a grin. As soon as I said it, my heart stopped. I'd seen a fish on a wall. And I'd seen a fish that was part of a medallion or a piece of jewelry in the crime scene photo. The images of the fish were identical. They were both primitive line drawings. "I've seen a fish on a wall," I said slowly.

"Where?" Ali stopped serving the pastries to stare at me. "At Beaux Reves?" she guessed.

"Yes, in the kitchen." My chest felt tight as I imagined the sunny kitchen and Lucy singing over the sink. There was a bright blue ceramic plaque hanging on the wall above her. It looked Mexican, and it had a line drawing of a fish that looked exactly like the item in the crime scene photo.

I grabbed a piece of paper and a Sharpie. "Here's what I saw at Beaux Reves. It was painted on a ceramic plaque hanging in the kitchen." I made two swift strokes with the pen and held up the image. "Can anyone identify this?"

"Yes, of course we can," Lucinda said in her schoolmarm voice. "That fish is an early Christian symbol. It's used very commonly in folk art. And it's quite popular with people who are religious."

People who are religious. The words hammered in my brain. Lucy Dargos was religious. She wore religious medals, she had a religious plaque above the sink, and she had argued with Osteroff because Abigail hadn't had a religious funeral.

It seemed probable to me that Lucy owned the piece of jewelry found on the landing in the crime scene photos. After all, it had a fish, a Christian symbol, on it. Who else would wear it? It might have ended up on the floor as she'd struggled to push Abigail down the stairs. Or she might have dropped it while she'd been cleaning the house and it had nothing to do with Abigail's death.

But did I really want to go down this road right now? I decided to bide my time and let the Dream Club continue. But Rose knew I was perplexed and called me on it.

"Is something bothering you, dear?" Rose asked in her shaky voice. "You look troubled."

24

"Nothing," I said quickly. "I was just thinking of something I need to check out tomorrow." I hadn't said a word about my visit to the mansion earlier today. There was no need to alarm the club members, and it would only distract them from discussing their dreams.

But Minerva has a steel-trap mind and remembered that I'd planned on doing inventory at Beaux Reves today. "How did you do with finding the items on the list?" she asked kindly. "Rose and I were worried about you rattling around that huge estate all by yourself. There are so many rooms, and there's so much to do. I wish we could have helped you, but we really can't do stairs anymore. Arthritis, you know." She patted her knee and gave a sweet smile.

"That's okay—I was fine," I said. I wanted to answer her question about the inventory quickly so we could move on to more dream material. "In fact, I took a photograph of one of the items, a painting called *Sunrise over All Saints Church*."

I whipped out my camera phone and passed it around. "According to the tag, it was painted by William Gilbert in 1932. Abigail must have acquired it shortly before her death. It was down in the storeroom; it hadn't been displayed yet."

I passed the phone around, and everyone admired the painting. All except Rose Harper. "This was painted by William Gilbert in 1932, you say?" She shook her head of fuzzy white hair. "There must be some mistake. Take a look at this, Minerva." She passed the phone to her sister, who took out her glasses to get a better look.

"Oh my. Well, it's All Saints Church, all right," Minerva said flatly. "Rather a nice landscape. I know Abigail was fond of William Gilbert's paintings, even though they're pricey. A similar William Gilbert landscape went on sale last week at Sotheby's for a quarter of a million dollars. And that was just the starting bid." She started to hand the phone back to her sister, who stopped her.

"Minerva, for heaven's sake, take a look at the church *steeple*, dear. The *steeple*!"

Minerva held the phone up to the light. "The steeple . . . oh yes, I see what you mean. It's all wrong, all wrong." She handed the phone back to me.

"What's wrong with the steeple?" I asked, baffled.

"Nothing's wrong with the steeple," Minerva said. "It's what's wrong with the painting. All Saints Church didn't *have a* steeple in 1932. Rose and I were both baptized there, and I have the photos to prove it."

"But it has a steeple now," Lucinda said. "My niece was married there. It was a lovely ceremony."

"And it had a steeple when it was constructed. But the church caught fire in 1928 and it took almost fifteen years to replace the steeple. It was the Depression and no one had money to spend on things like church steeples." Rose loves genealogy and has collected thousands of photos from years gone by.

"So," I said, trying to put the pieces together, "what you're saying is . . . "

"I'm saying this painting couldn't have been painted by William Gilbert, dear," Rose said flatly.

"She's right," Lucinda said. To my amazement, she'd pulled out an iPad and was tapping the keyboard with a tiny stylus. She read from the screen. "William Gilbert lived and painted in Savannah for a few short years before returning to England." She held up the iPad. "He was in Savannah from 1932 to 1935. The church didn't have a steeple in those days. That painting you photographed couldn't possibly be a William Gilbert. It's a fraud."

A fraud. There was a moment of silence while everyone digested this information. My thoughts were buzzing like bees in a hive.

Abigail had hired Angus to make an inventory of her possessions yet she'd asked us to find certain pieces. Was she suspicious? Did she realize things were missing? And who was responsible for new acquisitions?

Someone had bought a fake William Gilbert. Who? Was it an honest mistake, or something more sinister? Even reputable art experts can be taken in by a fraud, but I had a feeling this was different. My gut told me that money had changed hands with the sale of this phony painting.

The thefts, the inventory, the odd piece of jewelry with the religious symbol. It all came back to one person who was a constant. Who would notice if items disappeared? Who knew the placement of every antique because she dusts the house from top to bottom? Who had the most to lose if thefts are discovered and might be held accountable? Who stood to inherit thirty million dollars if Abigail died before she could change her will?

There was only one answer.

Lucy Dargos. "Lucy Dargos." When I said the name aloud everyone turned to me.

"Lucy Dargos?" Ali asked in surprise. Dead silence for a moment and then the phone rang. "Hold that thought!" she said, jumping up to answer it.

Persia sat back, her expression somber. I could see she didn't agree with me but didn't want to press the matter. After all, no one has a crystal ball, and we don't always agree on the course the investigation will take. There's usually not a consensus on the lineup of suspects or who heads the list. And since nothing is written in stone, we often change our minds several times before settling on a particular suspect.

I watched as Barney trotted out to the kitchen, winding his way around Ali's legs as she held the receiver to her ear. To my surprise, she ignored Barney and suddenly whirled to face me, her face deathly pale.

"What is it?" I half rose from my chair, nearly upsetting Scout, who'd curled up next to me, making snuffling noises in his sleep. Ali held up a hand as if to quiet me and spoke softly into the receiver. "I'll tell her." She hung up the receiver and stood stock-still for a moment. I knew she was taking a moment to compose herself, and that she was about to reveal something major.

But even I couldn't have guessed the next words out of her mouth.

"That was Noah," she said, making her way back to the living room. Her voice was flat and her face was expressionless as though she'd had a shock. "Something awful has happened at Beaux Reves."

"Sit here, my dear," Minerva said quickly, patting the seat

beside her. Ali was so white, I was afraid she was going to pass out. "What happened?" Minerva asked, her voice warm with concern. She clasped Ali's hand in her own and rubbed it as if to get the circulation going. I had the feeling Ali's hand had gone stone-cold as if her whole body had been shocked by the call. Her eyes had a dull, faraway look, and her lower lip was trembling. She was shivering and Minerva pulled a blue-and-white afghan over her legs. "Take a couple of deep breaths, my dear," Minerva said. "That will steady you. Don't try to talk until you're ready."

"It's Lucy," Ali blurted out. "Lucy Dargos." Ali's voice was a strangled cry and her eyes welled with tears. "She's dead." The last word came out in a whisper. She fluttered her hands help-lessly in the air in front of her and then let them fall into her lap.

"Lucy Dargos is dead?" I repeated. *Another death at Beaux Reves? How is that possible?* "An accident?" I man-aged to ask over a lump in my throat. *Surely not another fall down the stairs?* My mind was reeling.

I had just accused Lucy Dargos of murdering Abigail, and yet I felt distraught at the news of her death. Shock is a funny thing. It makes your body go numb and scatters your thoughts to the wind. Nothing makes sense as you struggle to take back control of your mind and your emotions.

Ali shook her head. She swallowed hard, and I could see she was trying to get her feelings under control. "Noah doesn't think it was an accident. She died in the mansion a couple of hours ago. Sam Stiles says it could be murder."

"Murder?" Rose said, her hand flying to her mouth as if she hadn't wanted the awful word to escape her lips.

"How did she die?" Sybil's tone was brisk. Sybil has something of a take-charge personality, and I was glad to turn the conversation over to her.

"I'm not sure," Ali said. She took a deep breath and exhaled slowly, obviously trying to calm herself. "Something about bathwater—maybe she drowned. I was so upset I couldn't take it all in."

"I told you I dreamt about water!" Etta Mae said excitedly. "The same thing happened to Desiree. Remember that dream you had, Lucinda? The one about a woman in a white evening dress walking along the Riverwalk?"

"Yes, but"—Lucinda hesitated, shaking her head—"I don't think there's a pool or a pond at Beaux Reves. So I don't see how this is connected to my dream about Desiree and the Riverwalk."

"Lucy may have drowned in the bathtub," Ali said flatly. She was sitting up straighter now, and had taken a few sips of strong tea. "At least that's what the first responders thought."

"How in the world could someone drown in the bathtub?" Rose asked.

"Don't you remember the Brides in the Bath murders?" Minerva replied. "Beautiful, healthy young women and they all were murdered the same way. They were all married to a bigamist, George Smith. He simply lifted up their ankles and they quickly slipped under the water," she said grimly. "Everyone was horrified and wondered how it could have happened. But it did."

"I've never heard that story," Etta Mae said. She looked entranced, her lips parted.

"It was a hundred years ago," Minerva said. "You can research the case, if you like. These days, with CSIs, he'd never get away with it."

"That's true," Persia added. "Back then, people didn't know much about forensics, and there wasn't any way to cross-reference suspected murders."

"Well, we won't know more until morning," Minerva said briskly, "so there's no sense in speculating."

"You're right," Rose piped up. "We shouldn't second-guess ourselves. This could be just a tragic accident. Do you suppose it will be in the papers tomorrow morning, Taylor?"

"I'm sure it will be online but not in the print edition. And I'm not sure how much information the police are releasing to the public. So for the moment, please don't reveal anything. Sam Stiles may have spoken to Noah in confidence."

"You're quite right," Persia spoke up. "It's wiser to say nothing for the moment. I'm sure I can find out more information at the practice tomorrow. I'll see what the associates are saying, and I'll fill everyone in." She gave a little sigh. "Lawyers love to gossip, you know, and I'm sure they'll have some theories about what happened."

No one had any more dreams to report, and the conversation sputtered and ground to a halt. Lucy's death had cast a pall over the evening, and Ali quickly wrapped up the meeting. There was a somber note in the air as the members made their way down the steps. Only Lucinda remained behind, helping Ali clear up the dishes.

"Are you feeling all right?" she asked Ali. "I was worried about you for a minute. You went dead white."

Ali gave a weak laugh. "I'm fine; it was just such a shock. All our attention was focused on Abigail, and then another death happens, right under our noses." She poured out the last of the tea and rinsed the pot. "Taylor, I nearly forgot. Noah wants you to call him. He's heading over to the mansion and asked if you'd like to meet him there."

I put down my coffee cup. "Is Sam going to let him inside?"

"I think so. As soon as the CSIs finish processing the place. I think she wants to hear his input."

"I'm on it," I said, grabbing my phone and my purse.

25

"I didn't know if you felt up to this," Noah said. I had just pulled in the driveway next to him at Beaux Reves. It was a beautiful summer evening, and petals from the magnolia blossoms were wafting in the soft night air. It was hard to believe that in a few seconds, I'd be stepping into a crime scene, fresh with the scent of death.

Noah reached over and plucked a blossom that had fallen on my head. He let his hand graze my cheek for a moment. "You don't have to do this, you know."

"I'm up for it," I told him. "At least I think I am. Ali wasn't, though. She wanted to come with me, but she was absolutely shattered by the news."

"I figured that. She sounded so upset on the phone. I hated to call during the Dream Club meeting, but I knew you'd want to hear the news right away."

"Yes, I did." Noah twined his fingers around mine and I

felt a little zing in my heart. "We wrapped up the meeting early. Everyone was thrown for a loop by your call."

I didn't admit I'd told the Dream Club that I suspected Lucy of Abigail's murder. And now Lucy was dead. Where did that leave the investigation? Had Lucy planned on blowing the whistle on someone? Did someone kill Lucy to silence her? Or was it just a tragic accident? First Desiree, then Abigail, and now Lucy. Three deaths, all unexpected. Was there a curse hanging over Beaux Reves?

As we walked up the oyster shell pathway, side by side, I tried to shake off the dark images roiling in my head. Noah seemed lost in his thoughts, and I figured he was developing his own theories about the murders.

I glanced at him. He was scanning the outside of the mansion; the portico, the winding drive, the edge of the patio peeking out to the left of the entrance. I always tell him he has "cop eyes"; they don't miss a trick.

It was hard to believe I'd had lunch on that patio just a few days ago with the mistress of Beaux Reves. My mind went back to that idyllic luncheon under the magnolia trees. We'd drunk wine, and Abigail had been so relieved to learn that her "death dream" might not be threatening at all. She'd laughed it off and made sure we all ate dessert. And now two deaths in a row. Abigail's premonition had come true after all. Death was clinging to the beautiful mansion like a shroud.

I wondered where Noah's thoughts were leading him and took another quick peek at his profile, his strong chin and finely chiseled features. He must have felt my gaze on him, because he turned and gave me a long, slow, intimate look.

He was wearing a navy blue Lacoste shirt with khakis, and in spite of the fact that we were on the way to a murder scene, he looked relaxed. "I didn't want to say too much to

Ali," he said, "because I was afraid she might blurt out some of the details."

"Probably a wise move. She was pretty shaken up. All she said was the Lucy had drowned in the bathtub and that Sam wasn't sure it was an accident."

Noah gave a wry laugh. "Wasn't sure? That's an understatement. Sam is looking at this like a murder, but it's odd." He paused. "And it wasn't death by drowning. It looks like Lucy was electrocuted."

I stopped dead in my tracks to face him as two CSIs emerged from the house with their kits and brushed past us. I spotted the ME's van starting to pull away from the side portico and I realized they'd already removed Lucy's body from the mansion. I tried not to shudder and forced myself to concentrate on the task at hand.

"How could she have been electrocuted?" I kept my voice low because a couple of uniforms were making their way back to their squad cars. I spotted Sam inside the mansion giving directions to one of the techs. She looked tired and frazzled but competent as always. Sam manages to control her emotions no matter what life throws at her. She's an excellent detective, and I have no doubt that she'll be a captain at the Savannah PD someday.

Sophie and Angus were walking down the path away from the house. Sam had nodded to the uniforms at the door to let them leave and I assumed they'd already been interviewed. Interesting that they both were at the mansion today. I wondered what they'd seen and heard. And more important, what they'd told Sam Stiles.

As the two passed us on the narrow walkway, I heard Sophie say to Angus, "Two deaths so close together? That'll be A-1 tomorrow for sure." She spotted me, gave me a cool nod, and continued down the path. *A-1?* Funny, Sara uses that expression all the time, and I never figured out exactly what it means. I made a mental note to ask her about it.

"What exactly happened here?" I was steeling myself for what I might see inside Beaux Reves. The more information I had, the better.

"I know it sounds crazy," Noah said quietly as we stepped into the foyer. "But wait till you see the crime scene. Lucy was taking a bath and apparently her boom box fell into the bathtub. On the surface, it looks like a freak accident. Why in the world she had a boom box in the bathroom is beyond me."

"Her *boom box*?" I suddenly remembered her dragging the clunky object with her as she worked. Her slacker son had neglected to buy a charger for her iPod, so she kept moving it from room to room, plugging it in each time. Music probably made the work go faster.

"Oh no," I said softly. "Suddenly it all makes sense." I quickly told Noah about the boom box Lucy had borrowed from her son, Nicky, and he raised his eyebrows. I was struck by a sudden thought and grabbed Noah's arm. "Nicky," I said urgently. "Does he know about his mother?"

Noah shook his head. "The police couldn't get ahold of him. He's spending the night somewhere in town, probably shacking up with a girlfriend. At least that's what Jeb Arnold told Sam."

Jeb Arnold! "How does Jeb Arnold fit into this?" I just realized I hadn't told Noah about Jeb trying to peddle artwork in town. Noah knew that Jeb had a gambling problem and might be dealing with some shady characters, but I hadn't mentioned my conversation with Gideon and Andre.

"He's the one who called it in," Noah said casually. "Jeb said he stopped in the kitchen to ask Lucy about some landscaping plans and he noticed water leaking from the ceiling. When he went upstairs to investigate, he found Lucy lying in an overflowing tub of water. The boom box was in the water with her. She must have been balancing it on the edge of the tub and somehow knocked it in."

"Poor Lucy," I said, feeling close to tears. Something about the boom box and the hardworking Lucy made me regret I had ever considered her as Abigail's murderer. But so many signs had pointed in that direction.

"Thanks for coming," Sam said to us, ushering us inside. The last of the crime scene techs were leaving. "Don't bother with booties," she said, brushing aside the box of blue paper slippers everyone puts over their shoes at a crime scene. "We've already gotten as much as we're going to get from this place."

She led the way upstairs, and we passed the second- and third-floor landings. Sam had a spring in her step even though I figured she'd been on duty for at least twelve hours.

"There's no elevator in this place," she said over her shoulder, "and Lucy's apartment is on the top floor." When we got to the fourth-floor landing, she guided us down a narrow hallway. It was in stark contrast to the rest of the house. The carpet was beige, strictly utilitarian, and there was no artwork on the cream-colored walls. "Did you take a look at Lucy's apartment when you were doing the inventory here?"

"No, I never got this far. I ran into a few problems downstairs," I said. "I'll tell you about it another time," I assured her.

Sam shot me a curious look. "Keep me in the loop," she said.

I nodded. I realized I needed to have a sit-down with Sam and tell her what I'd discovered about the phony William Gilbert painting, the fact that Jeb Arnold was spotted trying to peddle stolen property, and my mishap at the mansion today.

I couldn't stop thinking about the nightmarish experience in the tomb-like basement. Was someone trying to warn me off, or was it just a prank? Angus had made it clear he didn't like me, and I suspected he was capable of anything. I also needed to tell Sam I finally remembered where I'd seen a fish that looked like the one in the crime scene photo.

Usually, solving a crime is like a puzzle, and as you assemble more and more pieces, the picture comes into view. But this time it wasn't working that way. I was gathering bits of information here and there, but they didn't add up to a composite of the killer. Instead, I felt as though I were trapped in a labyrinth, blundering down blind alleys and reaching dead ends. The clues were coming fast and furious, but there was nothing cohesive about them.

"This is it," she said, leading the way into Lucy's private quarters. None of the glamour and elegance of the stately old mansion had made it up to the housekeeper's quarters. It reminded me of *Downton Abbey.* The maids' quarters are invariably tucked away out of sight; small, cramped little rooms that include only the basic necessities.

"Not as fancy as the downstairs, is it?" I murmured as we stepped into a tiny apartment. The living room was small and boxy with a beat-up brown leather sofa, two armchairs that had seen better days, and a TV on a small table.

"She kept it really clean, but it looks like all the furniture were cast-offs," Sam said. "Abigail didn't go out of her way to be generous with the help."

"Except for the thirty million dollars that Lucy stood to inherit," Noah pointed out.

"That's only if Abigail didn't get around to changing her will." I peeked into two identical small bedrooms. Each one had a single bed, and I assumed one was for Nicky on the nights that he slept at the mansion. "If Abigail changed the will in favor of Sophie, then all bets would be off and Lucy wouldn't inherit a penny. After thirty years of backbreaking work," I said.

I could feel indignation rising in me as I inspected the tiny bathroom. It was spotless, like the rest of the apartment, but the chipped tiles and cheap fiberboard cabinets were worn and ugly. Abigail was puzzling to me. She was generous to a fault with her friends and with charitable causes, but she let her loyal housekeeper live like someone who was destitute. Wouldn't this create a feeling of resentment and entitlement in Lucy? Could she have been angry enough to kill Abigail, as I'd originally thought?

"You think it was murder?" I said, taking another look into the bathroom. The water had been drained out of the tub, and I noticed there was no water on the floor.

"I'll know more when we get the autopsy report from the ME. It could be electrocution or it could be staged. I thought I saw bruises on her back, but I couldn't be sure."

"The bruises would mean that someone held her down?" I asked.

"Yes, and since there's no water on the floor, she probably didn't struggle. So someone could have pushed the boom box into the water and she was stunned but not dead. It would have been easy to keep her underwater if she was weakened from the electrical shock. At least that's my theory right now."

Noah and I looked around the bathroom. It was hard to believe a violent death had occurred here just a couple of hours earlier. "Where's the boom box?" he asked suddenly.

"It was taken away as evidence," Sam said. "We'll have the techs look it over and see if it shorted out."

"But it was in the water when you found her?" I looked at the narrow edge along the rim of the tub.

Sam nodded. "Absolutely. She must have had it balanced right here on the edge of the bathtub"—she ran her index finger over the porcelain—"because we spotted faint dark marks there. They matched the bottom of the boom box.

She must have plugged it in over there." She pointed to a wall outlet that was several feet away, above the counter.

I knew immediately that something was wrong with the scene. "The boom box," I said, thinking fast, "couldn't have been plugged in over there."

"But it must have been," Sam insisted. "There are only two plugs in the room, Taylor. And the other one is above the mirror. And that one doesn't work; we already tried it."

"I got a good look at the boom box when Lucy had it in the kitchen," I said firmly. "It had a very short cord. In fact, it was so short I was afraid it was going to fall in the kitchen sink while she was washing dishes. You can ask anyone. The cord was only a couple of feet long; it could never stretch from the wall socket to the bathtub," I said.

Sam looked puzzled. "Are you sure? The cord looked perfectly fine to me."

"No, it was short. You should ask Nicky about it. Lucy borrowed it from him. She needed a charger for her iPod, so Nicky loaned her the boom box. She used to lug it from room to room as she worked."

"I'll have the CSIs look into it right away," Sam said. "I'm glad you mentioned that. There was something about the crime scene that was bugging me, and I couldn't decide what it was. This is a sad case, isn't it?" She led the way back to the living room. "Not really much to see here. We went through the second bedroom—I assume that's Nicky's room, but I bet he doesn't spend much time here. It was immaculate."

"Maybe Lucy cleaned up after him," I suggested, remembering how she tended to make excuses for her slacker son. She probably waited on him hand and foot. I wondered how he would take the news of her death and what he would do if he had to leave Beaux Reves. With no job, no education, and no skills, he would be out on the street.

We spent a few more minutes in Lucy's apartment and decided there wasn't anything more to see. Sam already had uniforms posted at the front door who would alert her if Nicky returned to the mansion. If not, she'd have to try to track down the address of his girlfriend so someone could notify him about his mother's death.

"We're still going over that letter you found tucked away in Desiree's room," Sam said suddenly. "It's certainly interesting. If only the writer had signed it."

"That would make it too easy," I said ruefully. "I suppose Desiree had a lot of admirers. From what I heard, she was quite the girl about town."

"But she saved that particular letter, which tells me it was significant," Sam said. When we got to the first-floor foyer, she paused. "Anything else before we wrap things up here?"

The painting! I'd nearly forgotten the phony William Gilbert in the basement. I whipped out my camera phone. "Can you have someone bring this painting upstairs? You'll want to take it as evidence."

"Of course." Sam gave me a strange look. "Care to tell me what's going on?"

I took a deep breath. It was embarrassing to admit that I'd been creeped out by being locked in the basement a few hours earlier and had nearly panicked. But there was no way I could keep this from Sam.

Sam always says every single detail could be relevant, and it's important to tell the police everything. Sometimes one clue leads to another and cases have been closed on circumstantial evidence. So I fessed up to my phobia and told her how Angus had led me down to the basement to work on the inventory. Noah looked worried as I gave a quick version of the events. I tried to leave out the emotional part and concentrated on the painting and why it could be significant.

"It was all about the steeple," I said, wrapping up my story.

"So if it hadn't been for the Harper sisters, you never would have suspected the painting was a forgery?" Sam asked.

"Probably not. It looked legitimate to me, and I doubt anyone would send out every single painting to be appraised. This could be the tip of the iceberg. There may be dozens of other paintings here that are forgeries. Maybe someone was commissioned to paint the forgeries and they slowly were introduced into the mansion, one by one, replacing the original artwork. Or maybe someone was authorized to buy them as new acquisitions from a gallery and was getting a cut of the money Abigail laid out for them. It's just incredible that the Harper sisters remembered about the church fire and the missing steeple."

Sam laughed. "I think I need to get back to the Dream Club meetings more often. You ladies are going to take over my job. You've all turned into detectives."

"Not really," I told her. "We just come up with things from time to time." I suddenly remembered Dorien's dream about the fish. "And you know that fish symbol on the object you spotted in the crime scene photos?" Sam nodded. "Take a look above the kitchen sink before you leave. Lucy hung a blue ceramic plaque there. It has the same symbol as that shiny object in the crime scene photo. A line drawing of a fish."

I didn't bother telling her about Dorien's dream about Big Mouth Billy Bass. As far as I was concerned, it was sheer coincidence, and I was sure Sam would feel the same way. "The plot thickens," she muttered. "Thanks for the tip. I'll make sure we check it out before we leave."

Noah moved closer to me, his eyes dark with concern. "Do you think someone deliberately put that board there, blocking your escape?"

"I don't know." I shrugged. "At the time I did, but now it seems a little silly. I wasn't in any real danger, but maybe someone wanted me to mind my own business."

Sam motioned to a young officer and showed him my camera phone. "Go downstairs to the basement and find this. It's covered with a drop cloth, leaning against the wall. The entrance to the cellar is at the back of the house. It looks like the opening to a root cellar. Bring a flashlight and use gloves," she called as he headed outside. "We might be able to dust it for fingerprints." She thought for a moment. "Did Angus give you any idea who bought the painting?"

"No, not a word. He admitted it was a new acquisition. Of course, I'd already figured that out for myself because it didn't have any dust on it." I suddenly remembered the hidden passage in the alcove. "And Angus showed me a hidden staircase here in the house that goes down to the basement. It's right around the corner from where we're standing. Would you like to see it?"

"You know I would," Sam said, pulling on a pair of gloves. "You don't need to come with me, Taylor," she said, giving me a sympathetic glance. "You're looking a little peaked, as they say." She turned to Noah. "I think we're done here. Why don't you take her out for a nice cappuccino or a white wine?"

"I'm on it," Noah said, looping his arm around me.

26

"Cappuccino or white wine?" Noah asked. We were standing at the bar of a little restaurant down by the Riverwalk.

"Cappuccino, please, and make it to go. It's such a nice night, I'd like to take a stroll." I wandered back outside to wait while Noah ordered the drinks. It was one of those perfect early summer evenings when the air is sweet with the scent of magnolias and the breeze is soft as a caress. It was good to get away from the tragic scene at Beaux Reves. I could still feel the darkness and sense of evil; it was as though a malevolent presence was hanging over the once-dazzling mansion, and now it was somber as a tomb.

Noah appeared a few minutes later, and we strolled along the waterfront, lost in thought.

"You were pretty impressive back there at the mansion," he said, breaking the silence. He shot me a look, and his mouth quirked in a sexy little smile. "I think you missed your calling. If you ever want to join me in the detective agency, I could use a partner."

"Me, a detective?" I laughed and shook my head. "I don't think so. You should have seen me in the basement today when the lights went out. I was as frightened as a mouse."

"I can do the heavy lifting if you join the agency," he said, placing an arm around my shoulders. "You can do all of the analyzing, the strategizing. After all, you're the one with the MBA. I'm just an ex-Bureau guy trying to make a living as a detective."

We moved to one side of the walkway as a young couple with a double baby stroller passed by. *Twins.* Noah smiled at the parents, and I wondered if he and I would ever tie the knot and have a family someday.

"You notice things other people miss, Taylor," he said. He steered me to a bench under a banyan tree. The Riverwalk was crowded with tourists tonight, and a band was playing nearby, the sound of soft bluegrass drifting in the evening air. "The cord to the boom box could be the key to Lucy's death."

"I don't know," I said, suddenly wondering if my memory was correct. "Do you suppose I could have made a mistake?"

I'd been so sure I'd seen the boom box perched on the colorful tiles over the kitchen sink, and I'd been afraid it might tumble into the water. Or had I imagined the cord being short? Sometimes our minds play tricks on us and add details that aren't really there. Memories are as elusive as dreams. If Dorien heard my story about the boom box and the kitchen sink, she'd insist that I'd had a "premonition" that Lucy would be electrocuted. Dorien fancies herself a psychic and believes in precognition, the ability to foretell events that haven't happened yet.

"I don't think you made a mistake," Noah said. "Close your

eyes and picture the kitchen. Lucy is washing dishes at the sink and the boom box is on the counter. What do you see?"

I tried to bring the kitchen scene into focus. "I see the cord," I said. "And I'm amazed the boom box hasn't fallen into the sink yet. It looks dangerous."

"Then trust your instincts, Taylor." He leaned close and planted a kiss on my neck. "I know I do," he murmured in a husky voice.

"I thought we were here to talk about the case," I said, unconvincingly. I felt myself tingling just being near him and wished we were someplace private.

"Ah, the case," he said, pulling out his phone. "I got a text from a friend whose uncle went to college with Norman Osteroff. He scanned a page of the yearbook and sent it to me. Take a look."

I edged close to look at the screen and saw a much younger Norman Osteroff posing with his friends. Even as a young man, he looked austere, forbidding, his lips firmly pressed together. Did the man never crack a smile? I read the text aloud. "'Norman Osteroff. Career plans: future attorney. Clubs and hobbies: debate club, Adam Smith Society, Phi Beta Kappa, the rowing team. Astrological sign: Pisces.' No surprises here, except I didn't think he'd be involved in anything athletic." I started to pass the phone over to Noah when I gasped. "Wait a minute," I said, snatching the phone back. "Look at what his classmates called Norman. His nickname. I almost missed it."

Noah leaned over and his eyebrows shot up. "*Norman the Conquerer?* A bit pretentious, but maybe it refers to his debating skills."

"No, that's not it," I said excitedly. "Norman the Conquerer! Remember the love letter I found in Desiree's room?

The person signed it, 'your conquering hero.' That *can't* be a coincidence!"

"I'm not so sure," Noah said, his dark eyes earnest. "Norman and Desiree? I know they say opposites attract, but don't you think that's a bit of a stretch? He's a stuffy lawyer, and she was a girl who loved to drink and party, from what I've heard."

"It wouldn't have to be a love affair," I said. "At least, not on his part. Think about it. Desiree was an heiress. He might have pretended to be enchanted by her to use her in some way."

"How?" Noah drained the last of his coffee.

"I don't know. This seems to add another layer of complication to the case."

"We can check the financials again," Noah suggested. "Osteroff had a lot of power with that family, and if he could pull the wool over Desiree's eyes, maybe he fooled Abigail, too. I think at the end she might have lost trust in him and that's why she asked you and Ali to do the inventory."

"I think so, too." I felt as if the whole case had gone topsy-turvy. "Where do things stand right now with our suspect list?"

"If we take Norman out of the mix?" Noah sat back, resting his arm along the back of the bench. "Nothing's changed with the other suspects. What's the latest on Laura Howard? She stood to make a lot of money from the tontine."

"No, she didn't." I filled him in on my conversation with Laura about the Savannah real estate she'd won and how it wasn't the gold mine she'd expected it to be.

"But she didn't know about property values sinking until after Abigail's death, right?" he asked.

"Right. So she still could be a suspect, but somehow I just can't see her as a killer."

"You can't see past the white gloves and pearls," Noah teased me. "Some famous socialites have murdered people. Don't be fooled by their ladylike appearance."

"I know. If we take Laura Howard out as a suspect, we're left with Angus."

"You told Sam there's something shady about him," Noah said.

"I know there is. He and Lucy were upset when Ali and I were wandering around the mansion. I think they were afraid we'd find something that would incriminate them."

"And now Lucy's dead."

"I know. I have the feeling this is a game changer, but I can't figure out who would want to kill her."

"Someone who felt threatened by her," Noah offered. "Who stands to gain from her death?"

"Could it be her son, Nicky? He probably was helping himself to things from the mansion, but I don't think she would ever turn him in. And Angus wasn't threatened by her. I think they were involved in something together. They seemed thick as thieves." I paused. Sunset had passed, and a cool violet color was slowly taking over the evening sky. "I suppose we should consider Jeb Arnold, the estate manager. We know he was selling off antiques from Beaux Reves, or at least trying to."

Noah nodded. "I was glad you told Sam about what you heard from Gideon. They may be able to run a sting operation and catch Jeb. I just don't see him as a killer, though. And if he really was trying to peddle stolen goods, Lucy and her son must have been in on it. Lucy was there every single day, and she knew what came in and out of the mansion. So Jeb wouldn't have had any reason to kill her. Unless she was blackmailing him. Was that possible?"

"I don't think so; he was flat broke. He had awful gambling

debts and didn't have any funds to pay them off. So there wouldn't be any motive for Lucy to blackmail him. We have a wild card," I said. "Sophie Stanton."

"Sophie Stanton. Did anyone dig up anything on her?"

"The Harper sisters are on it," I said, "and Sara is calling in some favors to figure out if she's really who she says she is. There's just something about her that's a little off."

"As in crazy-killer off? She's not in any criminal database."

"No, she's probably not a killer. I just can't get a handle on her, and it's annoying to me." Noah glanced at his watch, and I knew we both were ready to wrap up the conversation. Noah had already told me he had to go back to the office to finish up some paperwork, and I wanted to get back home to talk with Ali. I knew she'd be waiting up, eager to hear what had happened at Beaux Reves.

"I always think of you telling me to 'follow the money' in any investigation," I said.

"I still stand by it." He smiled. "I'm flattered you remembered."

"It's a good strategy, but in this case, I don't see where it's leading us."

"I don't, either," he said, standing up and reaching out his hand. "The one thing I'm sure of is that it all goes back to Desiree. Somehow the three deaths are connected. If we can find out what happened to Desiree, we can find the killer."

* * * 27 * * *

"Somehow Abigail is the key to all this," Ali said. "I just know it."

"It may go all the way back to Desiree," I said, recalling Noah's words. "Until we figure out what happened to Desiree, we may never discover who murdered Abigail and Lucy."

It was the next day, and I was helping Ali and Dana set out coffee and pastries for the morning crowd. We decided to open the shop a little early today. The Harper sisters were dropping by to pick up candies for their nephew's class party, and Dorien wanted to see our tasting tray. I was sure she wanted to copy the idea for her own shop, and I didn't really mind. It's good to be neighborly, and there's room for both of us in the district.

Dorien has been having a hard time getting a foothold in the catering business, and she said she hoped we could "partner up" for some promotions. Offhand, I couldn't think of any way we could join forces. Her business isn't really much of a success and she's scrimping by with her part-time work as a tarot card reader. I feel sorry for her, but I don't want to jeopardize our own business by rushing into anything with her.

"I'm not so sure about Desiree," Ali countered. "What if it really was just an accident? Maybe she had too much to drink and fell into the river that night? She'd been spotted prancing along the edge of the pier, shoes in her hand, high as a kite. One misstep and she could have landed in the water. She probably couldn't swim in that floor-length cocktail dress, and she might have gone right under."

"That's a possibility, I guess." I found myself going back and forth on what happened to Desiree. Officially, the case was closed, but Noah had looked over all the police records and wasn't convinced that her death was due to natural causes. Abigail had certainly had her suspicions, at least after the fact. But why hadn't she pushed for a more aggressive investigation at the time? She had the money and connections to fund a deeper look into her sister's death.

Or could it be that she was too grief-stricken to think clearly, and she had let the opportunity pass her by? That was the only explanation that made sense to me. The only other possibility was that she was involved in her sister's death, and I simply didn't believe it. The two sisters were close, and Abigail felt her sister's loss very keenly.

I'd told Ali as much as I could about Lucy's death as soon as I got home last night. Just as I'd suspected, she'd been waiting up for me. She was upset, but was glad that I'd visited the crime scene with Noah. She'd become a little teary when I told her that Lucy may have been murdered, but she managed to control her emotions and ask all the right questions. At this point, she knew as much as I did.

The Harper sisters arrived a few minutes later, and I filled them in on the events at Beaux Reves. Both seemed upset at Lucy's death, particularly at the thought that she might have met with foul play.

"When will the police know for sure, dear?" Minerva asked me.

"I suppose after the autopsy," I said. I glanced at Ali. I didn't want to say too much in front of her. "There seems to be some question about whether she was actually electrocuted or just stunned and held underwater long enough to drown."

"Held underwater?" Rose blanched. "How would the police know that for certain?"

"There seemed to be bruises on her back," I said in a low voice. Ali was busying herself taking a tray of cinnamon rolls out of the oven. They're one of our most popular items, and we always seem to run short. "Sam said she thought she saw some suspicious marks on the body, but she couldn't be sure."

I didn't go into detail about my theory of the boom box and the cord. All that would be left up to the CSIs. Noah said I should trust my instincts. I was positive the cord was too short so Lucy couldn't have been balancing the boom box on the edge of the tub, but it was silly to speculate. "We should know something in the next few hours," I said with more certainty than I felt.

"I wish we knew what Abigail's inner life was like," Ali said, joining us.

Rose and Minerva exchanged a look. I'm sure they had no idea what Ali was talking about. "Inner life?" Rose asked.

"Her hopes and dreams, her fears, her goals. The sort of thing you'd put in a diary."

"I wish the police *had* found a diary," I said feelingly.

"Even a date book. Everything hinges on what Abigail was planning the night she died. What a pity she didn't keep one. We'd know if she had an appointment that night and who she was meeting."

"Oh, but she did keep a diary, Taylor," Minerva said. "She called it 'the book.' She mentioned it at lunch that day, do you remember? She was so surprised at the idea of dream interpretation that she said something like, '*This is one for the book.*'"

This is one for the book. "You know, I did notice that," I said slowly. It was all coming back to me. The happy, sun-splashed patio, the smile on Abigail's face as she realized she wasn't condemned to death by her dream. "And you're right, those are exactly the words she used. *The book.* I thought maybe she was writing a novel."

"A novel? Oh, good heavens, no," Minerva said. "That was just an expression. She always called it *the book*, and I assumed it was a diary of some kind. Or maybe an appointment book."

"Did you ever see it?" Ali asked eagerly. "This *book* of hers?" She quickly poured coffee for everyone and greeted Dorien, motioning her to a bar stool. "We're talking about whether or not Abigail kept a diary," she said, filling her in on the discussion.

Minerva pushed a plate of croissants toward Dorien and said, "No, I'm afraid I can't help you there. I never saw it, but I know it exists."

"But where is it?" Ali said, frustrated. "It's got to be some-where at Beaux Reves, but the place is so huge. Taylor and I have only had time to look in a few rooms."

"I have an idea," Dorien said, turning to Minerva. "You and Rose probably knew Abigail better than anyone. What was Abigail's favorite room in the mansion? Do you know?"

Minerva put down her coffee cup and rested her chin on her hand for a long moment. "It had to be the library," she said finally. "That was the room where she felt the happiest, surrounded by her beloved books, listening to a violin concerto. Sometimes she had Lucy light a fire for her, and she said she loved to look at the burning logs. She told me it was the most peaceful room in the house."

"The library," Dorien repeated. "That's interesting. I had a dream about Abigail last night, and she was in the library."

Ali and I exchanged a look. Was Dorien telling the truth or was this a shameless bid for attention?

"It must have been the library. It had walls and walls of books. It had a fireplace with a green marble mantelpiece and a maidenhair fern in a pot." Dorien was staring off into the distance as if she was lost in another dimension. Her voice became low, hypnotic. "There were two ceramic dogs guarding the fireplace. The room was dark, with heavy drapes. It had lots of mahogany paneling and what they call a 'tray ceiling.' I remember thinking it would look a lot better if someone let some light in. Abigail smiled and motioned to me to sit down. And then I woke up," she finished abruptly.

I could hardly contain my surprise and stared at Ali. What Dorien had described was the library at Beaux Reves. Her description was perfect, down to the last detail. How was this possible? I'd seen everything for myself: the green marble mantelpiece, the dark wood paneling. Even the ceramic dogs and the maidenhair fern. It was as though she had an exact image of the Beaux Reves library imprinted in her mind.

How had she described the room so perfectly? Had Dorien ever been inside the mansion? I doubted it. Of course, she could have seen a photograph of the Beaux Reves library, perhaps in a travel book. Some people have photographic memories and are able to recall a picture in complete detail. I don't have that ability, but I know it exists.

"That's very interesting," I said, keeping my voice neutral.

"Well, maybe that will put you on the right track," Dorien said, biting into a croissant. "Have you settled on a suspect yet?"

I shook my head. "Not really. Here's where we are." I took a few minutes to bring Minerva, Rose, and Dorien up to speed on the missing items from the mansion and our suspicion that more than one person might be involved.

"The trouble is, anyone could have been stealing from the mansion," Ali said. "Even Lucy."

"Surely not Lucy!" Rose said. "She was devoted to Abigail."

"I'm sure she was," I said gently, "but she could have been in dire straits. I suspect she might have had some financial difficulties. Her son seemed to be a complete drain on her. Of course, other people at Beaux Reves had access to valuables, too." I ticked off the possibilities on the fingers of one hand. "There is Nicky, her son. Angus, who was hired to do an inventory. Sophie, who is a bit of a mystery woman, and Jeb, the estate manager."

"You don't really think Jeb is involved in Lucy's murder?" Dorien put down her cup in surprise.

"Well," I said hesitantly, "probably not the murder, but I'm sure he's involved in the thefts."

"I don't buy it. I know his former sister-in-law, and she thinks he's a nice guy. He broke up with her sister, but he still comes by for dinner once in a while. He's got a bit of a drinking problem, but I guess you already knew that."

"Yes, I suspected it." I remembered smelling alcohol on his breath at Abigail's memorial service. I looked at Ali and raised my eyebrows. We should have asked Dorien about the suspects before. She might not be Miss Congeniality, but she has a certain shrewdness and knows a lot about what's going on in Savannah. As Noah said, "You never know where a tiny detail will lead you. Talk to everyone. You might get a nugget of information that you can put together with other clues to form the whole picture."

Ali poured more coffee for everyone. "Dorien, you said she considers him a nice guy. Why is that?"

"Well, she said he stops by to help her occasionally. She's single with two kids and runs a little farm outside Savannah. He picks up bales of hay for her and delivers them right to the paddock; those things are heavy and they weigh nearly a hundred pounds each. He's good with the horses. She really can't afford to keep the two mares, but the kids love them so much she can't part with them." She grinned. "And Jeb always brings pizza for the kids. He's a good guy."

I nodded. Jeb was great with horses and kids. Maybe he did have his good points after all, and in any case, I wasn't really looking at him as the killer. I flashed back to Sam's comment on the smudged handprint on the banister. She'd mentioned something that made me think of horses. What was it?

"And he does odd jobs for her, too," Dorien went on, breaking into my thoughts. "He's rewired the barn even though he's not licensed as an electrician. She could never afford to pay a real electrician to do what he does, so he really helps her out. He's had a few gambling debts, but he's doing the best he can. Everyone has secrets," she added glumly, staring into her coffee.

The breakfast crowd started trickling in then, and I quickly scooted off the bar stool. Dana had come in at the same time and was already seating them and handing out menus. "Do you want to see the tasting tray?" I asked Dorien, who nodded. I'd already put together Minerva's order for her nephew and Ali started to ring it up. I knew all Jason's favorite candies and had made sure I included them in the box.

"Did you add those little chocolate coins in the mesh bags?" Minerva asked, reaching for her purse. "He wants to make sure all his classmates get one to take home with them."

"Forty-three," Ali said. "And one for the teacher."

"Perfect!" Minerva and Rose said in unison.

28

Sara stopped by around eleven. The breakfast crowd had thinned out and I was glad we had a little downtime before lunch. I was eager to bring her up to speed on the investigation and share notes.

"Want a cinnamon roll?" I offered. "There's just one left. It must have your name on it." I put it on a plate and pushed it toward her.

Sara loves all pastries, but cinnamon rolls are her favorite. Ali rolls them in candied pecans before baking and adds a touch of real maple syrup in the batter. She found the recipe in an old church cookbook the Harpers gave her. The original recipe said "serves a hundred," and Ali had a laugh while trying to whittle down the ingredients.

"I'd better save it for later," she said, helping herself to hazelnut coffee. "Tell me about the crime scene last night," she said, whipping out her narrow little notebook. "I wish I could have been there. Everyone at the paper's talking about it, and the police have clammed up. They're saying that it's under investigation. Under investigation! That could mean anything." She nodded toward Ali. "Noah told me you were the only two outsiders at Beaux Reves last night."

"Ali doesn't handle crime scenes very well," I said protectively. "I'm afraid if she'd seen the bathtub, and imagined Lucy being pushed underwater, she'd have nightmares for weeks."

"She might," Sara agreed. She eyed the cinnamon roll, cut off a tiny piece, and popped it in her mouth. I knew what was going to happen next. She was going to slice off little slivers and eat them one by one until the entire roll was all gone. "Noah said something about a boom box?" She had her ballpoint pen poised over the notebook, and I hesitated.

"This is off the record, right?"

"Of course." She immediately put her pen down, looking aggrieved. I quickly explained about the short cord and that it was impossible for Lucy to have balanced the boom box on the edge of the tub. My guess was that someone had tossed the boom box into the water to make her death look accidental. "It certainly sounds suspicious," Sara said when I'd finished. "What's Noah's take on all this?"

"He's waiting for the coroner's report. Sam thought she saw bruises on Lucy's back, but that could fit either theory. Someone could have simply overpowered her, held her down and drowned her, or the killer may have shocked her first. She'd be easier to subdue that way." I gave a little shudder. "They could have flipped her over, facedown in the water, and applied enough pressure to her back to drown her."

"Who found the body?"

"Jeb Arnold. The estate manager."

"Really?" She glanced toward her notebook as if she was tempted to write something down, but restrained herself.

"That's odd. Why was he in the house?" I could see her hand creeping over toward her pen.

"You promised," I reminded her. "Off the record." We moved to a couple of armchairs so customers could have the bar stools at the counter.

"I know, don't worry. No notes. What happens in the candy shop stays in the candy shop," she said teasingly. "But was Lucy really alone in the mansion last night? Where was everyone else?"

"Lucy's son, Nicky, was in town, staying with his girl-friend. At least that's what Sam said. And as for Sophie and Angus, I know the police interviewed them at Beaux Reves, but I don't know if they were there when Lucy was murdered. They were just leaving when Noah and I arrived."

"There's something odd about those two," Sara said thought-fully. "Angus seems like someone out to make a buck, and Sophie is"—she hesitated—"well, I don't know what she is. I just can't figure her out. I think it's strange the way they covered for each other the night of Abigail's death, don't you?"

"Yes, I do. Angus got the name of the restaurant wrong, but Sophie quickly corrected him. If they're working to-gether, she's clearly the brains of the operation." I remem-bered how unemotional Sophie had been over Lucy's death when she and Angus passed us on the flagstone path leading up to the front door. "I've been meaning to ask you some-thing," I said. "I overheard Sophie saying that Lucy's death would be A-1. Does that expression mean anything to you?"

Sara blinked in surprise. "A-1? It's a term reporters use all the time. If something is really big, a breaking story, we might say, 'That's A-1.' It means it will make the front page of the paper. Where did you hear that?"

"Sophie said that to Angus. But most people wouldn't know what it meant, would they?"

"I don't think so. I've only heard it from reporters." She hesitated. "I doubt Angus has a journalism background, but do you think Sophie does? We know so little about her."

"All I know is that she was studying up on the south of France in case Abigail asked her anything about Sans Souci. I saw a guide book in the bottom of her tote bag. She'd highlighted certain phrases and she repeated them word for word. There's something going on there, I just know it."

I watched as Sara tapped her fingertip on the cover of her skinny little notebook. "And another thing. I guess it's a coincidence, but she carries one of those narrow little notebooks like you do."

"She carries a reporter's notebook?" she asked, leaning forward. "Are you sure?"

"I'm positive. It looks just like yours." *A reporter's notebook?* "Why do you call it that?"

Sara held up the notebook. "Because guys can fit them in their pockets," she said. "It goes back to the days when only men were journalists. It's just a tradition; we all carry them."

"So Sophie could be a reporter?" This put a totally different spin on things.

"It's possible," Sara said. "This is something I need to check out right away." She drained the last of her coffee. "Oh, by the way, I finally met up with that former society reporter, the one who covered the ball." Sara laughed. "I don't know whether to believe it or not, but she had quite a story to tell."

"About Desiree?"

"Yes, and her beau, as she insisted on calling him. You'll never guess who Desiree was dancing the night away with— Norman Osteroff!"

"Norman Osteroff?" I was stunned. "But he's so . . ." I groped for the right word.

"Boring? Stuffy? Awful?"

"All of the above. I just can't believe he could have had something going with Desiree. She was beautiful and vivacious, besides being filthy rich. She could have had anyone she wanted. Is this society reporter even credible?" I saw Ali ringing up some orders, and I knew she'd be joining us in a minute or two.

Sara nodded. "She's very credible. She's retired now, but she covered all the society events in Savannah, back in the day. She was something of a celebrity herself. Everyone invited her to their parties and they knew she would be the soul of discretion. Don't forget, nobody was writing tell-all books in those days. Quite a lot of hanky-panky went on, as the Harper sisters like to say. And none of it ever made the paper. People were more discreet back then."

"Interesting. But what exactly did she say about Norman and Desiree? I just can't imagine those two as a couple."

"I know it seems like a stretch, but she was quite definite about it," Ali said. "Did you suspect anything like this?"

I told Sara about the yearbook page Noah had shown me last night. "Norman was described as Norman the Conquerer in college," I said. "Hard to believe, isn't it? I assume it referred to his debating skills, not his way with women."

"*Norman the Conquerer?* Doesn't that remind you of that love letter you found hidden away in Desiree's room?"

"Yes, whoever wrote that note signed it, 'your conquering hero.' Of course, that could mean anything. I still can't get my head around the possibility that Norman and Desiree could have been romantically involved."

"Stranger things have happened," Sara said, glancing at her watch. "I've got to run. What are your plans for today?" She picked up her car keys, and I noticed she had a little charm hanging from them. It had two fish swimming in opposite directions and the word "Pisces" written underneath it. So Sara was a Pisces? Hadn't I come across someone else who was a Pisces? And wasn't there a fish involved? She gave me a puzzled look and shoved the car keys in her bag.

"I need to go back to Beaux Reves," I said firmly. "Minerva and Rose told me they were sure that Abigail kept a diary, or maybe an appointment book. She was afraid she was getting forgetful in her old age, so she made it a point to write everything down. Think of what it would mean if we could find it."

"Find what?"Ali asked, finally joining us.

"I was just telling Sara about Abigail's diary or date book. The Harper sisters seemed convinced that she had one. The police looked for it, but nothing turned up."

"It would be a gold mine if you could find it," Sara said, tucking her notebook and pen into her purse. "The key is in that book. If only you could figure out who she invited to the mansion that night, you'd have the killer. I'm sure of it." She started toward the door and then turned back. "Taylor, please be careful if you're going to the mansion alone today. Anything could happen." Just for a moment, a look of fear crossed her delicate features. "I'm worried about you and I don't know why." She laughed. "I sound like Sybil, but I swear I felt a dark shadow pass over you when you mentioned going back to that place."

"I'll be careful." I felt a tingling at the back of my neck at her words. I remembered when Ali and I had sat on the sun-splashed patio of Beaux Reves for lunch. I'd felt a dark presence sweep over the table as if the Angel of Death had dipped his wings into the air above us. A chill had gone over me in spite of the bright Savannah sunshine. I felt a quivery sensation right now. Was this some sort of premonition, or just a case of nerves? Maybe I was still shaken up from the crime scene visit last night. That would be the most rational explanation.

"You don't have to worry about her going alone, Sara," Ali said firmly. "We're both going to Beaux Reves today."

"Ali, are you sure? I didn't think you were up to it—"

"Not another word about it," Ali said. "We're in this together, sis. No matter what happens."

"The place to start is in the library," I said in a low voice to Ali. Sam Stiles had left a message that we were free to explore the mansion today and told us the front door would be open. Jeb Arnold was working somewhere on the estate, but he was nowhere in sight as we walked up the flagstone path.

I felt a little shiver go through me as I remembered the previous evening. I'd walked up that same path and been ushered into a crime scene. We entered the front hall, and I tried to dispel the creepy feeling that the scent of death hung over the place.

"The painting is still missing," Ali said. I nodded, looking at the blank space on the wall. Now that Lucy was dead, we might never find out where the painting had been taken. I didn't believe her story that it had been removed "for cleaning," and figured it was hidden away somewhere. Or sold. In any case, another piece of Beaux Reves's history, gone forever. Since I'd discovered the fake William Gilbert in the basement, the police had decided to turn over all the Beaux Reves paintings to the FBI's rapid deployment art crime team. An elite team of fourteen agents are assigned to cover art thefts and forgeries. They're the best in the business, and I had no doubt that they'd find a lot more forgeries in the

collection. It was sad to think Abigail had been chiseled out
of valuable pieces of art, probably by people she trusted.

A text from Noah came in as we stood in the hall. Sam
told me you were headed to Beaux Reves. Checked into Norman's financials. Large deposits transferred from Desiree's
account to his. Be careful. I quickly texted him back that I
had Ali with me and that I was fine. So there was some financial funny business going on with Desiree's money? I
tried to put this together with what Sara had told me about
Norman and Desiree being romantically involved. Nothing
made sense.

I heard a creaking noise nearby and froze. It could have
been a floorboard or it could have been a door closing. Was
someone prowling around upstairs or was my imagination
getting the better of me? I pulled Ali into the living room and
put a finger to my lips. "Did you hear that?" I whispered.

"Yes," she said, her eyes wide. "But it could just be the house
settling. Aren't there always strange noises in old houses?"

My mind was racing, and I suddenly remembered what
Sam had said about the smudged handprint on the banister.
It had contained a residue of saddle soap mixed in with other
ingredients. Saddle soap had made me think of horses, and
Dorien had said Jeb Arnold was good with horses. Why
hadn't I connected this before? Jeb was supposed to be on
the grounds at Beaux Reves today, but we hadn't seen him.
I thought about calling Sam but decided it might be a false
lead and it was better to get on with the work at hand.

We stood stock-still, and I mentally counted to twenty. I
started to relax and then a sharp thump split the air. I felt
an icy tingle go down my back and grabbed Ali's arm. That
was no creaking floorboard. I locked gazes with Ali for a
long moment, and then I looked past her at the living room
window and my whole body slumped with relief. I let out a

big whoosh of air; I hadn't even realized I'd been holding my breath.

"A shutter!" she said, her voice giddy with relief. "That's all it was." It was a windy day, and sure enough, one of the shutters had banged against the front of the house.

"Let's get started in the library," I said, suddenly eager to find Abigail's diary and get out of the mansion as quickly as we could.

29

"The library," Ali gasped. "It's exactly as Dorien described it in her dream. Even the two ceramic dogs by the fireplace. And the maidenhair fern." I'd forgotten Ali hadn't been in the Beaux Reves library before. The amount of detail that Dorien had included was startling. "Do you think she really had some sort of premonition?"

"She could have seen a picture in a guide book," I said flatly. "Anyway, whether she did or not, we have a lot of work to do." It was oddly chilly in the library. The windows were closed against the bright Savannah sunlight, and the dark green drapes were pulled tightly shut. It wasn't the warm, inviting place that Dorien had described. There were ashes in the fireplace and the room seemed dank and un-welcoming.

"How shall we start?" Ali asked. "It looks over-whelming." Books lined all four sides of the room, except for the areas taken up by the fireplace and the windows. The books were stacked from the floor to the ceiling, and there was a sliding wooden ladder for easy access to the top shelves.

"Let's divide the room up into sections," I suggested. "I don't know how big the diary is, so it could be tucked away behind one of the books. The bottom shelves will be easy to do. It looks like she kept oversized art books there. We should be able to reach behind them and see if she hid the diary."

"The top shelves will be more difficult," Ali said. "We'll have to go through them shelf by shelf. If only we knew what it looked like." She walked over to a round side table with claw feet. "It's got to be an antique," she said admiringly. "Expensive," she added, running her hand over the smooth surface. "There's a drawer," she said hopefully. She pulled it open and frowned. "Nothing."

"Let's concentrate on the bookshelves," I told her. "You start with the far wall, and I'll do this one. We can share the ladder."

"Do you feel a draft in here? Or is it my imagination?" Ali shivered and rubbed her hands over her arms.

"I think it's coming from this window." I peeked under the heavy dark green drapery. "They left this window wide-open, maybe to air the place out. Do you want me to try to close it?"

"No," she said. "It's musty in here. Just leave it. With the drapes closed, I won't feel the draft."

We worked steadily for over an hour. The search went more quickly than I'd anticipated. The books were neatly arranged by category. Abigail had been a voracious reader, it seemed, and the shelves were filled with books on art, history, and travel. She loved the classics, and I saw several French novels by Zola, Flaubert, and Victor Hugo. Her taste in modern novels tended toward bestsellers in contemporary mysteries and thrillers.

"What next?" Ali asked, taking a break and sinking into an armchair.

"We have to rethink our strategy," I told her. "The diary doesn't appear to be hidden anywhere in the room."

"The book," Ali said slowly. "Remember how Abigail referred to her diary as 'the book'?"

"Yes," I said encouragingly. "I figured she misspoke; I thought she meant to say, *This is one for the books.* And instead she said, *This is one for the* book." I didn't want to let Ali know how disappointed I was. If the library really had been Abigail's favorite room in the house, I could imagine her sitting by the fire every evening, writing in her diary. Where else should we try? The mansion was enormous.

Ali stood up suddenly and walked to the far wall. "What if 'the book' was a real book? And she used that expression for a reason?"

"I'm not following," I said, biting back a yawn. I thought I heard a faint creaking noise again, but I ignored it. Ali was right; old houses had lots of peculiar noises, and I wasn't going to jump like a rabbit every time I heard one.

"Look at this row of books on the bottom shelf," she said. "It makes sense that Abigail would choose the bottom shelf if she wanted to hide her diary. She was an old lady. I can't imagine her scrambling up on a ladder to retrieve it each time she wanted to make an entry."

"A good point."

"And this bottom shelf is devoted entirely to books about Savannah."

"Yes, and I ran my hand behind them a few minutes ago. There's no diary hiding back there," I said firmly. "I think you're on the wrong track."

"No, I'm on the *right* track," she insisted, her eyes glowing with excitement. "Taylor, we were looking at this all wrong. When anyone in Savannah talks about 'the book,' what do they mean? Anyone besides Abigail, I mean."

"The book? I don't know—" I said, and then stopped abruptly. It was like a lightbulb had gone off over my head. "When they say 'the book,' they mean *Midnight in the Garden of Good and Evil*, the novel by John Berendt."

"Exactly. It put Savannah on the map. It was on the *New York Times* bestseller list for over two hundred weeks. Everyone loves that book. It's all about eccentric people in Savannah and what happens when an antique dealer is charged with murder. It's so well-known everyone here calls it 'the book.'"

"So if Abigail had a copy . . ." I began, but Ali was already ahead of me. She was down on her hands and knees, scanning the contemporary novels I'd already checked on the bottom shelf.

"Not 'if,'" Ali said triumphantly, holding up a hardcover book. "She *did* have a copy, and here it is!" The dust jacket said *Midnight in the Garden of Good and Evil*, and it featured the famous Bird Girl sculpture on the cover. "And if my theory is right," she said, pulling off the dust cover, "*this* is Abigail's diary."

I gasped as she showed me a red leather diary inside the dust cover. The truth had been staring me in the face, and I had totally missed it.

She flipped open the cover to reveal pages and pages of notes written in a spidery hand. A flyleaf had Abigail's name, and Ali began to riffle through the diary. "It's part diary and part date book. All we need to do is find out what Abigail wrote about the visitor the night of her death. Who she was expecting at Beaux Reves, what they were going to discuss—"

"You don't need the diary, my dear. I could have told you that myself."

I recognized the voice, and it chilled me to the bone. Ali and I looked up in horror as Norman Osteroff emerged from the hidden passage near the fireplace. *Norman Osteroff?* He'd entered the library so quietly we hadn't heard him. His eyes glinted with an evil light and he reached out one gnarled hand for the book.

The other hand was holding a gun, and it was pointed straight at us. It's true what Noah once told me: when someone points a gun at you, you can't concentrate on anything else. It's like your brain goes into red alert, and all you can do is look at the gun. All the other details in a scene just fall away.

"Now, if you'll just pass that over," Osteroff said with a death's-head smile, "I'll be on my way."

Ali clutched the book to her chest and backed up so fast she nearly crashed into me. "You don't think I'll let you walk out of here with this?" She gave a high-pitched laugh, and I knew she was terrified. Brave but terrified.

"You won't care either way," he said with a sly chuckle. "You and your sister will both be dead. Dead girls don't talk."

"You won't get away with this," I said, forcing my voice to remain steady. "A lot of people know we came to the mansion today."

The lawyer's face twisted into a mock frown. "Yes, and they'll be so sad they didn't get here in time. Such sweet young girls. Another tragedy at Beaux Reves. Maybe there really *is* a curse hanging over this place." He chortled.

"They'll know you did it," Ali insisted.

"Not necessarily. I took the precaution of hiding my car in the woods, and I came up the back way. I entered the house through the root cellar. It was so easy."

"Jeb Arnold is working today," I said desperately. "He's somewhere on the grounds." I looked past the elderly lawyer and saw the bottom of the heavy green drapery move a few inches. It puffed out just a tad, like the jib on a sailing ship. Was it the Savannah wind coming in through the open window? Or were my nerves so jangled I imagined it?

Norman shook his head. "Oh, Taylor, how naïve you are." He waved the gun at Ali. "I thought you were the smarter one of the two, but maybe an MBA doesn't mean what it used to. Haven't you figured out that Jeb has been helping himself to artwork from the mansion for years?"

"So it was Jeb who killed Lucy?" The longer I could keep him talking, the better; I figured if I asked enough questions it would feed his massive ego.

He laughed, a thin, brittle sound. "Of course not. *I* killed Lucy. She was trying to blackmail me. That's the trouble with accomplices. You can never really trust them. They bite the hand that feeds them. So you have to put them down, like rabid dogs."

"Lucy was an accomplice to Abigail's murder?" I felt incredibly sad at the thought.

"Never. She didn't have the stomach for it. Stealing paintings was one thing, but she would never hurt Abigail. I had to do the dirty work."

"So you killed Abigail, too?" Ali's tone was incredulous, and her eyes welled with tears.

Norman nodded. "And Desiree." He raised the gun toward us. "And now you two."

"Wait," I said imploringly."At least tell us why you killed Desiree. I thought you were in love with her."

"In love? Never. I was in love with her money. Abigail was so shrewd, I couldn't put anything over on her, but

Desiree was like putty in my hands. All you have to do with a pretty girl is flatter her." He raised the gun again.

"But why kill her?"

"I had to," he said in a reasonable voice. "She'd turned over quite a bit of money to me, and I'd used it for my own investments. Bad investments. I'm sorry to say they tanked. There was no way I could repay her, and she'd threatened to go to Abigail. Abigail was my main client, my bread and butter for the last thirty years. I wasn't going to lose the golden goose, so I had to stop Desiree. A midnight stroll along the Riverwalk, one little push, and it was all over. Desiree was history. The water closed around her like she was a pebble. She didn't even scream."

"You're a monster," Ali said softly.

"And you killed Abigail because . . ." I hoped to keep him talking. I was sure I saw another movement behind the heavy drapery.

"I really hated to kill Abigail," he said regretfully. "She was a tough old bird. I actually had trouble pushing her down the stairs. I never expected her to put up such a fight. But somehow she'd figured out that Desiree had given me all that money, and I guess she'd put two and two together. She invited me over to the house to talk about it." He gave a harsh laugh. "'Talk about it'? What was there to say? I had to kill her. Sometimes we do things in life that are hard to do." He took a step closer and leveled the gun at Ali. "Like this." He raised the gun to take aim at her forehead, and several things happened at once.

Suddenly, Sam Stiles dove out from behind the curtains with a move worthy of Lara Croft. With her gun drawn, she hurled herself through the air and connected with the lawyer in a full-body tackle.

Osteroff's arm was jerked straight up in the air and his gun went off, blasting a hole in the fancy tray ceiling. Sam took him down in a classic karate move, and he was lying on his stomach grimacing in pain as she yanked one arm behind his back and pushed it up toward his shoulder blades.

"Cuffs!" she yelled to two uniformed detectives who seemed to appear out of nowhere. One of them quickly cuffed Osteroff, and the other jerked him to his feet. "Get him in the squad car and call it in," she ordered. She was panting a little and said to Ali in a gentler tone, "Are you okay?"

"I think I am," Ali said wanly. She looked deathly white, and I put my arms around her. She was trembling all over, and I gathered her in a tight hug. "I'm okay," she said after a minute. "How did you know to come here?" she asked Sam, who was dusting herself off and rubbing her wrist. I had the feeling she'd been bruised when she'd forced Osteroff to the floor.

"Noah told me you were on your way out here today, and I had a bad feeling about it." She laughed. "Now, don't go telling the Dream Club, or they'll think it was a premonition."

"You came because Noah told you we were in danger?"

"Not just that," she admitted. "Jeb Arnold spotted Osteroff's car in the woods and figured he was up to no good. He called the precinct and said we'd better send some cops out because there was bound to be trouble."

"So Jeb Arnold was looking out for us. I'm surprised," I said. "Osteroff told us Jeb was a thief."

"Yes, that he is," Sam told me. "Jeb and Osteroff and Lucy have been stealing from the mansion for years. I'm sure of it. But he's not a murderer. The DA will likely go easy on him. After all, he probably saved your lives."

"*You* saved our lives," I said feelingly.

Sam laughed. "Hey, that's what friends are for."

"Can we leave now?" Ali said in a small voice. "This place is creeping me out."

"We can leave right now," Sam said. "Let me just get some ice from the kitchen."

"Ice?" I asked.

She gave a rueful smile. "I think I broke my wrist. I guess I need to brush up on my takedown moves."

30

"I still think it was a premonition that brought you to Beaux Reves today," Sybil said placidly. The Dream Club was in full force tonight. It wasn't an official meeting but everyone gathered at our place, including Sam Stiles, who'd just given an abbreviated account of what had happened in the library.

"I knew this would happen," Sam said wryly. "Didn't I warn you, Taylor?" She helped herself to a cup of coffee and a couple of Russian tea cakes. Ali was experimenting with pastries once again, but this time with good results. A touch of hazelnut liqueur had jazzed up the sometimes-bland cookie and turned it into a masterpiece.

"Yes, you did." I scooped Barney up into my lap. He was making the rounds and had just greeted the Harper sisters, who'd brought him cat treats. I hate to think that his favors can be bought, but I'm afraid that's the case.

"Well, if it wasn't a premonition, what was it?" Dorien asked. She seemed subdued tonight. She had been in a sour mood since I'd shown her the tasting tray and Ali and I had given her a few marketing tips. Whether she didn't think our ideas were applicable to her struggling catering business or she had hoped for a full-out partnership, I wasn't sure. I felt satisfied we'd done enough. It's one thing to help a friend, but we couldn't jeopardize our own business, which was on something of an upswing.

"It was a confluence of events," Sam said thoughtfully. "Excellent tea cakes," she said to Ali, who beamed. "A lot of things happened at once," Sam went on. "It wasn't just the call from Noah, although that certainly nudged me in the right direction. He said he had a *feeling* that you were in danger out at the mansion."

I tried not to smile. Sam had grinned when she'd said the word "feeling," and I knew what she was thinking. Everyone believes that Noah is as cool and analytical as I am and that's why we're such a good match. They don't think Noah is capable of acting impulsively, or on sheer instinct or gut feelings, yet I know he is.

"There was the call from Jeb Arnold to the station house," she said, ticking off the items on her fingers. "He said Norman Osteroff was prowling around the grounds and had hidden his car in the woods behind the house. That was enough to make me sit up and take notice."

"How awful," Minerva said. "When I think of what that dreadful man could have done to you . . ."

"Saints preserve us," her sister Rose murmured. "You two would have been goners."

"And there was some forensic evidence that turned up yesterday," Sam said. "I didn't have a chance to tell you about it, Taylor, but I know you'll be interested."

"Go ahead," I urged her. Barney was getting restless, and

I placed him gently on the floor, where he curled up on my feet.

"Someone had tampered with the cord to the boom box," Sam said. "They'd replaced the original cord with a longer one. We checked it out with the manufacturer. You were right, Taylor. There's no way Lucy could have balanced the boom box on the edge of the tub. The cord was too short."

"So Osteroff tossed the boom box in the water to make it look like an accidental electrocution?"

Sam nodded. "Pretty clever. He figured he'd get away with it." She shook her head in amazement. "But he made one big mistake. He replaced the cord on the boom box with a new cord from the same manufacturer, but he didn't realize they'd changed the model. Lucy had an older version of the boom box, and it came with a short cord. That's how we knew he'd switched the cords."

"And he admitted it?" Lucinda asked. Lucinda was perched on the edge of her chair, her back ramrod straight. She told me she'd gone to a very strict boarding school in her youth, and young ladies were not allowed to "slouch back" in their chairs. The habit has stayed with her, all these years later.

"He had to admit it," Sam said. "We had him dead to rights. He must have noticed the boom box weeks earlier and bought the cord in case he had the opportunity to kill her. It was just sheer luck that she was taking a bath last night when he sneaked into the mansion. His original plan was to catch her with her hands in the kitchen sink when it was full of water. That was riskier because he wasn't sure the boom box would really electrocute her. The bathtub situation was perfect for him. She'd either be electrocuted or he could drown her."

"What an evil man," Sybil muttered. "To think he nearly got away with everything. Three people are dead because of him."

"There's more," Sam went on. "Do you remember that shiny object we spotted in the crime scene photos? The one with the fish?"

"Yes, of course. I wondered if it could have belonged to Lucy because she was religious and she had a fish symbol on her kitchen plaque."

"Well, as it turns out, it wasn't a religious symbol at all. It part of an expensive cuff link: solid gold with a fish design." She paused. "The fish represents Pisces, and the cuff links belonged to Osteroff. We found the other one when we searched his house. He probably had no idea Abigail had pulled it off when he'd struggled on the stairs with her."

"He *was* a Pisces," I said. "It said so on his college yearbook page."

"Isn't it amazing how it all comes together?" Persia said. "The word around my office is that Osteroff was making a big play for Desiree. No one really believed it because they were such a mismatched couple."

"But she had money and that's what he was after," Sara said. "My society reporter friend said the same thing. She was positive they were an item. She could see it in their photographs, the way they leaned into each other, the intimate looks."

I gave a little shudder. "Osteroff as a romantic hero is hard to imagine," I said. "As far as I can tell, the only good thing about him is that he likes horses."

"Horses! I knew there was something else," Sam said. Her voice was high, ecstatic. I was thinking that this must be a magical moment for her. A murderer was brought to justice.

All the clues were there, but no one had put them together until now.

"Jeb Arnold liked horses, too," I suddenly remembered. "You mentioned that to us, Dorien."

"Yes, I did. But how does this tie into the murders?" Ali passed Dorien the cookie tray, and she put a few on a napkin.

"Remember the saddle soap and lanolin on the banister?" Sam asked. "We couldn't figure out where the saddle soap came from. It was just a tiny amount, but it shouldn't have been there at all. No commercial cleaning product uses saddle soap, so we figured it must have come from the killer's hand. It was right there on the palm print."

"Norman Osteroff," Ali said. "His wife raises horses, and he helps out with them."

"If only we had seen all this before," Etta Mae said. "Maybe we could have saved poor Lucy."

Etta Mae is blunt sometimes, but she has a good heart, and I think she finds all this talk of murder distressing.

"We did what we could," I said gently. "Lucy made a big mistake when she blackmailed Osteroff. She practically signed her own death warrant. You can't tangle with a man like that. And if you do, you can't win."

"But tell us about the book," Sybil demanded. "I know Abigail had tucked her diary between the dust cover of *Midnight in the Garden of Good and Evil*, but what did it say? Did it lay out her suspicions about Osteroff?"

"Yes," Sam replied. "It had everything: names, dates, money transfers. She realized Osteroff had duped her sister, and she didn't want to believe he had murdered her, but all the evidence pointed that way. She invited him to the mansion in a last-ditch effort to to force him to explain himself. The next step was going to the police."

"But instead she ended up dead," Ali said sadly.

"Just as she had predicted that day at lunch," Minerva added.

I nodded. In all the excitement of Osteroff's arrest for three murders, I'd nearly forgotten Abigail's startling revelation at lunch.

"And we told her it was just a dream," Rose said in a tiny voice. She dabbed her eyes with a tissue. "We told her dreams could be explained in many ways, and there was no reason to think her death was imminent."

"You couldn't have known," Persia said. "None of us could. We don't offer answers in our dream interpretation work. Just possibilities."

"So there are no more surprises?" Sara asked. She was planning on writing an in-depth piece about the murders at Beaux Reves for a major news outlet.

"Well, just one or two," Sam said. "Do you remember how Sophie seemed so mysterious? She just appeared out of nowhere as a distant relative."

"I was suspicious of her from the start," I said. "There was something off about her, but I couldn't put my finger on it." I pointed to Sara's slender little notebook. She was balancing it on the arm of the chair while drinking tea and munching on cookies. "I wondered if she could be a reporter."

"Bingo," Sam said. "Her real name is Rachel Martin, and she was planning to write a tell-all book about Beaux Reves. She specializes in crime fiction writing and hoped to be the next Ann Rule. She wanted to spend time in Savannah researching Desiree's death, and she figured out a way to gain access to the mansion."

"By claiming to be a relative!" Sybil said.

"Exactly. Sadly, Abigail fell for her story and took her

in. Sophie covered her tracks and even had a fake passport printed up with her phony name." Sam paused and glanced at her watch. I knew she had to leave in a few minutes.

"What was her involvement with Angus?" I asked.

"Angus was on to her. He found out her true identity and threatened to go to Abigail unless Rachel looked the other way while he continued to steal from the mansion."

"So Angus was involved in the thefts, too?" Lucinda asked. "All that beautiful artwork, gone who knows where."

"Angus and Nicky were both involved. It seems everyone was stealing from Abigail. Taylor's theory was correct. They removed original paintings one by one and replaced them with forgeries. And sometimes they commissioned outright fakes." She turned to the Harper sisters. "Like that fake William Gilbert. If you hadn't noticed the steeple in the painting, we may never have caught on."

"What about that missing painting in the front hall?" Ali asked. "It was beautiful. I suppose they sold that, too?"

Sam stood up. "No, oddly enough, that painting is okay. It really *was* sent to a restorer in Savannah. Abigail sent it out herself. She made a notation about it in her diary."

"So it all comes back to the book," Ali said.

"It's all about the book," I chimed in.

The Harper sisters smiled at us. "Always, my dears, always."

"And who locked me in the basement?" I demanded. "Do we know?" I figured it had to be Angus or Jeb. Or possibly Lucy.

"It was a new gardener, and it was completely innocent. He misunderstood some instructions and barricaded the door to the root cellar. Nothing nefarious at all."

We broke up shortly afterward, and Ali decided to turn

in early. Barney and Scout scooted down the hall after her, so I was alone in the living room, finishing off the pot of tea. What an evening it had been! Full of surprises and revelations. Desiree, Abigail, and Lucy.

I was filled with a sense of sadness at their deaths, yet it was good to have closure to the case. The last thing Sam told us before she left was that Abigail had left Beaux Reves to the Magnolia Society in her will, so it would be preserved and enjoyed for generations to come.

I was stifling a yawn when the phone rang. Noah.

"Are you still up? I see your light is on."

I curled my feet under me on the sofa and hugged the phone to my ear. "The Dream Club left a while ago, after Sam brought everybody up to date. I'm just having a cup of tea and . . . Wait a minute," I said, scrambling to my feet and heading toward the window. The plantation shutters were open and the soft night air was drifting into the room. "How do you know the light's still on?"

Noah gave a low, sexy chuckle. "Because I'm parked right outside your building. Ready for a nightcap?" I peered out the window and saw his black BMW with the motor running.

"I'd like that. Do you want to come up?" I offered.

"Let's head down to the Riverwalk. There's a bluegrass band playing right now. I think we need to celebrate, don't you?"

"I do. Just give me a minute," I said, grabbing my purse and running a brush through my hair.

"I'll give you all the time you need, Taylor. I'll be here waiting for you. Always," he said in a husky tone.

I scribbled a quick note for Ali and grabbed my keys. I glanced out the window before I closed the plantation shutters. The moon was a golden crescent in a midnight blue sky, and the stars were twinkling. The night air was filled with the intoxicating scent of night-blooming jasmine, one of my favorite flowers. It seemed like an omen. This was a night to lay old ghosts to rest, to bury the past, to celebrate our successes. A night filled with magic, mystery, and promise.

And I was going to spend it with Noah.

Dream Symbol Guide

What are your dreams trying to tell you? Do you ever dream of being stranded in a strange city in the dead of night, alone and afraid? Do you dream of wandering through a beautiful house, discovering hidden rooms filled with treasures? Dreams are our passport to the unconscious and understanding dream symbols can help you unlock their secrets.

* Being lost and alone is a frequent theme in dreams and suggests that you feel powerless and vulnerable in some area of your waking life. You literally don't know where to turn, and there is usually a strong element of danger in these dreams.

* Finding yourself in a beautiful house, filled with hidden rooms, is another common theme. The hidden rooms represent your potential, parts of yourself that you have never explored, skills and talents you have never developed.

* Standing on the edge of a cliff is another well-known dream feature. You might be facing a turning point in your life, facing a momentous decision. Sometimes in

the "cliff" dream, you see a canyon across the way. The distance is insurmountable; there is no way you can bridge the gap. This usually means that there is an obstacle to an important goal in your waking life; the gap represents the barrier you must overcome.

* Dreaming of driving a car—or riding in a car—features prominently in dreams. Are you driving or is someone else driving? If the car is careening down the road, it could mean that some element of your life is spinning out of control and needs to be addressed. If you are in the backseat, or unable to reach the pedals, it could mean that you seriously doubt your ability to control your own life and destiny. You may be overly dependent on others to make decisions for you.

* Cellars in dreams represent the deepest level of your unconscious. There is usually an element of darkness and danger in these dreams. Dreaming of being in a cellar can signify there is something in your conscious life that is hidden, something that you are afraid to face.

* Drowning in dreams usually means you are having trouble "keeping your head above water," and water is a very powerful symbol of the unconscious. A flood represents the notion that you are about to be overwhelmed by a force more powerful than you are.

Symbols in dreams embody our greatest hopes and fears; understanding their significance can help uncover material that is useful in our waking lives. There is no single way to interpret your dreams because you are the architect of your life. Sharing your dreams in a dream club can offer valuable insights into dreams and the power of the unconscious.

Mary Kennedy

Nightmares Can Be Murder

A Dream Club Mystery

Business consultant Taylor Blake has returned to Savannah, Georgia, to help her sister Allison turn her dream of running an old-fashioned candy store into a reality. Allison is also interested in dream interpretation and invites Taylor to her Friday night Dream Club, where members meet once a week to share and analyze their dreams.

When a local dance instructor, Chico Hernandez, is found dead in his studio, and the murder scene has an eerie resemblance to one of the dreams shared at their meeting, Taylor can't help but be intrigued. And when her sister, who was briefly involved with the dance teacher, becomes the prime suspect, Taylor and their fellow club members can't be caught napping. It's up to them to dream up a solution to the murder before Allison faces a real-life nightmare.

Also in the Series
Dream a Little Scream
A Premonition of Murder